ANNEE LAWRENCE

Annee lives in Australia and has an interest in exploring cross-cultural connection and the way identity shape-shifts in an unfamiliar place and culture. She has close friendship and family ties in Indonesia and was the recipient of an Asialink Arts' inaugural Tulis Australian-Indonesian Writing Exchange in 2018. As a result, she had a six-week residency at Kommunitas Salihara in Jakarta and was invited to the Ubud Writers and Readers Festival.

Prior to becoming a tutor in literary and cultural studies at Western Sydney University in 2014, Annee worked as a writer, editor and community development worker in the areas of women's health, human rights and social justice. Two of her publications include: *I Always Wanted To Be A Tap Dancer: Women With Disabilities* and (with Nola Colefax on her memoir) *Signs of Change: My Autobiography and History of Australian Theatre of the Deaf 1973–1983*. In 1981 she was founding editor of *Healthright: A Journal of Women's Health, Family Planning and Sexuality*.

Annee has published articles in *New Writing, Griffith Review, Hecate* and *Cultural Studies Review. The Colour of Things Unseen* is her debut novel.

First published in the UK in 2019 by Aurora Metro Publications Ltd.

67 Grove Avenue, Twickenham, TW1 4HX

www.aurorametro.com   info@aurorametro.com

The Colour of Things Unseen copyright © 2019 Annee Lawrence

Cover image: © 2016 Pranoto Ahmad Rahji, Pranoto's Art Gallery, Ubud, Bali, Indonesia www.facebook.com/Pranotos-Art-Gallery

Cover design: © 2019 Aurora Metro Publications Ltd.

Editor: Cheryl Robson

Aurora Metro Books would like to thank Marina Tuffier, Taylor Gill, Didem Uzum, Maja Florczak

ISBNs:
978-1-912430-17-8 (print)
978-1-912430-18-5 (ebook)

The Colour Of Things Unseen

by

Annee Lawrence

AURORA METRO BOOKS

For Ida, Emil and Tahlia

Part One

A village, Central Java
1980s–1990s

Mama is making batik. She is drawing lines of wax on the creamy coloured cloth. I like the smell of it. Like the way the wispy grey smoke rises from the melted wax in the blackened dish. I even like the wash of heat on my face when I draw close to the hot coals.

The batik stand is at the front of our house, and when the doors are open you can see it from the street. My big sister Yanti says only girls make batik but I want to make batik too. I know I can.

Our village has only a few streets and our house is like all the other houses, wooden and with large doors at the front. In the daytime we open the doors and shutters so the light streams across the smooth, chocolate brown, earth floor where our family sits on a mat to eat, or drink tea with visitors. There are three bedrooms at the back and we have one black and white goat. I wish we had more goats, and a cow as well. I like cows.

Mama's eyes are soft and kind like a happy cow's. Yanti says there are no stars in Mama's eyes, but when she smiles I can see stars sparkling.

Mama is called Suriani. She is beautiful, even more beautiful than Princess Sita. Her hair is black as the darkest night and she has a thick plait with a curly pointy end that brushes the top of her sarong when she walks. Sometimes when Mama bends over, the plait leaps up and over her shoulder and she has to catch hold of it.

She scolds it as she tosses it back. "Very naughty to run away. Now home you must go," she says, and this makes me laugh.

Mama has pale half-moons at the top of her nails and I can see them when she holds the bamboo cane handle of the canting in her long fingers. The brass cup on the canting is no bigger than a rambutan seed and a minute spout bends over at the front of it. Mama dips the canting in the dish and fills it with the hot brown wax. She blows gently into the spout to clear the bubbles, and when she draws on the cloth with the wax, it sets in a creamy gold line on the fabric.

"Mama, please ... I want to make batik too."

Mama looks up and I see the stars sparkling in her eyes. "Alright Adi, she says. Now you are five, perhaps it is time for you to make batik too. Yes?"

"Yes, yes."

"Perhaps you would like to make a butterfly batik?" Mama says.

"Yes, yes," I say, and Mama finds a piece of cloth and draws a large butterfly on it with a pencil.

"Now you will learn to use the canting, but you must be very careful of the fire and the hot wax. Are you watching?"

So many times I have seen my mother, grandmother and aunts all making batik.

"I know, I know already," I yell.

"Pay attention, sweetheart. See, this is how you trace the outline of the butterfly with the wax."

I like the sound Mama makes when she blows into the tiny spout. I purse my lips and practise: Phew, phew. It tickles and I start to laugh. Phew, phew.

Mama lowers the canting to the cloth and begins tracing a fine even line of wax around the butterfly's wing.

"Let me," I yell again. "I can do it."

"Very well," Mama says and spreads out a scrap of cloth. "Have a try first on this until you get the hang of it, yes?"

I seize the canting and dip it into the hot wax, filling the little cup. Phew, phew, I blow into the spout just like Mama. I can do it.

Mama smiles and leans over me while I practise. She puts her face close to the top of my head and inhales.

"Very sweet," she says. "I think you are ready to begin now."

So I dip, blow, and tense my hand to keep it steady, but when I start to trace along the butterfly's wing, an ugly blob of wax goes plop! Right in the middle of it.

"Aduh!" I scream. It's ruined. Tears sting my eyes and cheeks, but Mama ignores them.

"It's nothing," she says, and picks off the honey-coloured scab with her fingernail.

The brown, cream and indigo patterns of our family's sarongs, kebayas and selendangs are as familiar as my own skin and I can see them always in my mind. Ever since I was baby, I have gone with my mother and aunts to the markets in Solo to sell batik, and even all the way on the train to the big market in Yogyakarta. Back then, Mama carried me in a selendang on her back or against her breast, and Yanti carried me in a selendang on her hip too.

When we hear the faint sound of the gamelan drifting across the rice fields, Mama and I look at one another and begin packing up.

"Quick Adi," Mama says. "It's time for the shadow puppet show. Where's Papa and the others?"

As Mama clears away the fire, wax and canting, Yanti and our two brothers, Budi and Ismoyo, arrive. Then Papa rushes in and says, "Hurry, hurry. It's time to go."

Chapter 1

Adi was just six when his mother Suriani died, but no one told him she had died or, if they did, he didn't hear, or perhaps he just couldn't bear it. She was just thirty-two. One day she was filling up his day, and then she was gone. First there was sunlight and laughter, and then thick clouds of ash crept into the house and layered the surface of family life, made everything grey, pressed down on them while they slept, and caused them to feel tired and cross when they awoke.

Adi looked for traces of her, but there were none. Her sarongs, kebayas, hair bands, and even her scent, had all gone.

When he asked where she was, his big sister Yanti said, "Mama has gone away." And when he begged her to help him find her, she just said, "That's not possible."

He waited and waited for her return and, when his sense of abandonment formed itself into a fist of pain where his heart's joy had been, he began thinking in colours. And then he found a little door to a place where flashes of memory were stored – fragments, moments of their shared times together – in vivid colours or sepia tones, and sometimes sharp-focused and sometimes blurred, and these slid across the events of his day, or into his dreams at night.

Slivers of memory lit up the things and people around him and connected him to his mother's presence as well as her absence. The press of her body, the softness of her voice, the ring of her laugh, and even the feeling of the weight of her plait could be triggered any time by scents, sounds, colours, and especially by patterns: the garuda wings on a sarong drying on a neighbour's clothesline, the jerking pointy end of a girl's long plait as she walked down the road, the cloud of yellow butterflies that rose unbidden from the rice field, the splash of a leaping frog.

Mostly these things reassured him and made him feel calm, but it seemed more and more that, as time passed, they were from another time, perhaps even from before he was born – and they were not just his own memories, but those of everyone he knew.

When their mother died, thirteen-year-old Yanti left school to take care of the family, all four of them – their father Totot, and Adi, Budi and Ismoyo who were six, eleven and eight. In the weeks and months that followed her death, Adi shadowed his big sister's every move, inserting himself onto her lap when she sat, squatting beside her at the fire when she cooked, sleeping alongside her at night. But if the family burned with small sudden fires of grief, he and his father were like volcanoes that seethed and rumbled and threatened to erupt without warning. And no matter what Yanti did, no matter how loving and kind she was, it was clear that there was only so much a young girl could do to tend to a loss like that.

As the years passed, a series of events swept into their lives like the floodwaters that flowed up and over the river bank, burst through the levee banks, and cast tree branches and trunks, fences, and the broken parts of bridges headlong before it. The first shock wave was Totot's decision to remarry which meant a new mother arrived to live with them.

As if adjustment to this new configuration was not hard enough, less than a year later a squalling baby brother was born, and then six months after that the rock that was Suriani's parents, and the children's grandparents who lived next door, shattered when they both died within three months of one another.

The marriage, birth and unforeseen deaths stretched the emotional fabric of the family to its limit, but then there came another marriage announcement and it was this that tore Adi's heart apart once again. For in the year he turned ten, his touchstone and great love, Yanti, got married to Goenawan, who also moved into the family compound. Banned from sleeping in his big sister's bed, Adi's old pain and sense of abandonment were reignited; the colour drained from his life and he became inconsolable.

No one knew what to do about Adi's burning rage. When accounts of his naughtiness began circulating in the village and beyond, the neighbours were forgiving, he was a child still grieving for his mama they said. But when the ten-year-old threw a bowl of rice at his sister Yanti, it became the talk of the village. After that he ran away and no one could catch him, for he did not stop running until he was vomiting so hard he could run no further. He became estranged from everyone and some days he disappeared and couldn't be found. Other days he refused to get out of bed and wouldn't eat. He even stopped going to school.

Adi was upsetting everyone and so Totot went all the way to Yogyakarta on the train to ask his uncle if Adi could move in and work for him in his batik department store. But the uncle said Adi was too young and suggested instead that he be sent to a rich family in Jakarta, a distant relative, who might take him on as a servant. Adi and his brothers knew nothing of this, but Yanti heard of the plan and became alarmed. She borrowed a neighbour's bicycle and rode to the village where their father's older sisters, Bude Kartini and Bude Nur, lived to ask for their help.

Of course the story of Adi's deteriorating behaviour had already reached the aunts, and when Yanti pleaded with them to stop their father from sending him away, they decided to act. First they consulted with their husbands, and then they asked Totot to let the boy come and live with them.

Totot agreed, and when Adi went to live with his aunts, the villagers, who had known and loved his mother, gathered him up and gave him a fresh start. And to everyone's surprise, a kind of peace drew down around him and his wild behaviour subsided. The aunts had time for him too and, because they were better off now than when their children were young, they insisted on him going to school. And, that's when the colour seeped back into his life.

At the end of his last year of primary school, the aunts decided to approach a wealthy man from the village who was a distant cousin and who had been a childhood playmate. He was the owner of two large batik department stores, one in Solo and one in Yogyakarta, and he and his wife lived in Solo. Like the aunts' own children, his were grown up, and when they asked if he could help them to secure Adi's high school education, he suggested that Adi could stay at his house in Solo, where he would do odd jobs in lieu of rent and meals while attending junior high school. He said he would pay Adi's school fees and even provide him a small allowance as long as he studied hard. If he turned out to be a good student, he would support him to go on to senior high school as well.

Chapter 2

From the moment he arrived in Solo, Adi found his time was consumed by work, school and homework. Most weeks he was visited by one of the aunts, or he called at the markets to see them at the stall where they sold children's clothing. During the holidays he sometimes travelled to the village for a day or two to see the family, but mostly he could go for no more than a few hours. When classes were scheduled in the afternoon, he spent the mornings sweeping the street or working in the house and garden. Every day there were floors to mop, grass to clip, garbage to dispose of, errands to run, or shopping to be done in the early morning market. When the family was away, and there was just the maid, the security guard and him, he could easily do his homework, but when they returned he had to do it late at night, and with a single candle when the electricity failed.

At the end of junior high school, Adi was grateful that there seemed to be no argument with him stepping up to senior high school. And now there was a new opportunity for him to study English with Pak Harto, whose English language skills were valued highly by the school. When Pak Harto made a request to run classes in art as an elective for interested students, the principal agreed on the condition that they take place outside the normal school hours. Adi and some of his friends were keen to study art but Adi first had to seek permission from his employer.

This was given after Pak Harto explained he would run the art classes in English, and when he began to get good marks in the subject, Adi's employer told him he could practise his English by helping out with the super-size busloads of tourists that pulled into the department store each day. He would continue to live with them and do odd jobs, but for the most part he would work two to three hours a day in the store. He would receive a higher wage for this, which would allow him to purchase the canvases, paints, brushes and other materials he needed.

In Pak Harto's art classes, the students spent six months drawing before moving onto oil painting. Pak Harto set weekly exercises and by the end of their first year they had learned to construct a frame, stretch and prime a canvas, mix oil paints to a magical number of colours and shades, and observe how the same colour might brighten or fade when placed next to a certain shade, or when seen in a different light. He also encouraged them to study how they responded with different parts of their bodies to certain colours and, depending on the lesson, there was always a row of prints by different artists pegged to a line of string that stretched along the top of the blackboard.

Some of these images would remain with Adi for life: Pablo Picasso's *Guernica* with its tortured and terrified animals, and bodies contorted with fear; Salvador Dali's *Burning Giraffe* which made him feel queer – what did the skinny frames of the women with rows of open drawers in their body mean, or the flaming orange back and neck of the standing giraffe in the background? What kind of person painted such things? Vincent van Gogh's *Starry Night* was a swirling universe that dwarfed the human, and Seurat's *Sunday Afternoon* (he could never remember the full name) thrilled him with its daubs of colour that shimmered and broke apart when you looked up close. There was African art, Islamic art, Australian Indigenous art, Dutch art, Japanese woodcuts, Inuit prints and Chinese art. And there were Brett Whiteley's Sydney Harbour paintings, and Georgia O'Keefe's *Black Iris* which glowed, and tugged him deep into its heart.

Pak Harto kept his art history books in a locked cupboard that was opened only during class. When a student asked what a painting meant or was about he would always say the same thing, "What do you see? How does it make you feel? How do you think it does this?"

Art led Adi and the other students to discover things about their own world and the world beyond; it connected them to landscapes, histories, places and cultures that were so different that they never could have imagined they even existed. And when Adi walked home after art classes, it was as if the streets and houses and people in them were paintings too. Colours were more intense, and he saw things he hadn't seen before. The design of a wall poster, an intricate moss garden the size of an egg yolk in a hole in the footpath, an oily rainbow in a puddle. Once, in the courtyard of a homestay, he glimpsed a nude statue of Venus whose head was wrapped in a real hijab.

Sometimes Pak Harto bundled them into several becak and took them to local artists' studios to see the paintings, sculptures or installations they were working on, or he took them on painting excursions to faraway villages where they slept the night. Sometimes he arranged for them to participate in local art exhibitions, and once they went to Yogyakarta in a small bus to see an exhibition of many different artists.

Pak Harto's enthusiasm for art making and practice was contagious and no one was at all surprised when, in their final weeks of senior school, five students announced they had been accepted to study art at the Institute of the Arts – ISI – in Yogyakarta. They were the lucky ones whose family could afford the fees, but for Adi this question of what to do next was not so straightforward. In his early days at high school he had considered becoming a religious teacher but this path had long since lost its appeal. Now, it seemed, almost everyone was ready to offer suggestions about his future; he could become a becak driver like his uncle, or a tailor like his brother-in-law, or get work in a batik factory, or use his English skills to work in a department store, or become a tour guide.

Chapter 3

On the day Pak Harto sent for him, Adi found his teacher wrestling with a large map of the world that insisted on rolling itself back into a cylinder. At Pak Harto's signal, Adi gathered books from a shelf and placed them at the outer edges of the map. When he finally had it tamed, Pak Harto beckoned him to look at the spot he was indicating with the long paint-stained nail of his right thumb.

"Java," he announced. Then he drew the thumbnail southwards to a large, odd-shaped island. "Australia," he said, "and this is Sydney."

Adi was puzzled. He had studied geography and knew that Sydney was a city of perhaps three million people, one of the biggest in Australia but not large by Indonesian standards.

Pak Harto gestured for him to sit down. "How would you like to go and study art in Sydney for three years?" he asked, and then waited to see Adi's reaction. "If I told you this was possible, would you be interested?"

Adi had no words. When he glanced up, Pak Harto began to speak even more slowly than usual as if to allow the words to sink in. "Well, I've asked you here to offer you this opportunity. I studied and also taught painting at this art school, and I think you would gain a lot from going there as well. You would have a Bachelor of Fine Arts if you completed the three years."

For Adi, it was as if a cloud of the deepest pink had floated into the room and was colouring everything in it – the walls, furniture and even Pak Harto's own abstract paintings, whose looming oversized figures appeared to be neither human nor non-human. As the cloud of colour began pouring into his entire being, Adi felt his mother's love was gathering him up and lifting him clear out of the room. Only when Pak Harto spoke again did Adi return to the room with a start. The teacher's voice seemed far off and he strained to catch his meaning, "The art school will waive your fees and I have secured a scholarship for you that will cover living expenses – rent, food, art materials, that sort of thing."

The way Pak Harto spoke Indonesian was different to almost everyone he knew, either in the village or in Solo. At first, when they heard him speaking like this, using bigger words and more complex verb constructions, the students found it difficult to understand, but as they got used to him they too began to follow his lead and use a more formal language, but only in the classroom. Outside it they mostly spoke Javanese, and if they did speak Indonesian they still spoke it in the normal way.

Despite his efforts to focus on what his teacher was saying, Adi found his attention drawn to a ceramic sculpture Pak Harto kept on his desk. It had a yellow cream glaze, with intricate red patterning over it, and writing in a script he did not recognise. The artist was an Australian sculptor whose name he did not know, or was she Iranian? For the first time in all the times he'd seen it there, he now recognised that its curving shape was like that of a woman's body. There was a knob at the top, small handles like tiny legs at the side, and three openings with a smooth black stone inserted into the bottom slit that suggested a deep dark opening.

Adi felt his body heating up in response to the sculpture's strong suggestion of sex, and it was with some effort that he dragged his eyes away. When he looked up and saw Pak Harto watching him, he blushed and turned his eyes back to the map to avoid eye contact.

Pak Harto was smiling, "It's an interesting piece, isn't it? Do you know, I think you're the first person who's really seen it?"

The offer of the scholarship was hard to absorb and Adi turned to the side to brush away the tears of gratitude that were leaking from the edges of his eyes and onto his cheeks. As soon as he agreed to the offer, Pak Harto gathered up his briefcase, locked the office door, and they went by taxi to his aunts' village. After Bude Kartini and Bude Nur had consented, they drove on to the family village to meet with Pak Totot and Mbak Yanti.

"The art school will waive its fees," Pak Harto explained, "and an organisation in Bali has agreed to provide basic living expenses for three years, as well as a return airfare. They do this for three or four students a year," he said. "Adi is not the first, nor will he be the last to receive such support."

Hearing this, Totot was moved to express his gratitude and he got up from the mat and exited the room. As Pak Harto was preparing to leave, Totot reappeared with a small brown-feathered chicken in a bamboo cage and tried to present it to the teacher. While Pak Harto was declining the live gift, Yanti slipped out of the room and – just as Pak Harto and Adi, minus the chicken, were getting back into the car – returned with a laden branch from a neighbour's rambutan tree and deposited it onto the back seat of the waiting taxi. Totot was relieved. No one, least of all him, would have been happy if the teacher had gone from their house empty-handed.

To many in the village, Totot's second marriage to Yuni had seemed intemperate and ill-matched, but it soothed his ongoing terror that – even with Yanti and Suriani's parents' help – he was incapable of adequately caring for his children on his own. He had been a broken man following Suriani's untimely death and, thanks be to God, the second marriage had not been entirely loveless. With time, the second family melded with the first and, with the exception of Adi who was still young, his and Suriani's children were all married now and had children of their own. They too were contributing to their community, tending the rice fields and other crops, and making sacrifices so their children could get an education.

When Adi went to live with his sisters, Totot felt relieved because each time he looked at the boy – who had Suriani's eyes, mouth and hands – it caused a fearful jarring in his heart. Some had been critical of Suriani's parents for giving their daughter such a powerful name, but they named her, they said, for the light and warmth she brought them when they no longer believed they would be gifted with a child. For Totot too, her vivacity, sense of humour and unequivocal love and affection for him and the children was like a joyful bubble. And just as her parents had failed to curb her exuberance, so he too had given in to her deep need for personal freedom. If he tried to correct or bend her, she simply dissolved his ambition by making him laugh.

At any one time as a girl, Suriani could appear gracious, refined even, and then came the break out, and with some action or shout she would transform into a daring rascal. On a whim she might shimmy up a tree to fetch a coconut or jump fully clothed into the river to cool off. She didn't care what people thought and, even after all this time, people in the market still recalled the time she stole a brand new bicycle and rode it round and round the market, ringing the bell and staying just out of reach of the pompous school teacher who owned it.

The depth of Suriani's love for Adi as a baby, and then as a child, had disturbed Totot and left him feeling a little jealous and insecure. So when their entwined life broke apart, the boy's demands for comfort compounded his own sense of loss. While he could not love him, and this haunted Totot and made him hard on the boy, he still cherished a hope that peace would blossom between them again one day.

As word spread of Adi's good fortune, Totot felt a deep gratitude that Suriani's youngest, and only the second generation after independence, had finished junior and senior high school, and was going to attend university in a faraway place. Adi would be the first in the family to go to university, or even overseas. Their society was changing. He could feel it and it made him happy, for he still cherished the memory of when he was a boy and President Soekarno came to their village in a black car with darkened windows to talk about independence.

On that day, when the news spread fast through the village and out into the rice fields and nearby villages that Bung Karno wished to speak to them, they came hurrying to the *alun-alun*. Men with bare torsos came direct from the fields, carrying a machete, scythe, or any other tool they had been using. Women changed into a clean kebaya, called out to their neighbours, and herded their children to stand in front of the makeshift stage that was still being erected next to the banyan tree. It was a subdued but excited crowd and people were still pouring in when Bung Karno climbed up onto the podium to address them. He spoke of freedom and independence, of the Pancasila – the five principles for the republic, and of the importance of education for all children, even the poorest.

Bung Karno sowed the seeds of the Pancasila that filled their hearts with the new republic's promises of social justice, democracy, belief in one God, respect for all religions, and a nation united. He promised them that education would be the keystone to a fair and just society.

"The Dutch educated the aristocracy," he boomed, "but not the ordinary people, and they educated them in Dutch. Now the Javanese will speak Javanese, but they will be Indonesian too and speak Bahasa Indonesia. And Indonesia's motto will be *Bhinneka tunggal ika*. Unity in diversity. Many but one. We will bring all our nation's many cultures, languages, peoples, islands together to form one strong, cohesive, self-governing and independent country: Indonesia."

How they clapped and cheered. Hardly anyone spoke of Bung Karno nowadays, but the Imam often repeated his message, "Educate the children, the rest will follow." And, "It is our spiritual duty to educate our children."

All of Totot's children studied the Pancasila at school and, while some in the village like his wife Yuni spoke Javanese only, most of the younger generations spoke Indonesian as well because they learned it at school.

No one wanted to learn or speak Dutch. Not anymore.

Chapter 1

Pak Harto's efforts to land the scholarship for Adi were based on his belief that the student had a naïve and driving curiosity. While this was an important quality in an artist, it was his steely determination that most recommended him to the teacher. He would face considerable obstacles in a place like Sydney, but they would be of a different nature to the ones he would face if he remained at home. Of course, as in the myth of Daedalus, he might err and end up flying too close to the sun, but it was a risk worth taking. Adi, and you didn't often see this, seemed to have been stamped an "artist" at birth.

Was he being idealistic, or plain unrealistic? Perhaps. But he knew that in his culture, as in many others, perhaps all others, an artist was a nobody, or a somebody in the same way that everyone was a somebody. It was not quite reputable as a profession and, unless Adi became very famous, it would do little to improve his social standing. Birth, family background and wealth were what determined a person's position in society, what you might do, how you might live, and when and whom you might marry. But while family connections mattered, and overseas study would not change his social or economic prospects, it might provide him a ladder.

This was what motivated and excited Pak Harto and he believed, rightly or wrongly, that Adi was at just the right age to benefit from the skills, stimulation and encouragement the art school could offer. He knew this because he had once been a student, and then a teacher, there himself.

There was also the matter of a social debt. Decades earlier, when he completed his studies at the Institute of the Arts in Yogyakarta, Pak Harto had gone to Bali and, like many other young artists there, the older artists had welcomed and occasionally fed him. They gave constructive criticism, helped him to sell his work, and treated him as an equal. Now he was in a position to offer the same belief to Adi, and it was his hope that when his student returned to Indonesia, he would in turn inspire and assist other younger artists. And if he remained in Australia, he would inspire them anyway because he would always be a Javanese, Indonesian artist.

***

On the day Adi was to fly from Yogyakarta to Denpasar, and Denpasar to Sydney, Pak Harto arrived in a taxi to take him to the airport. For the send-off, a slice of the community had assembled at Totot's house. As well as his father, there were Adi's stepmother Yuni, Yanti and her husband Goenawan and their children – seven-year-old Fitri and four-year-old Dimas, his brothers Budi and Ismoyo and their wives and children, and his younger sister and brothers. There were aunts, uncles and cousins, and almost all their near neighbours. They knew Adi was going a long way from Java and would be flying over the ocean for almost a whole day, and they knew that when he arrived he would be living and studying with *londo* – white people – and non-Muslims.

They had confidence in Pak Harto because he was a teacher, and he, in turn, felt honoured by their trust. For this reason, he had taken care when booking the airline tickets to ensure that family members would be reassured, when they consulted the Javanese calendar, to see that the day of Adi's departure was particularly propitious for making long journeys and starting a new project.

After greeting Totot, the aunts, Yanti and other family members he knew, Pak Harto settled back into the front seat of the car to wait while they wished Adi a safe journey, and even pressed crumpled rupiah notes into his hand. Throughout the whole affair, Totot watched and waited as Adi went through the motions of shaking hands or receiving a hug.

Adi was holding his body in a stiff pose to help maintain his calm, and he began focusing on small details such as what his father and brothers were wearing – their best sarongs and batik shirts, or that his stepmother, aunts, sisters and sisters-in-law had their hair covered and were wearing the outfits they usually wore on important occasions. He himself had on jeans, a tee-shirt and trainers, and Yanti had cut his hair to shoulder length the day before. As the minutes passed, Adi strained to fix a snapshot of the colours and patterns of the sarongs, shirts and other outfits in his mind as a souvenir to take with him on his journey.

When everyone else had had their turn, Totot stepped forward, "Goodbye son, and remember to always be a good Javanese." It was an instruction that made great sense and had real import for all who were present. And for Adi also. Then, just as Yanti was about to hand over his goodbye food parcel wrapped in banana leaves, a small figure flashed forward and launched herself upwards and into his arms, leaving him no choice but to swing up both arms to catch her. It was seven-year-old Fitri, and she almost succeeded in knocking him backwards onto the ground.

"Little uncle, please will you bring me back a kangaroo from Australia?"

"Of course, darling," he said, hugging her tight.

When Adi went to lower her to the ground, his niece tightened her grip on his neck and her small frame began to convulse with violent hiccups that ignited the cloud of sadness and dismay that had gathered over them all. Throats ached and there was a twitter of concern as Yanti struggled to unpeel her sobbing daughter's arms.

As soon as he was freed, Adi fled to the back seat of the car where the chill of the air conditioning closed in around him. The driver released the handbrake and nudged the car forward onto the deserted road and, as they accelerated towards the crossroads, Adi felt a distance opening up between him, the family, the village and his old life. It was as if he and they were each holding the ends of a length of elastic and, with every metre travelled, the strain and pressure of holding on grew more and more unbearable. Soon he would have to let go. But not yet. Not yet.

Now. Now. You must. And he did let go, and his entire body jolted as though struck by lightning. Adi swivelled around for one last look as the driver switched on the indicators to make a left turn. He saw that they all were still there on the road, still waving, or so it seemed. He could no longer make out the faces, and all he saw, or thought he remembered later, was a sunlit blur of disembodied, upraised arms.

On this trip to the airport, just a few months before his twenty-first birthday, Adi did not suspect that he would miss bundling into the *angkudes*, the small vans he caught for the journey from the village to Solo and back. Or miss the excursions with friends and Pak Harto to the great Hindu temple Prambanan or the Buddhist monument Borobodur, where they slept side by side in nearby villages and woke with the sun to sketch and paint the carved scenes in dull greens and grey oils. He did not wonder who would join him to break the daily fast during the month of Ramadan, or consider how he would ask the forgiveness of his father and stepmother at the end of the fasting month. If he'd thought for even a minute that it would be a decade before he heard the call to prayer from the village mosque again, or the barrage of morning sounds around the house, would he have gone?

Pak Harto hardly spoke throughout the journey, and neither of them said a word when Mount Merapi loomed like a live, towering giant, a rare sight at that time of the day when it was usually shrouded in grey cloud. He remembered how on a trip to Borobodur once, they saw a bright orange balloon, a full moon, slide out from behind the tip of the volcano and light up its chuffing dark puffs of gas.

I am thinking in colours, he told himself, and he allowed a flow of soft blue-greens and pale turquoise to wash over and protect him.

Was it car sickness or fear that was causing his gut to churn and a flush of fever to wet his forehead? He clenched both hands until they hurt, and then stretched out his fingers and began pulling on them one-by-one until the joints cracked. His backpack lay on the seat and he dragged it onto his lap and wrapped his arms around it for comfort. He thought of Prince Rama in the Ramayana, banished from the court and sent to live among wild animals in the jungle. But Prince Rama had his wife Princess Sita and brother Prince Laksmana to accompany him, whereas he, Adi, was setting out alone. He knew how to use a phone, having practised at Pak Harto's house, but Pak Harto said it was unlikely anyone at the art school would speak Indonesian – let alone Javanese – and he would find this hard at first. Even though Pak Harto was an excellent teacher of English. Everyone said so.

Adi had faltered when Fitri's sobs vibrated through him, but now he willed himself to sidestep the molten flow of anxiety that threatened to crash over him. Although grateful to Pak

Harto, there was also embarrassment at being the one chosen, and this had burst out of him when he went to see Yanti for the last time.

"Why did Pak Harto choose me out of everyone?" he asked and, as always, she stood and listened with her head on one side, the way she did when she was paying attention.

And then she squeezed his arm and said in a quiet, clear voice, "This is God's will. God wants you to do this, and God will take care of you."

Now, there in the back seat of the car that was speeding him away from all those he loved, he clung to this truth to keep him strong.

At the airport, the taxi driver handed Adi his bag, and Pak Harto presented him with a long parcel wrapped in brown paper. It was a gift, he said, as they walked towards the entrance doors.

"Have a safe journey," Pak Harto said as he shook his hand, "Work hard and try to do what the teachers ask. Be a good Muslim and don't be in a hurry to return. Stay for as long as you can."

And then, as an afterthought, he whispered with startling urgency, "Stay away from politics. There are spies. It's not safe for you to criticise the government there. Be careful. People will be watching."

Pak Harto pressed a hand down on his shoulder and propelled him towards the security doors. When he was through to the other side, Adi looked back and saw his teacher place the palm of his right hand to his heart. He returned the gesture, and then the gathering crowd began pressing him forward. When he turned to see his teacher one last time, Pak Harto had vanished.

Part Two

Sydney
1997–2001

Chapter 5

It was early in the morning when Adi caught his first glimpse of Sydney through the egg-shaped window of the plane. The sky was an electric blue colour he had not seen before, not even in a paint tube, and the absence of a single cloud moved him to feel that God was granting him a special gift for his arrival.

Below him, the city's vast spread of terracotta roofs was interlaced with straps of grey bitumen on which the specks of cars inched forward in different directions like minute ants. Occasionally, he caught sight of a large expanse of dark grey-green vegetation, a jungle perhaps.

The grid-like order of the city streets was like a child's drawing, with row upon row of houses set in neat rectangles with a green field at the back. In some, silver mirrors glistened like lonely rice fields waiting to be sown and, as well as one large building, there were often one or two smaller buildings, perhaps for other family members or servants he thought. Fences were dead straight as if drawn with a ruler and he puzzled about the pair of straight narrow strips that ran parallel down the side of the houses to a smaller building at the back.

Solo and Yogyakarta were his sole models of a city and he had imagined that Sydney too would be a collection of villages, with a main street like Jalan Malioboro that bustled day and night with people, cars, motorbikes and becak. In an instant he felt transported back into the streaming press of bodies that nudged him along the city's colonnaded footpath as he cast quick sideways glances at lowset stalls selling leather goods, wooden toys and souvenir tee-shirts on the road side, or into the stores stocked with stationery, clothes, fabrics and electrical goods on the other. Jalan Malioboro, where sad-faced toothless old women held out a cupped claw and whined until he gave up a few coins. They reminded him of the children's song, "Burung Kakatua," and with this thought he could hear Fitri singing the words of the song in a high, clear voice as she played with her friends:

Burung kakatua hinggap di jendela
nenek sudah tua giginya tinggal dua.
Tredung, tredung, tredung tra la la
Tredung, tredung, tredung tra la la
Tredung, tredung, tredung tra la la
Burung kakatua

The plane circled, turned on its side, and then straightened before sweeping down over an expanse of water. With gears and engines roaring and the whole vibrating, the plane seemed about to explode. He felt his body brace, fear gripped his bowels, and when he touched a hand to his forehead a layer of sweat dribbled onto his palm. Around him, the other passengers and crew remained calm while a small child across the aisle clung to an emerald green cloth elephant.

Adi slid both hands under his thighs and braced as the plane's great black wheels reached for the tarmac that was rushing up to meet them. The plane thumped down and thundered forwards as if it would never stop. He had had this experience before at Denpasar and he willed himself to breathe in and out until they glided to a standstill. When the engines were turned off, and people began rising from their seats, he felt seized by a deep trance-like desire to laugh like crazy, and leap up and down in a wild dance.

He had arrived. He was alive.

Chapter 6

The journey from the airport was a pastiche of colour, sound and speed as the taxi and traffic glided between the broken white lines. In the taxi, the seat felt soft and cool beneath him and there were odours: the smell of plastic and vinyl, and the soap the driver had used to bathe.

A cool breeze worried his face through the open window, and he saw cars and trucks, but no bicycles, becak or motorbikes. He saw car indicators winking red to signal a move from lane to lane, and traffic lights that commanded the vehicles to stop-start, stop-start. Enormous trucks with drivers seated high up above the traffic rattled to a halt beside them at the lights. Some dragged long, empty trailers that made a metallic racket as they passed, and some strained forward on the green light, roaring louder and louder as they gathered speed and worked their way up through the gears. As the taxi pulled away from them, he heard once again the crackled voices of the taxi radio and hum of the other traffic.

He was surprised at how quickly the traffic was moving. It was faster than he was used to, 80 km per hour, yet it was orderly and polite, like a fine gamelan orchestra in which everyone took their turn to perform. And just as he began to relax under the press of the seatbelt, a crashing roar from above smothered all other sound and made the car, and them in it, shudder. In fright, Adi pushed his body into the back of the seat to repulse the strongest urge to let go the seat belt and slide down onto the floor in front.

The driver turned to him, "Plane," he said, pointing upwards, and Adi looked out and saw the underbelly of a giant aeroplane whose wheels were folding up and under it like a rising waterbird's legs.

When his breath had steadied, Adi glanced at the car's clock and saw that it was almost seven o'clock. Throughout their journey the car windows had been down, but now he felt the sun turning up the heat on the bitumen blue road and concrete surfaces. As the sun inched higher in the sky, blinding sparks ricocheted off the rear car windows of the cars in front.

The taxi driver felt the change in temperature too, "Gunna be a hot one, they reckon. Might hit forty. Don't reckon it will, but. Early thirties maybe."

Adi nodded. He thought the driver might be referring to the heat.

"It summer?" he asked, looking up and noting the wisps of white cloud that brushed the intense blue. He must remember to mention that blue to Pak Harto when he wrote to him.

"That's right," the taxi driver said. "February is the last month of summer and the hottest. Hot and humid. Don't mind the heat, just can't stand the bloody humidity."

The taxi driver's hands were relaxed on the steering wheel, turning it slowly and lightly, causing the car to glide in any direction with just the slightest touch. Adi watched as the driver set off the clicking rhythm of the indicators, glanced into the rear or side mirrors, or jerked a look over his right shoulder to change lanes. After the speeds they had been travelling, he noticed that a string of red lights was forcing the traffic to slow down.

There was a puzzling empty neatness to the wide, sealed roads, gutters and footpaths, and the foliage on the roadside plants appeared faded and dusty, as if the rainy season had refused to arrive. Pak Harto had explained there were four seasons in Sydney, and no wet or dry season like he was used to, and when Adi heard this he wondered what it would be like to experience autumn, winter and spring.

Only once in his life had he experienced bitter cold, and that was when he and his friends had climbed the northern slopes of Mount Merapi in the early dawn. Then the cold had possessed them like a demon. It seeped into their skin and bones and did not leave them until they came down from the mountain and were right back in the village again. How their feet had ached as they slipped and slid on the damp mountain track in their sandals, and how their bodies shook. No matter how many sarongs they wrapped around them, they still could not get warm.

The taxi came to a halt in front of a three-storey terrace house with a sign, "Darlo Boarding House. Men Only. Apply Within" and, underneath it, there was another – "No Vacancies" – which swung on a pair of cup hooks. As the taxi pulled away, Adi picked up his bag, pushed open the black iron gate and stepped up to the concrete footpath that adjoined a rectangle of spiky damp grass. The front door of the house was painted a shiny red and next to it, on the narrow verandah, the slats of a wooden seat were painted red, yellow, green and blue. The collection of primary colours was so surprising that it struck him he had arrived at a magical place.

He knocked on one of the patterned panels of frosted glass set into the front door and saw a blur of movement on the other side. There was a clicking sound, the door opened, and he saw a tall, large-boned woman in a sleeveless summer dress. She was much taller and stronger than any woman he had ever seen and her pale skin was covered in faded orange freckles. Her short auburn-dyed hair was folded into tight rolls, and was so thin he could see her scalp.

Although she seemed stern, perhaps even cross, the words she spoke were kind, "Good morning, I'm Marj and you must be our guest."

She smiled at him and asked, "How do you say your name? Aye-dee, is it?"

Her voice was as booming as the revving trucks he'd seen from the taxi, and it took a moment to realise she was asking him a question.

"Ad-dee," he pronounced at length, taking care to keep his eyes down.

Marj stood to one side and gestured for him to enter. "Eddie. How about I call you Eddie? Come in love. C'mon, I'll take your bag."

He felt intimidated, and not just because of her loudness or the magnificence of her bare arms and ample breasts. She, Marj, was commanding, and when she held out a hand for his bag, he gave it up with only the slightest hesitation.

Marj hadn't been especially keen to take in another foreigner, not that she had any problems with Akira, and anyway you could only tell Akira was foreign by looking at him. But when she asked Akira and the Boys what they thought, Akira had said why not give him a go, and Archie and Bert said nothing. They'd been more concerned when she'd taken in Akira because the Japanese were the enemy in the war.

"Not sure you ought to be taking in a Jap, Marjie," Bert had said, and while Archie said nothing, Marj could see he agreed.

Ultimately, it was her decision and she was glad about that now because no one could be better than Akira. He was clean, thoughtful, quiet – well, except for the piano playing but that was alright. Seemed quiet now when he wasn't practising.

She had given Adi a good looking over when she opened the door and the first thing she noticed was the unusual stillness about him. He was probably about five foot eight, an inch or two shorter than her, but terribly thin, healthy but thin. He averted his eyes from her gaze but not before she noticed they were fringed with thick black lashes.

"Ya, ya." Adi murmured. He looked tired.

"Right you are then, Eddie, come on in. Wipe your feet, there's a good lad." Train them right from the start and you won't have any problems – that was Marj's motto.

Leaving Adi to close the door, Marj headed off up the stairs with his bag. "Room's just up here, love."

By the time he had closed the door, she was on the first landing and looking down. Seeing him still standing at the foot of the stairs, she called out, "C'mon dear. This way."

Once he was on his way, she turned right and went up several more steps to a second landing which was a hallway. She walked along the hallway, stopped at a turquoise door and turned the door knob, then stood aside for Adi to enter.

"Come in dear, these are your keys – one for the front door, one for the back, door that is, and one for your room. Everyone has a key so they can lock their door if they wish."

The light-filled room was simply furnished and had a faint smell of cleaning product that was not unpleasant. The warm white walls and high pressed-tin rose-patterned ceiling were freshly painted. The polished blue and white streaked linoleum was worn in patches and there was a navy chenille bedspread on the single bed. Marj pulled open the doors of a timber wardrobe to reveal hanging space on the left, and an open shelf and drawers on the right.

Some morning sun glanced through the single window that looked down an alleyway between the boarding house and the two-storey brick wall of the house next door. Adi glimpsed a backyard and saw men's shirts pinned by their tails to a square line. They were all khaki green or light blue and their long sleeves and arms lifted and shook as the contraption swung round and round.

When Marj broke the silence, Adi turned and gave her his full attention. "That's a Hills Hoist, love. Most backyards had them in the old days. Not so much now though. At least not in the city."

Marj's freckled hand was resting on the back of a brand new red desk chair that was pushed up under a wooden desk with drawers down one side. She patted the chair for emphasis and smiled, "Akira went and got you the chair and bookcase. He thought you'd need the bookcase for your books and art materials."

She gestured to the two-metre high pine board shelves next to the desk, and Adi followed her gaze to the armchair in front of the open window and waited for her to comment on that as well. Marj smiled at him once more and he saw a mass of deep lines crease outwards from the corners of her eyes.

She patted the top of the desk that was shiny and smelled of beeswax. "My son used to study at this desk when he was at the university. This was his room and he was a very good student. He's a lawyer now, y'know?"

There was a map folded up on the desk and Marj opened it and spread it out for Adi to see. Looking down and pointing to a large black "X", she said, "This is a map of the area. See, this is us here. And to get to the art school you just follow the arrows."

She traced her index finger along the series of arrows as she spoke, "It shows you where to go. You just go up here and across Oxford Street and then you're practically there."

She looked up and waved an arm towards the wardrobe, "It's down that way, and then you turn right. It's very close. Never mind, Aki's going to help you get ready for art school. That's Akira. Another student. He lives here too. The man at the art school says you have to go on Monday. Not tomorrow, next Monday."

Adi nodded. He felt lightheaded, as if he was in a dream.

"Now you get settled and in about half an hour come downstairs for breakfast. Half an hour. Downstairs," she repeated. "Alright? Half an hour. Eight-thirty, okay?"

When Marj reached the door she turned and said, "Oh, I almost forgot." She beckoned him onto the landing with her index finger, and the gesture was so rude he thought she must be angry.

"C'mon, I'll show you the bathroom. You'll be sharing with Aki and you both have to keep it clean, and keep the lid down on the toilet. Alright? You can have a shower now if you want. A good idea I think."

In the bathroom, there was a large freestanding iron bath with an overhead shower, a shiny pink pedestal hand basin, and a matching pink toilet with a black seat and lid. A mirrored wooden cupboard hung above the hand basin.

To his dismay, Marj led him to the toilet. "This is the toilet. Here's the paper."

Marj lifted the lid and seat of the toilet to indicate how it was to be used. "You stand and point into the toilet like this. Right?" Marj demonstrated. "If you want to do number two, you put the seat down and you sit. Right? No squatting on the seat. That's very bad for the toilet." She wagged a finger. "When you're finished you put the paper in the toilet and press the button here. It'll flush. See ..."

Marj pressed the button with a flourish, "You see, no standing on the toilet." She shook her head and finger in unison, back and forth, and looked down, "Then you put the lid down."

Adi looked at his feet for much of this performance. He was confused by Marj. Her body language and loudness suggested someone very *kasar* – unrefined, even angry. He thought perhaps she was joking with him, but she seemed serious.

The way she closed the toilet seat was loud too. Visually, he understood what she was communicating, but for what purpose he did not know and he contented himself and Marj by nodding, "Ya, ya." He did not want her to think him disrespectful.

Now Marj led him over to the shower.

He had encountered modern plumbing before and then, as now, he felt a sense of awe as Marj turned on the tap and the water flowed in a mass of single streams from the shower head. He reached out a hand to feel it on his skin and pulled it back when the water got too hot. The first time was in a new hotel in Yogyakarta where he and his classmates were attending an art exhibition. All of them had visited the men's bathrooms to observe the urinal and toilet cubicles, the flush toilets and marble tiling, the subdued lighting, expansive mirrors and porcelain; but of course Marj's bathroom was not nearly so large and grand as that.

When Marj returned him to his room, Adi took the towel from his bed, and went to take a shower and put on clean clothes. He had lain all his clothes on the bed and now he began putting them away – placing tee-shirts, sarongs and underwear into the newspaper-lined drawers of the wardrobe, and hanging the two pairs of jeans and a formal long-sleeved batik shirt on the coat hangers provided. Next he took the assortment of paintbrushes, paints, pencils and sketchpads from his suitcase and arranged them on the shelves of the bookcase.

At the very bottom of the suitcase, wrapped in a sarong, was an old *wayang kulit* puppet of the Tree of Life. Worn from long use, the leather *gunungan* was his most prized possession and, seeing a calendar, courtesy of the local butcher, hanging on a nail, he removed it and hung the puppet in its place.

Last of all, he undid the parcel Pak Harto had given him at the airport in Yogyakarta. It was a silk prayer rug, very fine, and woven in pale turquoise, soft browns and an earthy orange. As he opened it out on the bed, Adi saw a beautiful and sacred garden in a central panel, with the whole carpet bordered by a stylised pattern of flowers.

He wondered if Pak Harto had bought the rug when he went on Haj in Mecca and, as he skimmed the soft rich pile with his palm, it came to him with a rush of emptiness that he didn't know which direction to pray. He felt a flush of heat in his body and his eyes began to sting as he looked around and out the window to catch his bearings.

Where was he? What was he doing here? He didn't even know which way was north.

Chapter 1

The Darlo Boarding House was in a row of eight terrace houses and at the front it had the original wrought iron trimmed balcony with two pairs of French doors opening onto it from the upstairs bedroom. Above that, the building stretched to a third floor. It had five bedrooms and accommodated Marj and her four male boarders who each had their own room. At the back of the house there was an attached outside bathroom and toilet that were seldom used since Marj had converted two smaller bedrooms into bathrooms on the first and second floors.

On the ground floor there was an entry hall and staircase, with one large room off the hall that could be closed off into two separate rooms by some concertina doors that folded back against the wall. In the front room there was an upright piano and a formal dining table and chairs, and in the other there was a television, two armchairs and a lounge. Beyond that there was an informal dining room with one large table and long benches that could seat up to five people on each side.

When Adi came downstairs at eight-thirty, a young man with black hair pulled back in a ponytail was sitting at the long table. When he saw Adi he smiled and stood up.

"Hi, I'm Akira. You're Adi right?" Akira was holding out his hand and, after they shook hands, he gestured for him to sit down.

"Have a seat, mate. The Boys will be along soon. How hungry are you? Marj is cooking bacon and eggs for breakfast. That okay with you? I think she's got sausages on the go as well."

Adi scrambled in his brain for the English words and when he spoke his voice sounded hesitant, "I Muslim – not eat bacon."

Akira got up from the table, "Okay, then you'll probably want to steer clear of the sausages. They'll have pork in them. Will you have some eggs?"

Adi nodded.

"Alright, I'll let Marj know you'll have poached eggs on toast. Yeah?"

Akira left the room. For Adi it seemed curious that this young man reminded him of a cousin of his. He always liked that cousin and guessed that he and Akira were about the same age, but maybe Akira was older.

When Akira returned he was carrying two bowls and a box. He put them down and shook some dry yellow wavy shapes into the two bowls. "Cornflakes. Not sure if you'll like these, but you may as well give them a go."

He handed a bowl to Adi who watched as Akira added milk and sugar before picking up his spoon and eating. Adi followed suit and scooped up a mouthful. It was horrible, tasteless, and he didn't like the texture or the milk. With some effort, he managed to swallow the mouthful, and when it was gone he shook his head and put down the spoon.

Akira laughed. "Yeah, they don't serve rice for breakfast. You get used to it after a while … if you're hungry enough! But you know what, my mum gave me a rice cooker for my room that I've hardly ever used. But I'm sure Marj would be happy if we brought it downstairs and cooked rice in the morning. We can take it for lunch then as well. She's good value, Marj, really understanding."

Adi found Akira's Australian accent difficult to follow but thought he understood. "Yes, thank you. That good idea. And you? Is Mrs Marj your mother?"

Akira looked surprised. "No, she's not. She's my landlady – I've been boarding here for a year now. My room is next to yours."

Adi was puzzled because Akira sounded Australian even though he didn't look like *londo*. "You from where?"

"Originally? Japan. I'm Japanese. I came here with my family when I was ten. That's twelve years ago so you could say I'm Aussie now. My parents live in Canberra which is about three or four hour's drive from Sydney."

Akira spoke too fast for Adi to understand exactly what he was saying. "You study also?" he asked.

"Yes, I'm studying at the Conservatorium of Music. Jazz piano. That's my piano in the front room. You'll hear me practising. Marj and the Boys are pretty cool about that."

Akira looked up as two older men entered the room. One man was tall, perhaps six foot or more, and thin, a little stooped and with black hair and a bald patch on the top of his head. The other was shorter, wiry and strong looking, with a darker complexion and thick grey hair. Both were clean shaven.

"Oh, here they are now. Hey guys, meet Adi." Akira indicated the tall, thin man, "This is Bert," and then the shorter man, "And this is Archie. They board here as well. Marj and I, we tend to just call them 'the Boys'."

Adi shook the hands of both men. Hands that were strong, dry and calloused like a farmer's, with a band of deep wrinkles at the knuckles and wrists, and short clean fingernails. He hoped he could remember their names – that was something Pak Harto had warned him about.

"To begin with," he said, "it might be difficult to remember people's names because they are different to ours. And sometimes it might be hard to recognise them again, so try and think of a word – English or Indonesian – that goes with that person."

And so it was that he associated Bert with "bird," because he was tall and had long skinny legs like a water bird.

Chapter 8

On that first day in Sydney, Akira offered to be Adi's tour guide. Marj packed them a lunchbox each and, when they finished breakfast, they walked up to Oxford Street. The footpath was wide, smooth and empty of people and the lanes of traffic glided up and down the streets like choreographed robots.

"People, where?" Adi asked as he looked around.

Akira smiled, "You think this is quiet? You should see Canberra!"

When the pedestrian lights changed from the standing red figure to a walking green figure, Akira held onto his arm until the turning cars came to a stop.

"It's Sunday, a holiday. That's why it's so quiet," Akira said as they crossed over. "We're getting the bus to the Quay – that's Circular Quay. It's on the harbour."

On the bus, Akira bought tickets from the driver and, when they were seated, pointed to the red square button and explained how the bus driver only opened the door to pick up or set down at the designated bus stops. It was a different system – not like waiting by the side of the road until the van filled up, and no one hanging off the side calling for customers, or banging on the roof to tell the driver to drive off.

His brother Ismoyo had a job like that once, helping their uncle on the small van he leased from early in the morning to drive between the village and Solo several times a day, taking people to and from the market, work and school. Ismoyo's job was to collect fares and cram in as many passengers as he could, make them nurse their baskets to make room, or take their baskets when they got on, and hand them back after they were seated. The job only lasted a week because his uncle said he didn't get him enough passengers.

The bus continued down Oxford Street, turned right into Elizabeth Street and began heading north. Thanks to Akira, he was slowly getting his bearings. There were three traffic lanes and, between the red lights and forced stops to pick up or drop off, the bus made slow and steady progress. Akira pointed out the landmarks – Hyde Park, the City Circle Underground Station entrances – Museum, St James. On his left there were glass-fronted shops, all closed, and on the right a park with mown grass and trees whose thick wide canopies cast cool dark shadows on the ground.

When they got to the department store on the corner opposite St James Station, Akira told him that it was showcasing artworks by final year high school students in its shop windows.

"Every year they choose works by final year students across the state to put on exhibition at the Art Gallery, in regional art galleries and some shop windows in the city. You can see some of the artwork over there."

Adi turned to look but they had already moved on and were soon plunging down a steep hill. For this stretch the sky was blocked on both sides of the road by the tallest buildings Adi had ever seen. There were no other passengers on the bus now and when the bus stopped, the central door dragged open and they stepped down onto the footpath. Now, looking up, he saw skyscrapers, a crowd of red and yellow cranes, and then sharp slices of sky between buildings. He knew that north was straight ahead but, now that he was on the ground, the height of the buildings induced a kind of vertigo and fear that they were falling in on them. Added to that, the hill was so steep that it seemed to drop away beneath their feet, forcing them to walk in a strange jerking rhythm.

"Circular Quay," Akira announced, indicating the line of grey buildings that stretched from west to east in front of them.

Once again the streets seemed eerily quiet, but then the silence was racked by a deep rumbling overhead.

"Trains," Akira said, and pointed by way of explanation to the top level of the building.

At the Quay they crossed the road, passed through a gap in the buildings, and emerged at the ferry terminals. Here was noise, activity, crowds. And sea water – and an unfamiliar, but not unpleasant, smell. There was a holiday atmosphere too, like the sound of people who were happy and laughing. Overhead, the high summer sun split the air and was blinding in its intensity. He felt it burn through the fabric of his shirt and suck the moisture from his body. Thanks to Marj, he had been instructed to bring a hat, and he was grateful now to have it shade his face.

"Sydney Harbour," Akira said, and waved an arm at the animated jumble of colour, shapes and light.

It was difficult to focus. First the shifting crowds, then the wharf fingers stretching out into the water, and beyond all that – the sailing craft, motor boats, ships and ferries. And, overseeing it all, the giant charcoal-grey steel arch of Sydney Harbour Bridge. He had seen it many times in pictures, but now its sheer looming scale caused his heart to pound and his legs to weaken. Both the Bridge and the breadth of the harbour beneath it dwarfed all human activity.

Like a cheerful companion, the Bridge ducked and dived from view as they walked from one end of the ferry terminals to the other, as if overseeing all the to and fro in the harbour. Some wharves were empty, but on others the passengers flowed out of or onto ferries or catamarans. An enormous cargo ship loaded with red, yellow, blue and green containers glided from the right of the frame to the left until it passed under the Bridge and out of sight. Squat tugboats were on hand to guide it and they gave up deep-throated warnings like bulls muscling up for battle to any craft that looked like they might get in its way.

At a small park at the western edge of the Quay, they dropped onto the grass to watch the goings-on of the crowd. To Adi, the constant changing scenes on the harbour were like a full-colour, two-dimensional puppet show. On the water, a breeze blew up and began shaping the water into choppy ridges tinged with white and pushing forward a cluster of cream triangle-sailed boats – some with multi-coloured sails at the front – and when Adi stood up to get a better look, he saw that their crews were mostly young boys and girls.

Along the wharf, different-sized ferries sloshed into their berths, slapping rolls of wake against the massive anchoring posts of the jetties and, across from the Bridge, the Opera House curved up in a jumble of white ceramic edged waves from a tongue of land that poked out into the harbour.

"What's that smell?" he asked. He could even savour the saltiness of it on his tongue.

"Sea water – plus shell fish, seaweed maybe," Akira shrugged. "Do you like it? I love it."

The salty marine aroma mingled with the air and all memory of the earlier haunted emptiness of the city evaporated. Here the crowds were lingering, strolling or, like them, spread out on the grass. Behind them a group of young people, with pale faces and black clothes, sat in a circle. And to the side, a man, woman and two small children, all with cloth brimmed hats jammed down on their heads, took turns extracting food from a fat white paper parcel to eat. Every now and then one of the kids flung a morsel to red-legged seagulls and set off some ferocious squawking.

When it grew too hot on the grass, Adi and Akira joined the crowd along the foreshore to watch buskers doing acrobatics, fire-eating tricks or playing didgeridoo. On the way to the Opera House foreshore they dodged tourists taking group photos with the Bridge in the background, and then Akira led him across a vast square to the open gate of the Botanical Gardens, where a giant tree with dark-green glossy leaves and curtains of brown hairy aerial roots reminded him of banyan trees. Here, people and things – hills, grass, trees, picnic rugs – leaned or sloped, like the Opera House, towards the water, while the blaze of refracted colour off the harbour made the light so luminous that it felt like they had wandered into an impressionist painting.

Families were picnicking; children were playing with bats and balls, or rolling over and over down grassy slopes; and couples were lying on picnic rugs, reading or curled up in sleep. Akira led him on past exuberant flower beds, and along paths that divided or disappeared behind stands of palm trees. There were black sharp-faced bats, with soft rust-coloured body fur and black leather wings that wrapped tightly around them, hanging upside down from tree branches; and there was noise – a cacophony of birds calling, singing and laughing that took turns to be heard above raucous cicadas whose volume swelled and faded.

"Come this way, I want you to see something," Akira said. "I think you'll like it."

They were making their way up a straight, wide path that adjoined a stone wall and garden bed and, when they had almost reached the end, Akira took a right turn, and then a left, and they entered through an open gateway into a walled desert cactus garden in which succulent plants from all parts of the world grew and were labelled by name and place of origin.

In the surreal landscape, the stone walls and paved surfaces captured and stored heat to create a microclimate for the dark green and blue-grey cacti that carpeted the pink gravel in which they grew, or stretched sculptural limbs metres high into the air. Adi reached into his backpack for his sketchbook and, while Akira explored, began sketching all the strange textured foliage he could see from just one spot – spiked, clubbed, ballooning, chisel-shaped, disc-like, hairy and wavy-edged.

After leaving the desert garden, they came to an expanse of spongy grass that seemed like the earth had sprouted green hair and been given an all-over haircut. They kicked off their trainers and socks and laughed as their bare feet sank into the cool damp grass, and then went looking for a shady spot to sit and eat the sandwiches Marj had made for them. When they had finished eating, Akira left him to go and buy ice creams.

As Adi watched Akira walk over to where there was a building and disappear, a mist of doubt settled over him. He had felt fine looking at the new sights, but now he was beginning to feel overwhelmed – by the heat, colours, and myriad sensations. It was like being in a dream and he longed to wake up.

As the minutes ticked by and Akira still hadn't returned, Adi felt himself shrinking into the size and shape of a small lost child. What if Akira didn't come back? What if he left him adrift and alone in this alien city? How would he get back to Marj's? Was Marj, was this place, was any of it even real?

He pulled a sarong out of his backpack and spread it on the grass and when he lay down on top of it the earth's distinct smell – sweet and utterly foreign – seeped up through the pores of his skin and flowed into his body. He pulled their two backpacks towards him, curved his body around them and, with his face buried in the cloth of the sarong, slid into sleep.

Papa is ploughing the rice field with Pak Adji's water buffalo and he waves to Mama and me.

Mama says ploughing is hard work, but I think I'd like walking up and down in the squishy mud with my water buffalo.

Mama and I have a kite. We made it ourselves. A breeze bends the tops of the trees and little pieces of Mama's hair are flying around as she unwinds the string from the block.

I run away with the kite – holding it up, letting it go, watching it go up and up.

The kite bounces, waves and glides and Mama looks down and hands me the block with the string wound round it.

I hold tight, I feel it tugging, it lifts my arms, it wants to lift me up.

I cry out, "Mama."

"That's it, Adi," she says, laughing at the leaping kite that wants to carry me away.

Then all of a sudden the kite gives a funny twitch, leaps sideways, and dives. Splat.

It lands in Pak Adji's newly planted rice field and I start to wail because now the kite is all wet, but Mama seems almost pleased.

She pulls up her sarong, steps off the bank, and lets her feet sink into the mud. And then, catching her balance, she lifts up one foot and there's a sucking noise, and then another, and then another, and this makes her laugh as she moves along between the rows of green shoots to where the kite is.

At last Mama grabs hold of the kite and, holding it up high, climbs back up onto the edge of the rice field. When she comes back to me she has thick grey mud on her legs like the farmers and I cry even harder now because the kite is all soggy and broken.

"Don't worry," Mama says. "We can fix it."

She catches hold of my hand and we walk home along the road to our village.

And that's when I see them. "Look Mama, look at the yellow butterflies. They're following us."

Mama laughs and I can see her teeth. Her sarong is all wet and muddy but she doesn't care.

The yellow butterflies love Mama too.

Chapter 9

Leaving the Harbour Bridge, Lisa takes the western exit to Glebe, past the Fish Markets, up Bridge Road and, after bending away from Blackwattle Bay, swings the yellow Volkswagen the wrong way into a one-way street. She pulls up outside a large rundown terrace house, gives two short beeps of the horn, and watches as a tall, lanky young man emerges through the open front door.

Mack avoids eye contact as he pulls forward the back of the front seat and drops his bag onto the seat behind. He folds his long limbs into the front seat beside her and closes the door.

"Fuckin' late again," he growls.

Lisa laughs and gives his tangled blonde hair a rub with her hand, "Hey Mack, great to see you," she says, letting off the handbrake. The car putters forward, its engine chugging like a hotted-up lawnmower, and they head in the direction of Darlinghurst.

When they are close to the art school they circle the streets looking for a parking space. They are running late and so, when Lisa spots a car waiting to reverse into a vacant car space, she swings the beetle nose-first into the spot. The furious driver

55

beeps his horn, and gestures with two fingers out of his car window.

Before the engine has turned off, Mack opens his door, steps out of the car and retrieves his backpack.

"Not nice, but necessary," he says. "Quick, let's go before he jobs us."

They had a good half block to go up the steep hill to the art school and so they ran, flat out, as if they were racing one another.

Adi and Akira saw the blonde-haired couple running hand-in-hand along the footpath towards them, and then disappear. When they entered the art school the same woman was sitting on the cobbled stones of the courtyard and nursing a bloodied knee. The contents of her handbag lay all around and the young man was bending over to ask if she was alright. While this was happening, Adi and Akira began picking up the scattered items.

After assessing the damage to her knee Lisa looked up and, seeing Adi was about to pick up a tampon, leapt forward to snatch it up first. There was a violent crack as their heads collided and, holding her head, Lisa jumped up and began leaping from foot to foot.

"Shit, shit, shit, that hurt," she complained, as she took the tampon from his outstretched hand.

Adi's head was hurting too. "You okay? You hurt?" he asked. Lisa shook her head.

Mack was glancing at his watch, "Sorry guys, gotta go. Running late … C'mon Lisa." He took her by the elbow and began propelling her forward.

"Can you help us?" Akira asked. "We're looking for Building C for the Life Drawing class."

"Sure, that's where I'm heading. Lisa, you go on ahead."

Adi turned to Akira and raised a hand, and then fell in behind Mack who was striding off after Lisa. When he heard

Akira calling, Adi turned, "Hey, Adi, I'll meet you back here at 5 o'clock, yeah?"

Adi smiled and gave him a thumbs up, and then jogged a little to keep up with his guide.

It was his first day at the art school and Adi felt shaken by the close encounter with the young woman with pale mask-like skin, green eyes and full deep-red lips. Her halo of blonde frizzy curls, her faint smell of sweat and shampoo, and the whisper of her breath on his face had detonated in him a fantastic desire. Only in magazines had he seen such women and, even then, only rarely. There was a tightening in his groin and he felt slightly faint and disgusted with himself as they entered the Life Drawing class.

They were the last to arrive and the other students were already seated at their easels and had a large drawing pad open in front of them. Taking a lead from them, Adi put his pad on the easel and reached into his bag for his pencil case. It was quiet in the room and there was a sense of expectation. His hands were shaking.

The lecturer looked up from her watch. "Welcome to Life Drawing. My name is Jane Wilkins and I'm your teacher for the year. We're just waiting on the model who will be with us shortly I hope. You'll have two minutes per pose and I want you to focus on curves. We're not worried about proportion today – just curves."

All eyes turned to Lisa who was wearing a mauve embroidered silk kimono and had just entered through a side door. She was using the palms of both hands to push her hair up so she could secure it into a knot on the top of her head, and when that was done she took off the kimono and stepped up onto a low rectangular platform in the centre of the room.

The lecturer waited as she settled into a position. "Ready Lisa?"

Lisa nodded and Jane pressed her stopwatch. "Start drawing everyone … "

The platform elevated Lisa above the students. From where they stood, she seemed seven feet tall, and the mass of pale curls she'd just pinned was already loosening, so that a strand dangled in a corkscrew at the side of her face.

When Adi looked up, he saw that the model was facing him. Strong, muscular, she was holding the position as steady as a statue. He drunk in the broad shoulders and strong upper arms, the round firm breasts, the dark pink moons of her nipples, and her broad slightly tanned feet. Then he registered that it was the same woman they had encountered in the courtyard. Her pale skin glowed in the natural light and there was the bloody knee, red and angry-looking.

She was studying him through half-closed lids as if she was turning the tables, mirroring his gaze and fixing him with her own. Every time he looked up from his pad, she was still fixed on him. He blushed, became flustered, and struggled to regain his composure. It seemed as if she was laughing at him and he kept his head down to avoid any further possible eye contact.

Glancing around, he saw that the other students were unhesitating, concentrating, drawing – and he became seized with a great shame that he and his fellow students, whom he did not yet know, were staring at this woman and drawing her naked body. He picked up the pencil but his hand would not draw. He put it down. His heart was pounding and the rush of blood was making his head ache. No one, nothing, had prepared him for this. Had she no father, mother, brothers, sisters, aunts, uncles? What would they say if they knew? Maybe it's them, maybe they send her out to work like this?

When he could stand it no longer, he gathered up his pad and pencils, and the next thing he knew, he was in the courtyard and bending over a garden bed as if he might throw up. He felt confused. A memory surfaced. A child's drawing of a figure, an adult's face looming – his father's or was it a teacher's? And then his face stinging from being slapped so hard he felt his child's body lift up from the floor.

When the feeling of nausea passed he sat in the shade and began fingering the phone card Pak Harto had given him so he could call him at any time. But how could he tell his teacher about the encounter with the beautiful woman in the courtyard, or about her appearing naked for a whole room of men and women to draw. He could not admit this, and he could not go back to that class. Could not, would not.

At the front office, Adi spoke to Liz, the office administrator, and begged her to excuse him from the Life Drawing class.

Liz listened to all that he had to say and then shook her head, "I'm sorry, Adi, I can't excuse you. I think it best you speak with Phil Clarke, the Head of Drawing. I'll see if he can see you now."

She picked up the reception area phone, spoke briefly, hung up and then wrote a name and room number on a piece of paper.

She handed him the note, "Phil Clarke will see you in his office now," she said. "He's in Room 46. Just go down the corridor, it's the third door on the right. Good luck."

When Adi knocked on the door, there was no response. He knocked again, and this time he heard a command, "Come in. Come in."

He pushed open the door and saw a giant of a man leaning over a paper strewn desk. His high forehead and hairless head were smooth and shiny, and he was tracing the index finger of his right hand down the columns of figures on the sheet of paper in front of him. Without looking up, he shifted his attention to a large desk calculator and drummed at its keys with the fingers of his right hand.

"Come in, come in," he ordered, without looking up. "Close the door, sit down, I'll be with you in a minute."

Adi closed the door but remained standing. A minute passed before the man looked up from his paperwork, and Adi saw with alarm that his eyes were bloodshot, and his nose was a deep purple and pitted with holes. He felt his skin prickle.

"Sit down," he barked, and waved a hand at the chair in front of the desk.

Phil Clarke had been Head of Drawing for five years and while he didn't mind the administrative work he hated spreadsheets and budgets. If Liz hadn't been so insistent, he would've asked her to tell the young man to make an appointment for another time. Now he leant back in his chair and placed his fingertips together in front of him.

"Your name?" he asked.

"Adi." He spoke so softly that Phil had to strain to hear and he saw that, as a mark of respect, Adi was directing his gaze to the edge of the desk to avoid making eye contact.

In the morning light, Adi's shoulder length black hair seemed to emit deep indigo flashes and the draughtsman in Phil eyed with pleasure the thick eyelash-fringed eyes and almost perfectly drawn eyebrows. He remembered a visit to Bali, decades earlier, when he'd stayed at the house of an Australian artist, drawing and painting all day – he'd been so young then, probably the same age as this young man.

"Well, what can I do for you Adi?"

Beads of sweat caught the light on Adi's forehead as he strived to smile, gave up, and then let out a strangled giggle of anxiety. The English words tumbled out in a staccato rush, "The Life Drawing class. No good. Woman naked." He held out his hands, "I Muslim, must not draw. For me, this very big shame."

Phil remembered that he knew of this student, "You're the Indonesian student, right? Here on a scholarship right?"

"Yes, yes," Adi stammered, looking back to Phil who was beginning to stand up.

"Well, you have to do Life Drawing. No exceptions. Everyone has to do it – black, brown or brindle. You understand? If you're a student and you're a Muslim, you still have to do it. Get it?"

"The human body," Phil announced as he raised his six-foot-four tall body and grossly extended gut up from behind the desk, "is a beautiful thing."

He moved to the door and held it open for Adi to leave.

When Adi had gone, Phil called Liz to vent, "Whoever sends these kids should explain what they're here for. They should know life drawing is at the heart of what we do here."

Then, after receiving the required sympathy from Liz, he softened. "Poor bugger," he thought, "might've been a bit harsh – I'd better have a word with his lecturer tomorrow."

Chapter 10

Adi took the train to Lakemba on his own. He was to meet with the social worker at the Islamic Council of Churches, Pak Bambang, who suggested they get together after Friday prayers. Because it was his first time on the suburban train system, Akira walked him to Central Station, showed him where to buy a return ticket, and explained how the turnstiles worked.

Lakemba was a very different place to Darlinghurst and the inner city. Here there were Arabic signs on many of the shops and, inside them, he found spices and foods he'd not seen before. On the street, men stood casually chatting or drinking coffee at outside tables, and he was surprised to see so many women with their hair covered. One was even wearing a black niqab, something he'd not seen very often before in Solo.

It was his first time to enter a mosque since arriving in Australia, and it was a great relief to be joining in the prayers. There was carpet on the floor instead of tiles and he was pleased that Pak Bambang had told him not to bring his prayer mat. He would've felt like an outsider if he had. There he was, standing one among many, facing the Qiblat, ready and waiting to respond to the familiar Arabic words of prayer, "Allaahu Akbar". Through each of the familiar movements, bowing, his hands to his knees, then performing the sujud on his knees, his forehead kissing the earth, on and on through the first, second, third and fourth Rak'ah, and then the final greeting of Salaam from right to left, shared with the men beside him.

Bit by bit, the stress and anxiety of the past three weeks was released in prayer and, just as the canny social worker hoped, when he emerged back onto the street he felt a deep peace and sense of safety for the first time.

Adi liked Pak Bambang the moment he saw him, perhaps because he reminded him of his art teacher, Pak Harto. When they entered his office and were seated, Pak Bambang began by telling him his own story of how he arrived in Sydney at the age of ten when his father took up a position at the Indonesian Consulate, how he attended Sydney University to study social work, and how he returned to Indonesia to do a Master of Sociology at Gadjah Mada University in Yogyakarta.

After completing the degree, he had returned to Sydney to marry his Lebanese-Australian fiancée, Wafa. And now, he said, he and Wafa had three girls aged fourteen, seventeen and nineteen. Their eldest was at university, the middle one was in her final year of senior high school, and the youngest was attending junior high school.

Pak Bambang spoke both Indonesian and Javanese but said his Indonesian was better than his Javanese. It was relaxing to be speaking Indonesian again and when Pak Bambang finished giving a brief resumé of his own life, he encouraged Adi to tell him about his family, the village, where he attended junior and senior high school, and how he came to be in Australia. Finally, when he thought Adi was feeling at ease, he asked how he could help, and so, for the next half hour, Adi related the story of his encounter with the Life Drawing model, the subsequent discussion with the Head of Drawing who looked like a giant demon, and his fears that he might lose his scholarship.

The counsellor listened intently, nodding and repeating *terus, terus* to encourage him to unstop the dam of emotion and complaint inside him. It wasn't just the Life Drawing class, there were other things troubling him, impressions that made him wonder what kind of place he had come to. Out it came – all that he had seen and heard, the guilty judgements, the uncertainties, the confusions, and his interactions with people who seemed rude, and even angry. Even the Head of Drawing. They seemed out of control, and at times this made him feel nervous, even frightened.

He did not know what would become of him if he stayed in this place. Perhaps it would be better for him to return to Indonesia, even though he knew this would bring great shame on him and his family. His voice quavered and at times he struggled to maintain his composure. All the while Pak Bambang listened and murmured encouragement, even when he came to the final, most shameful of impressions – of prostitutes soliciting, of homosexuals drifting in and out of the bars on Oxford Street, of bondage displays in shop windows, of syringes scattered in the park. But most distressing of all to him were the homeless people, so many of them, young and old, women and men – sometimes abusive, drunk or on drugs – sleeping alone in parks or bus shelters. Why did no one care for them?

It was not quite three weeks since he had arrived but already it seemed such a long time, and he felt tired, so very tired with it all. His life had been filled with wild colours, jagged reds and oranges, purples and greens. All competing, setting him off balance, and it was as if his identity, and even his very soul, were under attack. The joyful naughty boy once loved by a whole village – that solid base – that sense of who he was and where he belonged, was gone, lost. He was lost, and he knew he didn't belong here. He'd known that the moment a very old, foul smelling man had abused him with alcohol breath – "Piss off, ya slant eye."

The wave of joy and ease at being able to express himself in Indonesian had swelled and carried him along, but now it left him stranded, and in the silence he felt the colour rise in his cheeks. It was rude to complain like this, what must Pak Bambang be thinking of him? But when he apologised, Pak Bambang simply said, "*Tidak apa-apa. Jangan khawatir.*" It's nothing, don't worry.

Throughout the monologue, Pak Bambang offered words of consolation, acknowledged how confronting these experiences were for a young man from the village, a very small village, and the courage it took to seize the opportunities offered, as he had done. At times, he also inserted words of compassion and concern for those who were homeless or driven to drugs or prostitution, and explained the multiple disadvantages of life for some people in big cities, even in a rich country like this. He described the ills caused by alcohol and explained that alcoholism was an illness. He talked about mental illness and how the society had still not found a way to properly look after people who suffered from it, not in Australia and not in Indonesia either.

Pak Bambang asked about Marj – what sort of person she was – the two men, Bert and Archie, Akira, his teachers at the art school, the librarians, the admin staff, the other students. In response, Adi found himself listing the many kindnesses he had experienced. Smoking with Bert in the back garden, helping Archie to prepare the garden beds for autumn planting, going with Akira to buy his art materials. When he came to Marj, he was surprised at how many things she did for him – cooking, cleaning his room, washing and ironing his clothes, enquiring about his studies, and even correcting his English.

At the art school, he was making friends with some of the other students, the ones he shared a studio with, and others who were in the same group as him. He learned too that some of them came from country towns and villages and were feeling shy and out of place in the big city, and how it fell to the more outgoing city students to draw them in – where are you from, where are you living, do you have family here?

Finally, the one remaining issue to be addressed was the one that had led him to Pak Bambang in the first place. Pak Bambang got up and asked him to wait, leaving him alone to sip his glass of tea. It was the real Indonesian tea he loved and he savoured the flavour as he sifted the stalks and leaves through his teeth.

On Pak Bambang's desk he saw framed photos of his wife and daughters at various ages and at first glance he felt there was something odd. What was it? Then he realised that in every photo they were smiling, all of them and even Pak Bambang. It was something he'd not seen before.

When Pak Bambang returned to the room he said, "I've spoken with the Imam and he says you are to continue with the Life Drawing class. It is a very great opportunity for you to have this scholarship and you must work hard and complete the course. Of course, Allah will understand that you do it with a pure heart. And, God willing, you will be a fine artist one day and will be able to help your brothers and sisters to educate their children as well."

Adi felt a great lightness of being as he walked to the station that afternoon, as if his feet were floating above the pavement. He could continue his studies with a clear conscience and he would not bring shame on his family.

On the station platform, the announcements over the loudspeakers were a slur of static. Is it English? he wondered. By the time the train entered the station, teenagers in school uniform had crowded onto the platform, ready to pour onto the train as soon as the doors opened. In his carriage, there were raucous, swearing boys seated at one end and, at the other, a group of girls chatted quietly. Soon he was the only one left in the carriage and he began sketching the train's interior. At each train stop he did quick sketches of scenes on the platform – a light post, a bench, steps – but no people. Not yet. That would wait.

As the train rattled through station after station without stopping, he felt a growing sense of curiosity, even excitement, about returning to the Life Drawing classes. Now, for the first time, he allowed a dream to take shape that he, Adi, might become an artist, perhaps even a famous one like Affandi. Perhaps one day his work would hang in an art gallery in Solo or Yogyakarta too.

Chapter 11

In the weekly three-hour Life Drawing class Adi scrutinised the human body. His first impressions were of the varying shades and textures of skin, then the effect of light and shadow on hair, angles and curves. Some people's skin seemed to welcome and absorb the colours around them, some glowed next to yellow, while others resisted or reflected or were drained of life by it.

Bodies were draped with fleshy curves, had curtains of flesh or puckering skin, ropey muscle and sinew; others were wizened, jagged, bony. Women's breasts pointed or drooped, were plump or wrinkled sacs, and the pubic hair of the women varied from soft orange curls that caught the light to straight matt black triangles. Nipples projected or lay flat, areolae were circular, sometimes elliptical, and all shades of yellow, pink, brown, almost black. Torsos curved in or ballooned at the waist.

The models varied from week to week. Some were regular fixtures so the students got to know them. Rose had been an artist's model for more than fifty years: "I like it, it keeps me in touch with the young ones – money doesn't go astray either," she used to say. Bill was a thin wiry streak in his sixties, with steel grey body hair and concave buttocks; and there was red-haired Sally, whose immense bosom and multiple rippling folds of creamy white belly vibrated whenever she moved or laughed.

Occasionally, there was a pregnant woman or young women with strong masculine type bodies in Adi's eyes. Among the male models there were corpulent breasted giants, muscled narcissistic types with all over tans, outdoor labourers with roughened hands, and men with tight bulging guts. There was a black man too.

Adi studied bodies like some people study the weather. He saw similarities and differences and slowly came to experience the uniqueness of each person. He pondered the concept of beauty and wondered how the individual shapes, textures and colour of different parts of a body could influence how you felt about a person – from revulsion to attraction, and even lust.

Details were important to him – the length of fingers or the shapes of finger nails or toenails, dimples in a chin or cheeks, the way faces and eyes glowed when someone smiled or laughed, tiny blonde hairs on a freckled arm, a black furry chest or back, the arch of the foot or eyebrow. Smells too – of shampooed hair, a person's breath, sweat, perfume, aftershave. All these and the way people moved – how they sat, got up, stood, walked – could pull on his emotions and influence the marks made on the page.

His teacher, Jane Wilkins, was a practising artist and she directed Adi to study the drawings of other artists like da Vinci, Rubens, Picasso, Braque, Whiteley. For a while he became obsessed with studies of Michelangelo's painting on the ceiling of the Sistine Chapel in which the bodies of the women were muscular and masculine, with breasts seemingly added as an afterthought. It puzzled him that such a famous and revered painting could have this flaw and when he discussed it with Akira, Akira sympathised.

"Yeah, it's like when I heard Joe Hodges didn't always play in time. I was shocked. I mean, like, he's one of the most famous jazz drummers in Sydney."

As he drew the naked bodies of men and women, Adi was drawn back to his childhood when he had been used to seeing women and men working bare from the waist up and wearing just a sarong – especially the older people who removed their kebaya or shirt to stay cool, or spare their clothes. No one seemed to mind that a woman's breasts, after raising so many children, sagged like skinny pouches as they bathed in the river or squatted to grind spices in the family compound.

But things had changed in the village, and more and more of the women covered up now, especially when they went out or for formal occasions, wearing pants and long sleeved tops with their *jilbab* – the scarves that covered their hair and shoulders and were pinned under the chin. They were called a hijab in Sydney, but he could not remember his own mother wearing one. In his memory, she was always wearing the traditional sarong and kebaya, and her long hair was either in a plait or rolled into a ball on the back of her head.

On the way to the shadow puppet show in my aunts' village, we see Pak Adji and his new rooster with the shining copper feathers.

I don't like the rooster, it pecks, but I like the birdcage. Pak Adji bought it at the Bird Market in Yogya and it's made of bamboo, with a round roof, and carved butterflies for the feet.

I want to go to the Bird Market too, and Mama says she and Papa will take us there one day.

Pak Adji has a cow. It is a soft yellow colour and he lets me pat her any time I want. I like the smell of the grass Pak Adji cuts for her, and the way she makes a funny gnawing sound when she chews.

"Good evening, Pak," Mama says.

"Yes, and to you, Mas and Mbak. Where are you going Adi?"

"The Ramayana, Pak."

He gives me a thumbs up. He always does that.

"Very good, little one," he says. "Perhaps the cruel Ravana will beat Rama tonight?"

"Oh no, Pak. No."

Yanti squeezes my arm. "Pak Adji is joking, Adi."

Mama likes a happy ending and that's why she and I like the Ramayana. She likes Sita the best, and I like Hanoman.

Papa likes the Mahabharata stories and my brothers do too, but Yanti likes everything.

The dalang is Mama's uncle and he lets me help him sometimes.

At the edge of the village there's an arched sign that says "Selamat Jalan." I read it to Mama, "Have a Safe Journey," and she smiles and takes my hand. On the other side it says "Selamat Datang" and I read that too, "Welcome."

We're going through the rice fields to save time. At first we have to go in single file on the little path and Papa leads the way, then Yanti, Budi and Ismoyo. Mama and I go last because we like to look at things.

Whenever a farmer comes along we have to stop and let him pass. Sometimes they carry a machete on their shoulder, and sometimes they tuck it into the back of their sarong. Papa has one too but he won't let me touch it.

The music is getting louder now but we have to stop to let some women pass. They're very old and from our village, and we can hardly see their faces because they have a big pile of grass loaded on their back. They're bent right over at the waist, and they have a stick in each hand so they won't fall over when they walk.

Chapter 12

On each day in his new life Adi was absorbing a river of new sensations, and responding to the intense emotions they incited. But alongside the raw aliveness of being in all the strangeness, there was the weight of sadness of missing his family and village, and of shame when he could not understand or be understood.

Something was changing inside him, and he sensed the sink holes that were opening up, and through which everything he felt or discovered was flowing right on into his art making. All of it was there in the painting, you couldn't see it but it was there, and on the outside he, Adi, appeared as still as an ocean pool at low tide, all clear right through to the sandy bottom, no dark places and no sea monsters lurking.

In the constant effort to stay afloat, to manage the anxieties of being in a foreign place, Adi found himself buoyed by two things: his studies at the art school and his adopted family at the Darlo Boarding House, where Marj was radiant in her role as head of the household. She ruled and protected, asked questions – learned when assignments were due, insisted on knowing results.

Marj knew more about their everyday lives than anyone because she listened and never judged or criticised, although she did give advice if she thought it was needed. She cooked, kept the house spotlessly clean, and the linoleum and the pot plants shone. The rooms were freshly painted and her decorating style was pure kitsch, with flying ducks on the wall, black ballet dancers holding up pleated pink plastic lampshades, Fler chairs, and even a framed Tretchikoff print. Akira dubbed it a retro collector's treasure trove.

"Marj," he said, but not in her hearing, "is so far out she's in."

On their birthdays she cooked a special meal, usually a roast followed by her specialty, lemon meringue pie, and a birthday cake, complete with candles – one for each year of their life. And there was a card signed by her, Archie and Bert, with a twenty-dollar note inside.

Ever alert, in late April Marj surmised that Adi was already feeling the cold and she took him around to various charity shops where they bought thick woollen jumpers and a jacket, wool socks and mittens, long johns and an electric blanket. It was his first winter in Sydney, and if it hadn't been for Marj, he would've suffered even more than he did. There was no central heating in the boarding house or the art school and, by May, he was already coughing and sneezing and struggling with the whole notion of using tissues.

From May until late November he wore a black woollen beret, a birthday gift from Akira, and only when the temperature reached thirty degrees for two days running did he concede that summer was imminent and he could retire the beret in favour of a cream straw hat bequeathed him by Archie from his "days of sartorial splendour".

When Adi began to paint, a drop sheet appeared on the floor of his room. At least weekly, his paint stained glass jars and plates were removed, washed and returned –

refreshed, cleaned, erased – and like an invitation, a nod of encouragement, to keep painting.

Even though he lived as cheaply as he could, he found the scholarship inadequate to live on and buy artists' materials, so a few nights a week he worked as a kitchen hand in a Japanese restaurant at Kings Cross. Akira was a waiter there and it was on their walks home together from Kings Cross to Darlinghurst that he saw a darker side of the city, one in which Akira had an almost uncanny ability to avoid aggression, either by spotting its potential and side stepping it, or by being so self-assured that even the drunks let them be. They walked this route three times a week, late at night, as if invisible, passing without challenge through the drug dealers, the prostitutes – male and female, the desperate, the psychotic, and those with no home to go to. There were cruising men, streetwalkers, fun seekers and backpackers on the streets too, but the most dangerous were the occasional alcohol-fuelled packs of young men.

Different times of the day brought a different crowd onto the streets. In the daytime, the sun shone, birds flew in and out of giant trees, and well-dressed people took to the streets – visiting the bars and cafes, meeting for coffee or a meal, shopping, or passing by on their way to and from work.

***

Akira's piano had pride of place in the house and if Marj, Archie and Bert were driven mad by the sound of him practising for three, four or even five hours a day, they never said so, and Adi grew to love the way the music was absorbed into the fabric of not just the rooms of the house, but their lives and bodies as well. It was present even when Akira was out, or no longer playing.

The first time he heard the piano's mournful cry, sounding like five instruments at once, it filled his body with a strange and thrilling melancholy. He had never felt the tug of music like this before and he sat on the stairs to listen as Akira played a tune he came to know as an old jazz standard called *Summertime*. It would always remind him of his first summer in the city.

He waited for Akira to stop playing and joined him at the piano. "I never hear music like this before. It sounds like many people playing. What do you call this music?"

"Oh hi Adi, been there long? It's jazz piano. Want to see?" Akira opened the top of the piano and he and Adi peered down at the wooden pieces and strings inside.

"You watch while I play." Akira played some scales and chords. "It's actually a percussion instrument, y'know, like drums. You've never seen a piano before?"

"My teacher had a piano in his house but I never hear him play. When you play, I feel it in here," he said, putting his hand over his heart.

Akira lowered the top of the piano and sat back down at the keyboard. "I'm jamming at a mate's place tonight with a few people – why don't you come too?"

A group of young musicians met weekly on the third floor of a city warehouse near Central Station where some of them lived. There was a creaking lift whose walls were painted in crazy bright swirls of colour and, on the landing, a door opened into a large room. At one end of the room there was a baby grand piano, a double bass lying on its side, and a drum kit. Lounges of all sizes, shapes and colours lined the walls and a square of lime-green carpet covered the floor. The lift artists had been at work on the walls of this room as well.

The core of the group were three jazz students from the Conservatorium of Music – Akira on piano, Zoë on drums and Jacquie on double bass. Sometimes they were accompanied by Matthew on clarinets and saxophones, or Claire on vocals, or

Josh on trombone. After his first visit, Adi began attending every week, listening and watching the musicians take turns to improvise, or improvising together, observing the different ways they marked the rhythm and beat with their bodies, the flashes of joy or laughter at the lines they individually or collectively laid down, or when they played their way into a corner and then back out again.

The way they improvised astonished him and he was buoyed by the richness and passion of the sounds, and the generosity and encouragement they gave each other. Sometimes, as the music washed over him, he felt his heart or chest expand, or his legs became so restless he'd have to stand, move around, or go outside to the narrow bridgeway for a cigarette. On most nights, time became elastic, stretched by the music, and his whole being was transported with it.

Akira was the main composer for the group and he often played his latest composition to Adi at home, explaining that it was the structure on which the musicians individually, collectively, and spontaneously fused their own listening and interpretation. Later, when he heard them improvising on their different instruments, and supporting the others as they took turns to play, Adi realised that each was wringing their own truth and beauty from the composition.

Hearing Akira practising alone was one thing, but what happened when they came together was quite another. As Akira put it once – said he read it somewhere – improvising was like three or four people stepping off a cliff to express their souls together. Jamming was their way of practising and, as the months went by, Adi sensed their growing skill and confidence. As Akira himself explained, "I 'play' the piano, the others 'play' their instruments, and when we come together we muck around."

Adi loved their playful approach, envied it even, and was inspired to approach his own work in the same way. The important thing he learned from being around them was that you had to risk everything, throw everything you had into it, even when you didn't yet know what it was. As an artist he wanted to emulate the concentration and pure pleasure they wove into their songs. It was okay to dare. Failing didn't matter, daring did, and no matter what happened, the reward was that they could always surprise themselves and each other.

He wondered if what he was witnessing – the sheer joyful collaboration and free ranging self-expression – was unique to the world of music or was it just jazz improvisation? To trust each other so implicitly, to bend and flow with, against and around one another like that. There was great spirit and openness in what they did. And respect. And later, he saw the same thing with the more experienced musicians – older guys and the small but growing number of women. Saw the same roiling effects of the music in their bodies and faces, whether playing or listening, or both at the same time, and they didn't care who saw them shaking, nodding, twitching, tapping, grimacing – whether in joy or pain he could hardly tell. Sometimes they just laughed with pure joy. Not everyone though. There were different personalities and just as some were light, still others were dark, moody, cranky almost.

On the nights he listened to them play, Adi absorbed the colours of the music and later, when he returned home, he painted them. Dancing the rainbow he called it, and he would work and work until all the music and all the colours were transferred from out of his body and onto the canvas. Only then did he sleep, and sometimes that was not till dawn, or lunchtime the next day.

In response to Adi's curiosity, Akira began playing him recordings of some of the great musicians, especially the jazz pianists – Duke Ellington, Abdullah Ibrahim, Herbie Hancock, Jessica Williams; and some Australians too like his jazz piano teachers; and jazz musicians from other places like Scotland

and Japan. They went to a music shop to see the instruments and hear their sound. Then, at Adi's request, when they listened to different tracks, Akira called out the names of the different instruments – saxophone, double bass, bass guitar, trumpet, trombone – or their combinations.

As Akira described how jazz first drew on the African rhythms brought by the slaves who were transported, centuries earlier, from Africa to North America, Adi began to imagine the world through the lens of a geography of music and rhythm. In one of these sessions, Akira began talking about the Civil Rights Movement in America during the 1960s, and the often violent struggle of African Americans for civil rights and non-segregated education, health care and public transport.

When he spoke of the way African Americans had been denied entry to everyday places like shops, restaurants, parks and swimming pools and described the impacts on the lives of musicians he revered, Adi heard Pak Harto's whispered words, "Stay away from politics," echo in his mind. In an instant, he felt himself recoil. It was an involuntary reaction, as if his body was putting up a wall, and sensing this, Akira said, "Sorry mate, I hope I'm not boring you."

Adi shook his head and told him no, but something had changed and they didn't continue with the Sunday sessions. Yet it had been enough for Adi to realise that, for him, painting was similar to jazz improvisation. And he soon learned – when he discovered the American artist Jackson Pollock, whose paintings invoked the passion and intensity of jazz, and even its repeat notes and riffs – that he wasn't the first to make this connection. For this is what he knew – like the twelve bar melody, you take a subject or palette of colours and you improvise, you take the basic rhythms, tones, textures and markings, and you mix them up to create something fresh – a new sensibility, a new way of seeing.

Chapter 13

The tingling pleasure of being immersed in the high tide wash of waves that broke over the rocky edge of the ocean baths at Coogee spoke to Adi of life and art. Swimming in the moody rock pool, where the only option was to get into the water and see what he could find in and of himself, reminded him to enjoy, be responsive, and be on guard. Depending on the tides, the waves either slipped over the edge and spread out in ripples across the pool, or they whipped the surface and unleashed a fizzing swirl that dragged at his body and threatened to drown him; and then he had to tread and flap his arms and legs to stay afloat.

When he worked on his art it was the same – past, present and future melded, time bent or stood still, doubt and judgement were suspended. An exhilarating sense of playfulness and discovery drove him on until everything that was within him flowed onto the canvas, and when that was done he felt emptied and satisfied. It was addictive, this feeling, and he sought it again and again. Not just the doing, but the feeling after the doing.

The transition to living in the city, in a new country, and attending art school would not have been possible without the lifeguards who gathered around him. There were the admin staff, teachers and librarians at the art school, some of the students, Pak Bambang, but most important were his housemates at the Darlo Boarding House and, month by month, he grew closer to them and learned about their lives.

Marj had raised her son, William, or Billy as she still called him, as a single parent. She had worked as a barmaid to support them until Billy turned ten and Marj received the news that a favourite customer had died and left his entire estate to her in his will. There was a house and a significant amount of cash and so Marj was able to give up work, and move herself and Billy into the house. By spending some of the cash, Marj converted the house into the Darlo Boarding House. Archie and Bert were invited to move in as tenants and, when Billy turned twelve, Marj sent him as a day pupil to a nearby elite private boys' school. Now Billy was married with two daughters, whom Marj rarely saw, but there was a series of framed studio portraits of them at different ages on the sideboard in the lounge room.

Marj's windfall had provided Archie and Bert with a secure roof over their heads, and who knows where they might have ended up if it weren't for her. Although he knew that they had been alcoholics, Adi seldom saw either of them drink alcohol, and while it was possible that one or both had been, or still were, Marj's lovers, Adi didn't think it respectful to give it much thought, and neither he nor Akira ever discussed it.

As the only smokers in the house, Adi and Bert often retired to a bench in the backyard that was reserved for their smokos.

"Smoko," Bert would say, and it was during these moments together that Bert began telling him stories of growing up in the bush and, once or twice, the time he served in the army in New Guinea in World War II. There was also mention of a failed marriage after the war, and Marj had once confided, but without referring to Bert directly, "A lot of the alkies – you know, alcoholics – were in the war. Never the same afterwards. I don't think their families understood what they went through. As a barmaid you saw them struggle, saw the damage."

Brought up on a farm, Bert knew how to fix things and the old laundry at the back of the house was his shed. It housed his work bench and tools, many of which hung on the wall in a spot marked by the tool's outline. He was fastidious about properly cleaning, oiling and maintaining his tools and machines and, when it came to fixing things, he would sit tinkering for hours, even days, until he worked out what to do. When he scratched his head and announced, "I'm stumped," it meant having a chat with Old Jim and the fellows in the local hardware shop to see what they suggested.

For Adi, Bert really came into his own during the second semester when he began the sculpture elective at the art school. It was Bert who instructed him on the functions of the different power tools – drill, sander, circular saw, jigsaw – and showed him how to weld. And he was the one who advised him when it came to constructing the things Adi saw in his imagination or sketched on paper.

No matter what he was doing, Bert was always listening to the radio – parliamentary debates, current affairs, the races. He read the paper every day, usually the *Sydney Morning Herald*, ("I wouldn't even wrap my fish n' chips in that other lot after what that man did to Gough Whitlam," Bert once told him, referring to the Murdoch-owned press). Most race days he went to Randwick Racecourse and Marj admitted she didn't mind an occasional flutter at the races either.

Archie said Bert was a "serious punter" though, and if you named any horse he would be able to tell you who the dam and sire were. When Adi asked Bert about this, he said his father used to train and race trotting horses, but he, Bert, was into gallopers, and he saw to it that Adi was "educated" to know the difference.

There were six kids in Bert's family and the youngest was his brother Jack who took care of his finances. Marj had a soft spot for Jack. "He's a good bloke," she told Adi. "Comes to Sydney every Easter for the Royal Agricultural Show and sees Bert then. Jack makes sure Bert's got money and when he comes to visit he always brings me a bunch of flowers and a pound of prawns."

Adi smiled. He liked the juxtaposition.

"What you gotta understand about Bert is he's very kind and he'd give all his money away to anyone who asked. So Jack makes sure the rent is paid and gives him a weekly allowance – enough for a couple of beers whenever he wants. And he's given me five hundred dollars in case Bert needs tools or has to go to the doctor or something. But Bert doesn't know anything about that so don't you go saying anything, will you?"

It was also Bert who kept Adi up-to-date on the volatile situation in Indonesia, and called him to the television as the worsening economy, rising petrol prices and collapse of the rupiah led to widespread, sometimes violent, demonstrations across the archipelago from late 1997. The images so alarmed Adi that he bought a phone card and called Pak Harto to find out if his family was managing alright. Pak Harto promised to find out, and suggested he phone every first Sunday of the month until things quietened down.

If Bert was the handyman, Archie was the gardener. He had the whole of Marj's backyard divided into rectangular raised garden beds that were filled with rich composted soil and the horse manure he brought from nearby stables in a wheelbarrow. Adi thought the wheelbarrow a brilliant invention and was disappointed to learn that neither Bert nor Archie was the inventor. Throughout the year, Archie grew and harvested vegetables and Marj stored what couldn't be eaten in the freezer, either cooking it first or simply freezing it. There were fruit trees too – two kinds of lemon, some banana trees, a persimmon, a fig and passionfruit vines.

Every now and then Marj had a "quiet word" to Adi or Akira to prompt them to ask Archie if he needed a hand with anything, and this was how Adi became familiar with the seasonal work of the garden – digging manure and compost into the soil, layering it with straw, nurturing and planting seedlings. It was from Archie that he learned the English names of the vegetables – even those he'd not known before such as capsicum, zucchini, eggplant, broccoli; and with every crop, Archie harvested the seeds of the healthiest and strongest plants and stored them in labelled containers, ready to be planted the following spring or autumn.

While Archie insisted Adi and Akira wear gloves when they helped him in the garden, he himself never did and they saw that he seemed to relish plunging his worn rough hands into the dark soil. Often, as they worked side by side, Archie would hand Adi some fresh picked peas to eat, or extract a carrot from the soil, wash it and urge him to taste the difference.

Archie had no family, he said, but he grew up in Balmain during the Depression and this was where his passion for growing vegetables took hold.

"Back then we had this old Italian bloke living next door, and he had a big garden. He even had chooks. And I used to hang about in there 'cos me mum and dad was always down at the pub and I guess they took me in, him and his missus, felt sorry for me I s'pose, an only child and being left on me own all the time."

Archie had to keep busy even when he was talking, and he drew his finger in a line down the garden bed. "I'd give him a hand and they'd feed me. Pretty fair exchange, eh?" Adi nodded. "Y'know what though? I never tasted tomatoes like what he grew. I keep tryin' different varieties but I still can't get 'em to taste like what he grew."

Archie was silent for a while, and when he spoke his voice was raspy, "Yes, they was very good to me and I always called them Mr and Mrs Rosso, not first names like nowadays. See them persimmons, they're in memory of them."

One by one, Archie began dropping beans into the drill he'd made and Adi followed, pushing the soil over them and watering them with the watering can. "I left 'ome at fourteen and went to sea as a merchant seaman, working in the kitchen." Archie wiped his forehead with his sleeve, "I never went back and saw the Rossos and I never saw me old man or me mum again neither. I ran into a bloke – musta been about twenty years ago now – went to school with 'im, and he said he heard they was dead, said Dad got hit by a train, drunk I s'pose. And me Mum – well he thought she mighta got married again."

Archie didn't like him asking too many questions when he talked like this, and so Adi moved on to thinning a crowded line of carrot seedlings.

"Water under the bridge," Archie said, and then to change the subject, "You got the same vegetables in Indonesia?"

Adi nodded, "Rice, onions, garlic, ginger, many things the same. Tomatoes, beans, cucumbers, carrots. But mainly different."

He didn't know how to describe the many varieties of fruits and vegetables in Indonesia because there was no comparison, and he only knew their Indonesian or Javanese names. Here, he thought, there was not the same variety because the food people ate came with all the different migrants. It was not what Indigenous people ate.

"Marj reckons you're one of them Javos. That right?" Adi nodded. "Yeah well I knowed some Javos back in the war y'know? They were seamen too."

Adi was surprised. "Were they here in Sydney?"

"Too right. They were crew on the Dutch merchant ships – y'know KLM and the like. They were held up here because of the war. I was a member of the Seamen's Union of Australia and when we found out the poor wages and conditions they had to put up with, we said we'd back them if they wanted to go on strike. So they walked off the ships. About two thousand of them."

"What happened to them?" Adi asked.

"Well, the Dutch had them locked up in Long Bay Gaol, and then when that filled up they sent them to Cowra Prisoner of War Camp."

Archie washed his hands under the tap and, after drying them on a faded towel, sat down on a garden bench. He seemed to have forgotten all about the gardening.

"Yes, he said, they just wanted the same conditions and pay that other seamen like the Dutch and Australians were getting in the war. Danger money, proper cabins and food, warm clothes. They were getting none of that. Well, it turned out the Dutch had to give them what they wanted because no other seamen would take their place."

"So they got out of gaol?"

"Too right, and it was a big bloody victory. They were owed wages too and that was paid, but then some refused to go back to the ships. They took on other war work instead."

They'd resumed planting, and Adi gathered up the emptied seed trays and began adding loose straw to the bed while Archie refilled the watering can.

"Later on the seamen formed their own trade union in Australia," Archie said.

"What's a trade union?" Adi asked.

"It's when workers, like seamen or waterside workers or teachers or nurses say, form an organisation to try to improve their wages or protect jobs. Sometimes, if the employer doesn't give them what they want, or they don't treat the workers fairly, they go on strike. They stop work until they get what they want."

Adi was surprised. "They can do that?" he asked.

"Yes. Many people in Australia belong to a union. They make sure wages are fair. And just so you know, the Indonesian crews walked off the ships again after the war because they refused to crew any ships that were taking arms and munitions to Indonesia. I was working on the wharves by then, and our union voted to stop loading them as well. We were on the Indonesian side by that time."

"I don't know this," Adi said as he began curling up the hose to hang it back in its place.

"Well the Javos was pretty damned organised as it turned out. They knew the Dutch would want to go back to the good life like before, and they were out to stop them. We just did what they asked, that's all. Can you pass me that fork? Good man."

Adi passed him the fork and Archie dug out two stubborn weeds.

It was the longest conversation Adi had had with Archie. Usually they worked in silence, or he explained how to do things like pruning or thinning seedlings, or he pointed out what he called the "gardener's friends" – a ladybird beetle, native snail or praying mantis eggs.

"Well, I'll be buggered. You're one o' them, like them Javos. Marjie said you was."

Adi did not know about this sliver of shared history, and he felt there was more to it. This often happened with Archie, he would begin a story and in its telling he, Adi, would find himself filling up with questions. Then, when he asked a question, he never knew if Archie would continue. Now he wanted to know more about these seamen who had been here waiting for the war to end so they could return to Indonesia.

Was it just these seamen? Or were there others? And what of his own family during wartime too? More and more he was sensing there were gaps in his country's history, things he did not know, or might never know, and they were like the missing pieces of a puzzle.

There'd been a few spots of rain and they still had to mulch and water in the rows of lettuce seedlings planted earlier. The straight lines of green recalled newly planted rice seedlings, and this brought a jolt of longing for the rice fields and the village.

When we hear the singing, the other kids push past Papa and run ahead. No one waits for me but Mama says, "Look Adi!"

There are two white waterbirds – one is standing in the water and the other is its reflection. I click my fingers and whistle and it turns its head. It sees Mama and me watching, then lifts its wings and rises up out of the water with two long thin legs dangling. It floats up into the sky like a kite, turns on a wing and fades into the distance.

Papa is calling us to hurry up. It's getting dark and I can see the wayang kulit screen up ahead. It's under the hairy old banyan tree near Bude Kartini's house, and the gamelan orchestra is in front and at the side. There are lots of people, and candles and kerosene lanterns, and big tubs of food on mats on the ground, and some people have mobile carts with glass cases.

I can smell the satays and corn cobs cooking, and there's rujak, Yanti's favourite. Mama and I made rujak once from green fruit salad, palm sugar and shredded green coconut. It was very delicious.

The Tree of Life puppet glimmers on the lit-up screen. Everyone is talking, but some are just eating. Papa unrolls a mat on the ground next to my aunts, and he and Budi go to buy food. I know where Yanti is and I want to be with her. Mama leads me through the groups of people sitting all around and I bend over and drop my right hand down like her to be polite.

Yanti is behind the screen watching the dalang get ready. He's Mama's big uncle and very famous. Mama sits down next to Yanti and I sit in her lap. It's a special privilege to sit behind the screen like a king. I call the dalang uncle, and when he sees me he gives a signal with a blink of his eye. I can see the puppets – Prince Rama, Princess Sita, Prince Laksmana and all the others. I look for Hanoman, the White Monkey general. There he is.

Papa brings food as the play begins. The dalang is funny, and makes everyone laugh. Sometimes I fall asleep but tonight I'm going to stay awake the whole night. I wait and wait, and when the roosters crow I'm fidgeting, ready and waiting for Pakde to let me help put the gunungan into the banana trunk at the bottom of the screen.

When this is done the show is over and it's time to go home, even though the gamelan is still playing. When Papa sees us coming he picks up Ismoyo and carries him.

Yanti and Budi are very sleepy, but Mama and I are not sleepy at all. When we reach the rice fields the sun is a fire ball floating up and Mama puts her hand over my eyes to stop me looking at it. We wait for the rice fields to catch fire, and then a noisy flock of ducks comes gabbling along the track and skives off, beaks first, into the water, legs paddling.

Mama and I laugh and laugh, and then we see the white waterbird again – walking around, lifting its skinny stick legs up and stretching them out one at a time like a silly soldier. I try to walk like the bird and Mama laughs and pulls up her sarong and tries too. *Yanti is too sleepy and leans on Mama's arm while we walk.*

In the village the women are scratching the roads clean with their stick brooms and burning off little piles of rubbish. Thin trails of smoke curl up to greet us as we enter, "Selamat datang," they say. "Welcome home."

Chapter 14

Adi couldn't explain why the city was female to him, but during those first years of being a student, he made friends with her moods, expressions and poses, and gave himself up to her beauty. He also took in her underbelly of crass commercialism, grieved when eye-catching graffiti was removed, and treasured her trash. In her labyrinth of back lanes, he studied the objects put out for garbage collection; some of it he brought home, but mostly he left it where it was, or photographed it as he found it.

At different times of the day or night, and in different seasons, he was out walking, exploring, sketching, painting and photographing. He returned again and again to favourite spots – harbour wharves and islands, headlands and beaches, forests and foreshores, parks and reserves.

In Darlinghurst, he registered the suffering on the faces of the homeless men and women who inhabited the crooked streets, or took shelter in the parks under giant Moreton Bay Figs, with their shopping trolley or meagre plastic bags of possessions. Sometimes they seemed familiar, like someone he knew – a relative or friend from the village perhaps – and this caused him to feel that all and everything were connected in some way. Not just people and people, but people and animals, trees, plants, soil, water and air. Even the trash.

***

In the entire student body there was only a handful of students that could be called "Asian" – two from Japan, one born in Vietnam, two Koreans, a Chinese, and he was the only Indonesian. He didn't feel Asian and couldn't even say for sure what that was. He didn't feel particularly Indonesian either, unless someone drew attention to it.

When he saw Asian students or people in the street or on a train he sometimes saw them as different because, most of the time, he was just a student like all the rest, sometimes sure of himself and sometimes unsure or anxious, especially when it came to writing essays – even though he had been matched with a tutor for help with this.

The real differences between students were their age and experience – about thirty per cent came straight from school, but the rest were in their mid- to late-twenties, thirties, right up to their sixties, and at least one was seventy. Some had children still in school, some were having a first or second child, some had studied or worked as graphic designers, lawyers, teachers, fashion designers, miners, sign-writers. A small number had been artists all their lives.

The first-year students studied art history on Mondays, still life and life drawing on Tuesdays and Wednesdays, and completed six-week courses in painting, printmaking, ceramics, sculpture and photography on Thursdays and Fridays. Midway through the second semester they were told they had to select two disciplines to focus on in their second year, and at first Adi found it difficult to choose. Unlike some who knew exactly what they wanted to do, and who resented being made to study anything else, he would've been happy to keep doing them all.

When he shared the problem with Marj, she suggested a dining-table talk with herself, the Boys and Akira, and it was as a result of this discussion that he decided to narrow his focus in second year to the two first year subjects he did best and worst in. The best was a high distinction for printmaking and the worst a credit for painting.

In their second year, Mack and Adi had studios on the same floor and, although Adi had not forgotten his encounter with Lisa, their paths did not cross again until she returned as a model towards the end of that year. It had been more than a year and a half since their first encounter and he was relieved there was no trace of the emotions that had crushed him back then. There had been a shift in perspective for him as well. Now it was the line on the page, not the model, that was the subject, and this absorbing process – the flow from the body and eye to the hand, to the charcoal or pencil marks on the page – happened in a zone that permitted no other exchange – no thoughts, no connections – in fact a state of not knowing. White light.

Jane Wilkins had continued as Adi's Life Drawing teacher and, at her prompts, Lisa adopted a different pose. She recognised Adi and, now that she was facing him, saw that he was working as if in a trance. The teacher was circulating, looking at each student's work, offering feedback and encouragement. When she came to Adi, she paused. It was involuntary – as if the work insisted she give it closer attention, or allow herself some felt emotion or sense of recognition in regard to it.

All that week the Head of Drawing had been visiting the drawing classes and Jane had been advised that he would attend her class that morning. When Phil Clarke slipped into the room, he nodded in her direction and moved from one student to the next, looking over their shoulder as they drew. Like Jane, he paused when he reached Adi, moved away, and then returned at the end of the class to ask to look at his earlier work. Adi handed over his sketchpad and began packing away his pencils as the teacher flipped through the pages.

He handed the sketchpad back to Adi. "Good work," he said. "Good to see. Keep it up." And then he turned and headed out of the room with Jane.

"That's the young man who begged to be let off Life Drawing at the beginning of last year, said it was against his religion. I told him he had to do it," Phil told her.

Jane never did find out why Adi missed those classes, "Oh that's right, he missed a few classes early on, but he's not missed a beat since then. In fact, I'm very pleased to be teaching him again this year."

Phil was relieved it had all worked out. "I was a bit rough on him, but he seems to have carried on. Impressive – it's going to be interesting to watch his progress."

"I expect he'll top the class," Jane said. It wasn't just his work she liked, it was his passion – it was contagious and made the whole class a pleasure to teach.

"I'd like to see him do drawing in an honours year," Phil said. "What's his major?"

"I'm not sure. Painting I think."

"Painting." Phil almost spat the word out. "I don't get why so many students choose painting, do you? In fact," he sighed, "I just don't get painting."

Phil was an installation artist and it wasn't the first time Jane had heard him say that. "He could still choose drawing for honours if he wants," she said, "but he's got a year to go before he has to make up his mind. We'll see."

Lisa had agreed to meet Mack at a nearby cafe after the class but there was no sign of him when she arrived. She joined the queue and, while she waited, a group of schoolboys filed in behind her and, as the line edged forward, the boy behind her was bumped into her by his friends. The first time it happened the boy apologised. It happened again, and this time his friends burst out laughing.

Lisa scowled and said nothing, but when it happened a third time she swung around to face them. "Look here," she said, "cut it out!"

Rather than restore them to their normal inhibitions and habits of courtesy, this seemed to incite an override in the boys, who momentarily became a pack. Embarrassed, the boy in the front moved to the back of the group so that another boy was standing next to Lisa. Then this boy was pushed into her.

This time Lisa yelled, "Just quit it, okay?"

The boys' laughter subsided into guilty silence and Adi, who was ordering his lunch at the front of the queue, turned to see what was happening. He left his tray on the counter and walked up to Lisa, took her by the arm and steered her to the front of the line. He gestured for her to order and then made room for her salad on his tray.

When they got to the cashier, Adi handed over the money, and they made their way to an empty table.

"Thanks for that – I was getting ready to cripple those guys. But, hey, you shouldn't have paid. Here … "

Lisa tried to hand Adi the money but he waved it away, shaking his head.

"C'mon," she said, "we're all students. You can't afford … " She stopped mid-sentence; she did not want to offend him.

Adi set the tray down and placed her plate and cutlery in front of her.

"I'm Indonesian … We don't do the Dutch treat," he said.

Lisa laughed and put up her hands in surrender, "Okay, I won't argue with that. Thanks."

"Please … " he said and gestured for her to begin eating.

Adi ate his lunch without making any attempt at conversation and she saw that his fingers were long and slender, the skin fine textured. While the nails on his right hand looked almost manicured, although completely discoloured with paint, the nails on his left were cut short. Oddly, though, his thumbnail remained a good inch in length.

Around them, the cafe was becoming quieter as people finished their lunch and went back to work or study, so when Mack and three other students came in, they infected the place with the noise of the street outside.

Lisa waved to catch Mack's attention and he strode over and kissed her on both cheeks, "Hey Lise."

"Everyone, this is Adi," she said. She'd met Mack's friends before but didn't remember their names.

"Yeah we know," said Mack, "he was in our group last year. How ya goin' mate? Hey Lise, d'you wanna hear a joke? There's this magician on a ship, right? And every day when he does his tricks, the Captain's parrot gives him a hard time."

Mack mimics the voice of the bird. "He's not really sawing that lady in half, there's two ladies in that box … " Or, "That box has a false bottom … "

"Every time the magician's doing his show, the Captain's parrot is there, and every day he ruins the show by telling the audience how the magician does his tricks. Like, the audience loves it, thinks it's all a part of the act, but the magician is getting seriously pissed off."

Adi had got to know Mack over the past two years but he still found him hard to understand. Something to do with the way he hardly moved his lips when he spoke, and his use of idiom. Also, while he could mostly understand conversations one on one, he often found it more difficult in a group. And if he was feeling tired, or he judged that what was being talked about wasn't important, he just switched off. This was one of those times.

"This goes on day after day and the magician's getting really fed up. Then one day the ship hits an iceberg and sinks. The magician finds himself in the water, and when a plank of wood floats by he grabs hold of it."

To Lisa, Mack's exuberant loudness seemed to accentuate Adi's stillness and she looked first at Mack, and then at Adi. Both were attractive, but they were a study in contrasts. On the one hand, the muscular, tanned surfie with his knotted tangle of blonde hair, blue eyes, day-old beard, dry sunburnt lips and large hands; and on the other, Adi's dark brown eyes, high cheekbones, wispy beard and sensual mouth, and arms that were a soft brown colour and smooth, except for some scattered longish black hairs.

Mack's friends were waiting for the punch line.

"The magician clings to the plank of wood, and when he looks up he sees the Captain's parrot sitting at the other end. Day and night they drift together, and neither of them says a word."

Adi looked up and saw Lisa looking at him. He returned her smile.

"Finally," Mack said, "the parrot couldn't take it anymore. "Okay," he said, "I give in ... What did you do with the ship?""

Mack's friends laughed, and then walked away to order their lunch.

Adi said, "The life modelling? Is that the work you do?"

Lisa laughed. "No, I just do that for fun. I'm a full-time student, studying fine arts at uni. This is my first year. I want to be a curator or a gallerist but we'll see.'

Lisa nodded towards Adi's sketchpad, "Would you mind if I had a look?"

He handed it over and looked on as she began turning the pages. She saw that he had magnified her curves and body shape, and given them a voluptuousness that, in her mind, was reminiscent of Greek sculpture. For Adi, though, they were in the tradition of the stone carving on the great monuments of Central Java.

"Do you think I'm fat?" she asked.

"Not at all," he replied, and when she gave back the sketchpad, he picked up his bag and got up to leave as Mack and the others returned with plates that were piled high with food. He saluted Lisa, and left the café.

"He's a bit odd isn't he?" Mack said to Lisa who was watching Adi cross the road to the art school.

"I like him," she replied.

"He's a bloody good artist. Has a bit of a problem with the language, I think, tends to keep to himself. But he's improving."

"He shouted me lunch and when I tried to pay him back he said he didn't go in for a Dutch treat. It took me a minute to get the joke," Lisa said.

Mack looked puzzled, 'So, what's the joke?"

Mack's friend Jordan rolled his eyes, "Like derr? Indonesians were colonised by the Dutch. Also it's customary to shout if you invite someone to eat with you."

Mack paused before biting into his hamburger. "But if you had to shout everyone you invited to lunch you'd go broke," he said. "I don't think that'd work."

The crops have failed and lots of people are getting sick. Some babies have died and my little cousin died too. Mama was very sad and so was Papa. Me too, I miss him.

Now Pak Adji who always lets me pat his cow is ill. Mama says it's because there isn't enough food.

Sometimes I feel very hungry and Budi and Ismoyo show me how to eat the shoots of the banana flowers. We catch grasshoppers and fry them on tiny fires made with dried cow dung.

At night we make a lantern to catch larons in a bucket. It's exciting when they swarm towards the light, and Mama makes us wrap selendangs around our heads so the larons can't get in our ears.

The neighbours come and help and everyone is laughing and even Papa thinks it's funny. After that Mama makes patties with the larons and they're very crunchy.

Mama is serving rice and we each have a spoonful on a banana leaf. Mama has an egg and it's very exciting when she is peeling off the shell. Then she cuts it into six tiny portions and serves a small piece of the cooked white and a fraction of the yellow yolk to Papa, Yanti, Budi, Ismoyo and me, and then the last little bit is for her.

We all wait and then we mix the egg in the rice and eat it. It's yummy.

Chapter 15

The Art Gallery of New South Wales was a favourite place for Adi and it was free. He could spend a day there or just a few hours. Sometimes he visited a single section or exhibition, other times a single painting. There were free films, talks, a bookshop. Nearby, and just a stroll across the green expanse of the Domain, there was the State Library which also had free exhibitions. He occasionally went to the Museum of Contemporary Art too, and to other museums if they weren't too expensive.

Posters around the art school notified the students of exhibitions in commercial galleries and he also discovered artworks in odd places around the city – in city squares, gardens or the foyers of buildings. Someone told him about a street in St Peters where street artists regularly painted the factory walls and he visited it often. And there was the street in Glebe where a sculptor had placed his sculptures in his neighbours' gardens. Different councils, too, held mural competitions and sometimes friends co-opted him to help paint their murals.

At the beginning of each year, the students went to Cockatoo Island by ferry to draw, or they camped at North Head where there was a colony of little penguins and the harbour opened out to the ocean. There was the annual event of Sculpture by the Sea, too, where sculptors exhibited work on the cliff tops and beaches to the south of the harbour, from Tamarama to Bondi.

Adi's sketchbooks were a record of where he went, what he saw, and how he was feeling. He liked to catch a random bus, or just let his feet lead until he found a place to sit and sketch. Sometimes he went into a rail station at peak hour to catch quick sketches of people rushing to work, or waiting to go home at the end of the day. He studied their facial expressions, the way they wrapped themselves into their bodies if they were waiting for a bus or train, and how their posture changed if they met someone they knew. He imagined he could tell just by the way they were sitting or standing if someone was smiling or not. On Sundays he often gravitated to Circular Quay where he'd find a spot to sketch, paint or pretend to fish while he idly took note of the life swirling around him – the day-trippers interacting with the buskers, the movement of boats, the dancing light patterns on the water.

***

It was early April in Adi's third year in Sydney, and a flush of autumn coolness had driven lots of people outdoors to enjoy the warmth of the sun. At Circular Quay, he was doing some watercolour studies of the wash created by the ferries that came and went from the wharf when he heard a female voice call out his name. When he looked up, he saw it was Lisa.

"Hey Adi, are you fishing?"

"Oh hi Lisa – fishing, yes. Just a minute … " He continued painting until he was satisfied, and then placed the brush in a jar of water.

"Mind if I join you?"

He waved an invitation for her to sit.

Lisa removed her hat and lowered herself onto the edge of the jetty. As she did so, a gust of wind blew her hair forward over her face and, laughing, she brushed it back and jammed the hat down on the springy mess.

"There," she said, and turned her whole body towards him.

Even under the hat her face and eyes seemed to radiate warmth and light, as though the sun had slid out from behind a cloud, and when he glanced up at the sky, he saw that the clouds had indeed slipped away and the sky was an intense autumn blue.

"Catch anything?" she asked.

"Not yet," he said, pulling in the line that had a hook, sinker and ... "No bait!"

Lisa laughed as he dropped the line back into the water. She glanced at the drying watercolour and then swivelled around to watch the passers-by. Adi followed her lead and, together, they watched two older men in mismatching polyester checked pants and jackets escorting a woman wearing gold hooped earrings, tight stretch jeans and running shoes. A man with a cockatoo on his shoulder had a trail of bird shit down his back. Some punks with elaborate spiked cockies' combs on otherwise shaved heads glided by in silence. Behind them came a neat and tidy mum and dad with three children, all wearing their public school hats and licking different coloured ice creams in cones. The family paused in front of a couple of buskers in colonial dress who were coated in thick silver paint and still as statues. Along from them, three small children began playing child-sized violins next to a cardboard sign that read, "Saving for Japan tour with the Children's Orchestra".

Lisa sensed that Adi was studying each of the passing scenes with objective interest, but for her, sitting next to him, the familiar and ordinary scenes began to seem staged. A pageant named "Sunday Arvo at the Quay". As each scene unfolded, she felt that same gnawing sense of hilarity she experienced when watching Jacques Tati's Monsieur Hulot films, where the simplest familiar actions and sounds became overwhelmingly strange and more hilariously funny the more they repeated over and over again.

Finally, when two men turned up wearing black on white spotted costumes that matched their pair of Dalmatian dogs, Adi spoke.

"Many kinds of Australians … " he said flatly.

That was it, the trigger that set her off, and she burst out laughing. The laughter rose again and again, wave after wave, until she was groaning from the ache in her belly. Every time she tried to stop, her body refused to obey and she was off again. It was wild laughter, and she could feel Adi's concerned gaze on her as she tried to slow her breathing and calm herself.

What did he think of her? she wondered, recalling the day when he got up and suddenly left the Life Drawing class. At the time it felt like a small victory, but it dawned on her later that she'd misread the wall of reserve he gathered around him. Now she wanted to experience more of his sense of humour, to be a friend if nothing else.

"Are you okay?" he asked. He had begun winding in the fishing line, and was removing a piece of seaweed that had attached itself to the hook.

"Yes, I'm fine." She felt calm now and was savouring the joyous feeling the laughter had left in her body.

"There's something I've been thinking about," she said. "Do you know Grove Gallery? Gerardo Pettini owns it. He's a friend of mine and I think he might be interested in your work."

Adi stopped packing away his sketchpad and paints and gave her his full attention.

Lisa said, "I wondered if I could maybe come by and see your work at the art school so I can get a sense of what you're working on before I mention you to him. What do you think? Would that be alright?"

The following week, Lisa and Adi met up at Adi's studio at the art school, and then later that day she called in at the Darlo Boarding House to see the work there. When she rang the doorbell, there was a brief wait before Adi opened the door, and then as she stepped inside she could hear someone playing the piano.

The house was cool and there was a faint smell of fresh paint, and when she glanced into the front room, she saw part of a piano keyboard, and then a hand crashed down loud on the deepest of the bass notes.

"Who's that playing the piano?" she asked.

"Akira. He lives here too," Adi said, closing the door. He held out a hand to direct her up the stairs. "The studio's upstairs. Please."

When they reached his room, Lisa saw that every surface was taken up with canvases, paints, brushes and other paraphernalia such as library books, ring binder folders and sketchpads. The walls were papered with postcards, theatre and exhibition posters, cuttings from magazines, photographs of friends and fellow students, press clippings.

"Wow, how does your landlady feel about having an artist-in-residence?" she said as Adi cleared a space on the bed for her to sit.

Adi stood back and indicated the cleared space, "Please, sit down. Marj is cool. Just cleans around."

"She cleans your room?" Lisa was curious about the household and for a minute or two the questions flowed. Who owned the house, who else lived there, were they students too, what did they do, what else did Marj do for him?

She had a particular interest in Marj. "She does your laundry and ironing? Does she cook for you as well?"

"Oh yes, she cooks the dinner. Sometimes she makes lunch." Adi began pulling out canvases and arranging them around the room for Lisa to look at.

"Wow! It sounds amazing – like a home away from home for artists. Do you think I could move in too?"

Adi's eyes widened.

"Just kidding," she said, laughing.

After pulling out the canvases, Adi left Lisa to look through his sketchbooks and continued spreading metallic greys, rust and deep broody blues onto a large canvas with a palette knife, and then inserting spot lathers of yellow that glowed dully like lamps in a fog. It was part of a series of industrial dockland and harbour views he was working on and the smell of oil paints hung heavy in the air despite the open door and window. He wondered if she found the smell unpleasant.

Downstairs Akira had begun playing a lyrical piece. Single notes, right hand, an upbeat joyful melody, repeated over and over, then joined by a rich layer of chords. Adi looked up from his painting and saw Lisa sitting very still by the window. There was nothing but the music, and when Akira stopped playing the notes hung suspended in the air.

Lisa looked up, shook her head, and then looked back down. Neither of them wanted to be the first to speak but a knock on the open door pulled them back into the room and they saw Akira standing in the doorway.

"Hey man, you ready to head off? Oh, sorry mate, didn't know you had visitors? Lisa isn't it?"

Adi stood up to introduce them.

"Hi Akira, I really enjoyed hearing you play. Did you compose that last piece?" Lisa asked.

"Yes," Akira said. "Excuse me Lisa, just checking with Adi, do you still want to go and eat? We've done the sound check already but we gotta be there by eight. I reckon we should head off in five. That suit you?"

The air was warm and humid when they left the Darlo Boarding House and they saw a bank of thick dark clouds gathering in the direction of the city. Lisa had agreed to meet them later at the venue and so the two men set off downhill to their favourite noodle bar.

The Jazz Collective was an artist-run affair that sponsored and organised weekly gigs for up-and-coming jazz musicians. The gigs were an opportunity to play their own compositions in a fifty-minute set with a line-up of one, two or three established jazz musicians. Tonight Akira was teamed with a well-known double bass player and percussionist, both of whom performed as sidemen or band leaders at different venues around the city.

It was a big night for Akira, and Adi wanted to be there to support him. Looking around the room he recognised a number of older musicians in the audience, there to be impressed by the younger artists' skill, confidence, and musicality. Like any community, the jazz community's colour emanated from its rich variety of thoughtful introverts, intellectuals, flighty show offs, smart arses, cool Christians, drug and alcohol abusers, gay and straight dudes and petulant narcissists. What bound them together was their respect for superb musicianship, along with the grace, generosity, and sense of humour they shared with one another.

The venue entrance was on a busy, main road. Inside there was a small stage, and seats for the audience were a colourful assortment of lounges that had most likely been gifted or found in second-hand shops or on the street. Adi and Akira had arrived early enough to claim one of these and Lisa joined them soon after. There were a lot of young people in the audience and they were possibly fellow students and friends of the performers. No one spoke during the performance, but at the end of each song there were whoops, yeahs and clapping.

As Akira's band played, the siren of an occasional police car or ambulance rose and fell just metres from where they sat, and when that happened the music somehow stretched out from the room to absorb the sounds of the city. At the end of the set the musicians made to leave the stage but then settled back behind their instruments to play an encore.

Afterwards, by the time Akira got to Lisa and Adi, he had a drink in hand and was feeling relaxed and relieved.

Lisa was enthusiastic. "That was great Akira. You must be so happy. What was the name of the last piece you played? It was magic hearing it this afternoon and the version you just played was extraordinary too."

"It's called *Rainy Day At Marj's* – I wrote it for a composition assignment last year and a few people asked if they could play it. This is the first time I've played it for an audience myself, but I was pretty happy with how it went."

"So what's more important to you – composing or performing?" Lisa asked.

"Well, I like it all I guess. Improvising and performing and composing – they all tend to feed into each other."

Adi left them to buy more drinks and returned just as the emcee was introducing the next band. The room darkened and this time the line-up was a bass guitarist who was joined by a well-known drummer and saxophone player. Two women and a man. The room hushed.

When Adi, Akira and Lisa emerged from the venue it had been raining. The reflections of street lights and neon signs shimmered in the wet surfaces of the streets and, picking up where the music left off, the swishing sound of passing cars latched onto the rhythmic beat of the city. They located Lisa's car in the canyons of warehouses, old factories and office buildings near Central Station and she was soon chugging away, a retreating dash of yellow in the shadowy dripping streetscape.

With Adi's *kretek* cigarette leaving a trail of sweet clove scent, they made the uphill trek to Darlinghurst in silence. By the time they hit Flinders Street, a thin misty rain was blurring the glow of the street lights and dampening their clothes and hair. Life brimmed with possibility. They were euphoric.

Chapter 16

The annual Graduate Show showcased the work of the final year art students to the industry and general public. As well as having works in the curated exhibition, each of the graduating artists had a studio exhibition where anyone could meet them and see more of their work. Having finished their third year final assessments in early November, the students set about preparing for the exhibition later that month. A range of scholarships, residencies and cash prizes was offered to selected students in the lead up to the event, and gallery owners saw it as an opportunity to identify new talent.

Adi had topped his year in painting and, with the encouragement of his teachers, had applied for and been granted a visa extension as well as a scholarship to do an honours year. Mack had done well too, and had decided to enrol in a graphic design course with a view to getting a job in advertising.

On the day before the opening, Adi ran into Lisa outside the art school.

"Hey, Adi – do you want to have a coffee?"

"Can't, sorry – have to finish getting the studio exhibition ready." He held out a small box of business cards. "I just picked these up."

"Okay, I'll see you at the opening then," Lisa said and turned to go.

"You're coming?" he called after her.

She turned back to him, "Sure, I wouldn't miss it. My parents are coming too. They're friends with Mack's mum and dad. I'll introduce you. Yeah?"

***

Mack and Adi had been delegated to stand at the entrance to the art school to welcome guests, hand out maps, and direct visitors to a bar where free drinks and snacks were being served. It was evening and a pink light still suffused the sky when Akira, Marj, Archie and Bert arrived. They spotted Adi and made their way over to him.

Marj was wearing the pale mauve satin dress with matching jacket she'd last worn to Bert's nephew's wedding. She had stopped dyeing her hair about a year after Adi arrived in Australia, and her brand new perm twirled her thin grey hair into fluffed rolls. Akira had on indigo dyed batik pants and a loose jacket, and his long black hair was pulled back in a ponytail. Archie and Bert were done up in wool ties, creased pants and tweed sports jackets. They were freshly shaved and Marj had given them both haircuts. The three men waited while Marj gave Adi a kiss and a hug, and then one-by-one they shook his hand.

Marj said, "We're all real proud of you, aren't we Boys? Real proud. We'll go and have a good look round. Don't you worry about us, Aki'll look after us and we'll see you later."

Adi handed them a map and they agreed to meet at his studio after the official proceedings.

Soon Lisa arrived with her parents, "Mum, Dad, this is Adi. Adi, my parents Helen and Ian. Adi's one of the stars here tonight … "

Helen and Ian went through the motions of shaking hands with Adi and then turned their attention to Mack who said, "Oh yeah, thanks a lot … "

"I said *one* of the stars. They already think you're one!"

"Congratulations Mack dear, I can't wait to see your work. Are Robert and Elizabeth here yet?" Helen asked.

"They said they'd wait for you at the bar," Mack said. "I'll take you to them." And he led them through the crowd.

Lisa turned to Adi. "I'm sorry about that," she offered, embarrassed that both parents had failed to take any interest in him.

Adi looked at her and shrugged, "Many kinds of Australians … "

It was his line from the time they had sat watching the passing crowd at Circular Quay and she smiled in recognition.

There was still the official opening to get through and when this part of the night was over, a small queue formed to purchase catalogues that included a photo of the artists alongside a picture of the artwork that had been selected for the curated exhibition. All the graduates, including Adi, were wearing a laminated name tag that also featured the artwork.

Adi was on his way to his studio when he heard Lisa call out to him. When he turned, he saw that she was with a stylish man in his forties who looked vaguely familiar.

"Hi Adi. D'you have a minute? This is Gerardo Pettini from Grove Gallery – he's the gallerist I told you about."

Gerardo greeted him warmly, "Pleased to meet you Adi. I just bought your painting. Heard so much about you from Lisa, and from some of your lecturers as well. I hear you're going on to do honours. Well done."

Lisa excused herself and left Gerardo to accompany Adi back to his studio. As Gerardo looked at each of the paintings,

Adi was impressed by the attention he gave to them, and the intelligent questions he asked about influences, references, the artists he most admired, and what he felt he'd gained from studying at the art school.

Finally, Gerardo said, "Lisa tells me you've got more work at home. I won't look at that now, but I can give you a space in my Summer Group Show if you're interested. There'll be some big names showing so it will expose you to some fairly astute collectors. I can take one large piece or a couple of smaller pieces."

Adi nodded.

"You can? Good. Bring over what you've got on Saturday and we'll decide what to hang. Here's my card."

He patted Adi's arm. "Must fly … good to meet you."

When Gerardo left his studio, Adi tried to take in what had just happened. He'd often visited exhibitions at Grove Gallery, and Gerardo Pettini was a familiar figure at graduate shows. He had a reputation for being ethical, generous, and a strong advocate for everyone in his stable of artists. When he took on an emerging artist it was understood they had a strong future.

An hour later when Lisa arrived at Adi's studio she was excited and curious. "How'd it go? What did he say?"

"He asked me to bring over some work on Saturday – for a group exhibition in December."

"That's fantastic. You know that gallery don't you, Grove Gallery? It's probably number one in Sydney, perhaps in the country."

They walked downstairs and out into the main courtyard to where Akira was waiting for him.

"I put Marj and the Boys in a taxi. I think they were pretty impressed. You probably noticed that Marj insisted on us dressing up for the occasion."

Lisa signalled to a passing waiter. "Here," she said. "Let's celebrate." She took a glass of prosecco from the tray and handed it to Adi.

Adi took the glass, "Er, um … no thanks."

"Oh … what would you like? Let me get it," she said.

Akira said, "Not to worry, I'll take that one."

Adi handed the glass to Akira. "Wait," he said and headed in the direction of the bar.

Lisa said, "Gerardo Pettini from Grove Gallery just offered Adi a place in his annual group exhibition."

Akira said, "Cool. By the way, Adi doesn't drink. He's a Muslim."

When Adi returned with a glass of sparkling mineral water, Akira raised his glass, "Here's to ya mate! Lisa just told me about Grove Gallery. It's bloody good news."

Later that night when Adi and Akira arrived back at the boarding house, they made coffee and went to Adi's room. As well as selling his painting and securing a spot in Grove Gallery's annual group show, he had won an honours scholarship and a $500 voucher for art materials from a fine arts shop he often went to for paints, brushes and canvases.

The scholarship meant he could remain in the country and continue his studies. More than all his other good fortune, this was the most significant for it meant he could stop worrying about the future for one more year.

Akira picked up the guitar and began to pick out some notes while Adi set to work on a dock scene he hoped Gerardo would take for the group exhibition.

"What's with you and Lisa?" Akira asked.

Adi was surprised. It was uncharacteristic of Akira to ask such a direct question.

"What do you mean?"

"C'mon, mate – it's pretty obvious she's keen on you."

"No ... I don't think ... "

"Too right ... Don't tell me you haven't noticed."

Adi looked at the palette in front of him, "I think she's in love with Mack."

"She's interested in you, mate. Can't you see that?"

The question unleashed a flood of unacknowledged longing in Adi and he put down the blade he'd just loaded with thick yellow paint and joined Akira on the bed. He picked up a bamboo flute and began handling it. He lifted it to his lips and played a few bars of an Indonesian ballad. Then, feeling too agitated to play any more, he got up off the bed.

"What can I do?" he said. "I'm just a poor man, I have nothing." He wanted to move, but the space was too crowded with canvases and art materials. "I cannot dream to marry someone like Lisa. We are from different worlds and my future is uncertain. If I want a teaching job I must pay, and this is not possible. Even if I borrow the money, I could not repay the loan."

He looked down at his outstretched empty hands and then at Akira who said, "Mate, I'm not talking about marriage – you don't have to marry her to go out with her. Anyway, I'm not sure she'd be too interested in marriage."

"But I'm a Muslim ... " Adi said.

The excitement and sense of hope stimulated by the successes of the night had dimmed. As he saw it, they gave him relief from thinking about the future for now, but the things Akira took for granted were not for him.

To his dismay, Akira continued, "It's how it is here, mate. It's like you have a relationship, you get to know someone, maybe it works out that you marry them, or maybe you don't. It's open. You can live with them or not, marry or not. It's up to two people, what they agree is fair and right, what they feel comfortable with."

Adi looked unconvinced and Akira continued, "If Lisa's keen, why not enjoy her company for the time being and leave the rest for later?"

After a minute of cold silence, Adi declared, "I'm a village boy – I'm from the village and I will return to the village."

He felt angry with Akira and wanted him to leave him alone but Akira was not letting up.

"I've seen the way she looks at you … and the funny thing is I bet part of the attraction is that you're not trying to get into bed with her. She's probably wondering if you're gay."

Adi was offended, "I'm not gay. How can you say this? I'm a Muslim."

"So, there are no gay Muslims?" Akira asked.

When Adi first came to Sydney he had attended the Gay and Lesbian Mardi Gras Parade with Akira. It wasn't what he expected – lots of men, especially, showing off their bulging muscles, wearing strips of leather on their crotch and little else, or in elaborate sparkling evening dresses with high heels and hairstyles.

Mardi Gras was colourful, festive, theatrical. Everyone was having a good time, but when he saw parents with children of all ages watching on, it was shocking to him. And when he discussed this with Pak Bambang, the social worker explained the history of Mardi Gras, the gay rights' movement, and how gay men and women had been discriminated against, bashed, and even killed. He spoke about the AIDS epidemic and how the early marches tried to raise awareness of safe sex practices to stop the spread of infection.

The effect of this chat was that Adi, despite his friendships with openly gay artists at the art school, began to associate being gay with danger.

After Akira left his room, he found he could no longer paint. His head was crowded with thoughts, admonitions and arguments against the views put by Akira. To have a relationship with Lisa without intending to marry her was, in his mind, disrespectful. She was not used to living the way he was used to. And if they did not marry and were to have a child? What then? The child would not be a part of his family.

He willed himself to put the tangle of thoughts from his mind, but sleep escaped him and he got up from the bed and began selecting only the colours that soothed him to paint with.

Mama and I are bathing in the river. Just the two of us. Mama is washing her hair and her eyes are shut tight to stop the shampoo stinging. The shampoo is from a little packet she bought at Lik Mud's shop and it smells sweet, like jasmine.

Mama has so much hair and she pushes it up and around with her hands to make it all soapy. Mama's sarong has fallen to her waist. I can see her boobies and I want to drink from them again but I'm too old. I put out my hand in a little cup for Mama's boobie and Mama gets a fright.

"Aduh!" she says, and smacks my hand away.

That hurts, and I stop laughing. Now I am crying and cannot stop because Mama hurt me. I try to run away but the water won't let me.

Mama calls, "Darling, darling," but I keep trying to get out of the water. Mama catches me by the waist and tries to hug me to her in the river, laughing while I wriggle and squirm.

"You frightened me, that's all," she says. "It's nothing, don't worry."

I fight, kick, and finally I'm free. Free of Mama, free of the water. I run up the steep path beside the river and hide behind some bushes. Mama is calling and calling, but I keep on hiding because I'm feeling very sad.

Chapter 17

At Grove Gallery's Summer Group Show, all three of Adi's paintings sold to collectors who prided themselves on spotting up-and-coming talent. Gerardo had twenty to thirty committed collectors keen to acquire works by emerging artists but the interest in Adi on the night was such that he thought he might be forced to auction one of the works.

To resolve the situation, Gerardo made a promise to the loser that he would be granted a preview of Adi's forthcoming solo exhibition. The only problem was that Grove Gallery exhibitions were booked at least two years ahead and he had only just met Adi. Also, while the group show was an opportunity for an emerging artist, it was Gerardo's policy not to take anyone on while they were studying. It put them under too much pressure.

The white lie had been a way out of a tricky situation but now the client kept asking him for the dates of the exhibition for his diary. So, when Madrill, a major artist, announced he was moving to New York and wanted to cancel his next scheduled exhibition, Gerardo decided to assess whether Adi had work of sufficient quality and strength on hand for a solo exhibition. If so, he knew he could reduce some of the pressure on the newcomer by having a more experienced artist take up half of the space, possibly a sculptor, or someone so well-established they wouldn't be worried about the possibility of being upstaged.

On the day Gerardo came to the Darlo Boarding House, Marj let him in. She told him Adi was expecting him, but when she called out up the stairs there was no reply, and so she invited Gerardo to go on up. When Adi returned to his room, he found Gerardo examining the brands of the tubes of paint on Adi's desk, and nodding his head in approval, "Good to see you've not been cutting corners on materials. It's always disappointing when artists do that," he said.

Adi looked on as Gerardo began pulling out and setting aside canvases that caught his eye. He was curious about which paintings he selected, the way he arranged them side by side, or stepped back to view them from a distance. It wasn't easy to do in the crowded bedroom so Gerardo picked up five of the canvases and began lining them up in the adjoining hallway.

"Well it seems you'll have plenty to give me for an exhibition. I can see why some of your teachers were enthusiastic about your work. You've clearly worked very hard."

Gerardo was particularly taken with the industrial dockyard scenes. "Okay, you need three things. A studio, materials and, tell me if I'm wrong, some cash to keep you going? Am I right?"

Adi opened his mouth but no sound came out. He nodded.

Gerardo continued, "Madrill is leaving for New York – he has a studio in Surry Hills and he wants to hang onto it in case it doesn't work out over there. It's not flash but it would do, and you could live there as well. I think Madrill would be pleased to have someone in there till he makes up his mind."

As it turned out the studio occupied half of the fourth floor of a rundown warehouse in Surry Hills, not far from where Adi used to go to the jazz jam sessions with Akira. He had asked Akira to go with him and when they stepped out of the building's creaking old style lift they found Gerardo already waiting for them.

In their eyes the studio was enormous and light-filled. It had fourteen-foot high ceilings and a row of eight-foot high sash windows along the northern side. A long table covered with painting paraphernalia dominated the workspace and some thirty giant-sized canvases – some finished paintings and some blank – sloped against the walls. At one end, there was a small kitchen with a bar fridge, sink, stove and a fifties-style red laminate and chrome table, and six red vinyl dining chairs.

A door painted in Rousseau-inspired green foliage led to a bathroom with a claw foot bath and shower, hand basin and toilet. By the windows there was a double bed mattress on a raised wooden platform and, near that, an old green lounge suite – a couch and two armchairs – was arranged around a large square coffee table constructed from timber pallets. The coffee table was strewn with art books, including one on the artist himself. Two black painted bookcases housed Madrill's much prized jazz and blues vinyl collection.

At this level, the rumble of traffic on Elizabeth Street was just a low hum, and from the windows there were sweeping views of Central Station clock tower, and glimpses of Belmore Park and the railway tracks where the City Circle trains plunged underground.

Adi was blushing with gratitude. "This is very good. Thank you."

"Don't mention it. Self-interest okay? I want good work from you for the March exhibition. For now, just concentrate on your studies, but you can move in as soon as I organise with Madrill about storing his paintings and the vinyl collection. Give me a month. That alright? It'll give you time to get things sorted out with your landlady as well, yeah?"

***

Packing up his room at the Darlo Boarding House felt like a betrayal and Adi felt guilty about it, and hesitated to make a start. He feared that Marj, the Boys and Akira would feel rejected, and that they would think he didn't appreciate everything they had done together as a family. Finally Marj took matters in hand by sending the Boys out to get boxes so that she, Akira and Adi could begin packing up his room. Some student friends turned up with a van and, within three hours, everything he owned had been transferred to the studio. By the time they brought it all up in the lift, Marj and Akira had been and cleaned the place up so that everything could be put away as soon as it arrived. When that was done, they returned to the Darlo Boarding House for a baked dinner.

It was strange at first to be there by himself at night, but within a couple of weeks the studio had become a common room for fellow students, and he turned no one away. After that he was rarely alone, even at night.

When Akira asked why he didn't just shut the door to keep everyone from dropping in, he said, "I like it. People come, I feel good. Not so lonely."

Adi painted steadily. Day or night. He enjoyed the buzz of people but rarely responded, even when they asked questions or expressed an opinion, such as that he really should do something about the cockroaches. In time the visitors stopped complaining that the milk was off or the sugar had run out. They made their own tea or coffee and bought more if supplies ran out; they entertained themselves – read his library books, played Scrabble, argued about politics or the arts, swapped notes on which exhibitions, movies or plays to see. They even put up signs to remind one another to wash up.

Week by week and month by month, the stack of new blank canvases and paintings resting against the walls multiplied and, on the floor, piles of art books and reference books rose like miniature skyscrapers. When Lisa visited the studio for the first time, she found Akira, Mack and a young woman she didn't know playing Scrabble. They looked up as she entered, and Mack got up to give her a kiss on both cheeks.

"Hey Lisa, do you want to play? We could start again seeing they're wiping the floor with me."

"No thanks Mack. Hi Akira. I'll just say hi to Adi."

Adi nodded to Lisa and she said, "Hi, just came by to see how you're going," and when he didn't respond, she added, "Mind if I look around?"

She saw that he was glancing at an object that was hanging on the wall as he painted, and recognised that it was a recurring image in a few of the paintings propped against the walls.

"Hey Adi, what's this?" she asked.

Adi looked up, "It's a Tree of Life shadow play puppet. The puppet master puts it on the screen at the beginning and end of the shadow puppet play. We call it a *gunungan*."

Adi took down the leaf-shaped puppet from the wall. It was very old and fragile and she noticed the careful, loving way he handled it. He held it out for her to examine and she saw that, while the leather was worn, it was intricately carved, and there were minute faded specks of colour that suggested it had once been brightly painted.

He pointed out the traces of some steps leading to a pair of double doors, "These are the gates to the temple. They are the giants that guard them," he said.

She could just make out the temple doors and the guards poised with shield and sword at the ready. She pointed to the heads of two large creatures on either side of the temple roof. "What are they? Dragons?"

"Garuda. Like the eagle. They mean freedom," he said.

She traced her finger upwards, "So here's the Tree of Life, and what is this?"

She pointed to a fearsome face, and then a snake weaving itself up the trunk of the tree towards the flower at the top.

"Banaspati guides and protects from danger. Naga is a kind of dragon. This is like the path in life, how in different lifetimes, human beings grow in spirit. At the top is the flower – *tunjung* – which means wisdom, holiness."

"I see," she said. 'So the Tree of Life promises freedom and wisdom, like the Buddhist nirvana, yes?"

Adi nodded, "The Tree of Life is like the family that has many branches. It includes all creatures, not just humans. All joined together. What is the word in English?"

"Co-existence? Interdependent?"

"Yes, you understand. See the Naga's tail – reaches all the way down to bottom, to the earth."

Adi turned the puppet over to where the second side presented a demon face with an open mouth, red tongue hanging out, and eyes bulging. Its head was framed with flames.

"Oh, two sides. What is this one?" asked Lisa.

"First one, good energy. This one, bad energy."

"Oh."

"On this side there is evil, bad things, destruction. But there is a third side too."

Lisa frowned. "Oh really, how is that?"

"The third side is the shadow on the screen in the shadow puppet play, which is seen when the light shines from behind. This is the ancestor spirit. It does not change."

"It looks very old. Where did you get it?"

"Yes, it is. A puppet master gave it to me. I call him uncle and he is still alive, but very old now. As a kid I loved the wayang kulit and so did my mother, and he often let me sit behind the screen to watch him perform."

Adi hung the Tree of Life back on the wall with the positive side facing into the room and went back to his painting. Then, as if suddenly remembering it was her first visit, he said, "You want coffee?"

Lisa looked at her watch, "No, no. It's okay. I just came by to invite you to our party. On Saturday. It's a vermilion party ... red, everyone has to wear red. Can you come?"

Adi said he would and Lisa left an invitation on the coffee table, and handed one to Mack, Akira and some other students who were just arriving.

"Any time after nine ... the theme is vermilion. Okay everyone?"

When she reached the door of the studio, Lisa turned and saw that Adi was once more completely absorbed in his painting.

Chapter 18

Music, bodies and the sweet smell of weed spilled out of the redbrick semi-detached Bondi bungalow. The house was about three blocks from the beach and the majority of guests were past and present students of the art school, as well as the occasional lecturer. It was a warm summer's night and about a dozen people were at the front of the house, on the lawn and footpath, or sitting on the low brick fence.

Most had made some effort to dress in red, or shades of pink. A couple had on matching red and white checked retro swimming costumes. There was an overheated devil in an all-in-one suit with crescent shaped horns, and a woman who was wearing a shift with a child's paintbox painted on it that displayed different shades of red. A bored cattle-dog-cross lay on its belly on the footpath, its chin resting on its paws. Its owner had dyed its coat red and it sported a red and white op-art kerchief around its neck.

The front door of the house opened into a short hall that led into a large living room. All furniture had been removed and there were mattresses and cushions spread around the walls for people to sit on. The place was throbbing like a giant's heartbeat and under the stairs a group of people, including

Lisa and Mack, were lounging, talking and laughing. The party was still warming up and people streamed past them, going back and forth to the dining room and kitchen at the back where their drinks had been deposited in tubs of ice.

When a taxi pulled up out the front of the house, the partygoers saw two men in masks get out and cross the road. They were slim, brown-skinned and bare-footed, and when they reached the pavement they froze.

One was wearing a white carved mask and his bare torso was rubbed all over with red powder. A pair of intricately patterned gold leather wings was strapped to his upper arms and, around his hips, he wore a deep red sarong that fell in folds to the ground at the front. On his head, an elaborate gold metal headdress, which was decorated with red hibiscus flowers, jittered every time he moved his head.

His companion's mask was demonic, with stiff bunches of coarse black hair protruding from two large carved nostrils. A long red and gold tongue hung from the open mouth to his knees, and two creamy fangs curved up on either side. Coarse straight black hair covered his back from the top of the mask to his knees, and he carried a small drum under his left arm. When he started playing a steady beat on the drum, his companion began responding to the rhythm.

The white-masked dancer was standing on his left leg which was bent at the knee, with the foot turned out slightly and flat to the ground. His right leg was bent forward and rested lightly on the toes. At the end of his outstretched arms, the fingers were pointing down and pulsing. He caught up a strand of the scarf in his right thumb and index finger, drew it out to the side, and let it drop as his body began to flow in slow curves, the movement extending down into the wrists, hands and fingertips. The mask moved back and forth at the neck, left to right, right to left. At times it seemed menacing, at times benign; sometimes young and playful, sometimes ancient.

The partygoers were mesmerised. "Who's that?"

"Dunno."

"Maybe Adi?"

"Yeah, gotta be."

"Hey Adi, is that you?"

The one playing the drum was the puppet master, and the dancer was his puppet, gathering up and extending one strand of the scarf, dropping it, and then repeating the movement on the other side. As they inched forward, making their way down the path and into the house, the guests saw that they were both wearing a large brass-handled knife that was held in place at the back by the scarf around their waist.

A young dark-haired woman had entered the house earlier with two backpacks and asked the DJ to fade the music. In the living room, people pressed themselves around the edges of the room, and Lisa and Mack, who were sitting under the stairs, suddenly found themselves hemmed in by a wall of legs. They scrambled out and stood up to get a better view of what was going on.

The dance lasted several minutes and during the performance the music grew more insistent and intense. It was a mashup of dances Adi had known as a boy and, sensing his audience was wanting more, he turned to Lisa with his arms and hands outstretched, and beckoned her with nods and dancing downward pointing fingers. At first she resisted, pressing herself back against Mack.

"Go on," Mack whispered. "I think it's Adi."

He nudged her forward and, as she begun to follow the masked dancer, the drummer began escalating the rhythms into a vibrating wave of sound. She moved awkwardly at first, but then her body succumbed to the call and response of their bodies, with each taking a turn to lead and follow. Finally, when the throbbing tension of sound and energy seemed poised to wash them clean away, there was an abrupt change. All froze. Silence, and then the echo of notes still lingering.

As a roar of applause erupted, Lisa slipped away, and Adi and Akira paused a moment before removing the masks, and then the headdresses. A small group gathered around to ask about the rhythms and the dance itself, but their conversation was soon drowned out by the DJ.

When Adi looked around, he saw Mack pull a joint out of his shirt pocket and light it. Lisa was looking up at him as he inhaled deeply and then passed it to her. She repeated the action and held it out to Adi who shook his head. She handed the joint to Mack who began whispering something in her ear that made them both begin to giggle. Still laughing, they moved to the mattress under the stairs, leaned momentarily against the other, and fell down in a heap. When Lisa looked up at Adi and patted for him to sit next to her, he turned away. The room was filled with sexual energy, and it began to gnaw at him. He felt strange, out of place. He wanted to get away.

Akira was dancing with Lisbeth, the young woman who had earlier carried their bags into the house. Adi spoke to him and then retrieved his backpack, the drum, masks and headdresses from under the DJ's table. He found his way out past the kitchen to the backyard and through tangled kikuyu grass to the back gate. The fragrance of lemon-scented gum hung in the night air, and when he stumbled on some exposed tree roots, a couple on a makeshift bench pressed pause on an argument about an exhibition to tell him to go easy.

Beyond the Hills Hoist clothesline he caught a whiff of damp rotting vegetable matter and, somewhere in the shadows, he heard groans, urgent whispers and small cries. When he came to the back gate he flicked his lighter and, seeing there was no lock, pulled back the bolt and dragged it open. In the back lane a cone of light fell unimpeded from a streetlight and the sudden glare made him blink. Sensing his presence, a dog in a nearby yard emitted menacing growls that triggered a moment of gut-turning-fear in his belly.

As he walked away from the party, Adi tried to shake the image of the intimacy between Lisa and Mack from his mind. He gulped in the cool night air but the tears came anyway, a sign of grief over a fading dream he had hardly even recognised. It would soon be time for him to leave Sydney, but he still could not picture the life that awaited him. Whenever he tried, the here and now of his present life enveloped him with such vitality that all other possible lives appeared colourless, like shadows.

Slowly, the work awaiting him in the studio came into focus and propelled him to get up from the kerb where he had been sitting. He pulled pants and a tee-shirt from his backpack and put them on, and then wrapped Akira's sarong around the mask and keris daggers before placing them in the backpack. With the other sarong wrapped around his shoulders for warmth, he set off, carrying the headdresses in one hand and the drum in the other. Uphill towards Bondi Junction, along Oxford Street, and past Centennial Park. He calculated it would take an hour for him to get home but he didn't mind.

It was past midnight and the city appeared like an Edward Hopper painting, empty of people but beautiful in its colours, shapes and design. Even the cars seemed subdued as they passed by the illuminated mannequins in Paddington's luxury boutiques. To him, the fashionable, expensive clothing seemed alien and tasteless, and he imagined them as museum exhibits in some far off time.

At Paddington Town Hall his stride began to lengthen as the road sloped down past the sandstone walls and palm trees of the army barracks. The bookshop windows caught his eye, then the cinema posters, a men's clothing store. At this hour, only the gay bars and colour-bright windows of adult sex, toy and leather shops seemed animated, and their familiar presence was a sure sign that he was close to home.

Home. Yes, the studio was home. The thought jolted and a blast of sadness and grief pressed down once more on his shoulders. He quickened his pace, he wanted to sleep, but if sleep wouldn't come he'd paint.

"Hey, mate. S'bit early for Mardi Gras, idn't it?"

He vaguely recognised the night club bouncer, a box of a man with thick fuzzy hair, flattened nose and large soft lips. He was balanced on the balls of his feet with arms hung loose to accommodate bulging biceps. Ready for anything but a quiet night.

Adi saluted him with a grin, and an upwards nod of the chin. In the moment there was just the two of them, and he felt the warmth of the exchange go with him as he walked the remaining few blocks.

***

The day after the party, Adi heard a knock at the open door and looked up from his painting. Lisa was standing in the doorway and there was a strange look on her face, as if she had just been given some bad news.

"Hi Lisa, is something the matter?" He had not seen her like this before.

"You left the party without saying goodbye," she said.

He was perplexed, "Sorry. I didn't think you'd notice."

"What d'you mean?" she asked.

Adi didn't reply. He was confused, and a little afraid of the aggression in her voice.

"Come on Adi … what's that supposed to mean?"

He felt something snap, as Lisa's anger uncapped a surge of rage and self-pity in him. For a moment he was overwhelmed by a desire to make her see and feel the distance in their lives as he did, a student on a visa, someone whose time was running out. Everything was coming to an end. They would go on without him and, whatever the future held, he had to accept that Lisa would have no part in it.

He looked down at the mix of paints on the palette and pushed them around a little with a flat rounded spatula. Then he looked at her, "Why are you here Lisa? What you want?"

She met his gaze. "I'm here because I care about you, about being friends with you. I know the exhibition is important but it's okay to chill occasionally." She tried to smile, but then looked as though she might cry. She was like a ghost.

Adi had become very still. Silent. She waited for him to speak.

"Lisa, I paint, and that is all I know."

He wanted to tell her that he was just a poor man from the village, but his pride would not allow it.

"That's not all you know, Adi. There's so much more."

Adi turned away. He could no longer bear to see her like this.

When he did this, Lisa's hands clenched into fists by her sides. She raised them and watched her fingers stretch out, one by one, and when that was done, she let her hands drop to her sides, glanced around at the stacked canvases, the Tree of Life puppet on the wall, the brooding dark green foliage of the bathroom door, the dishevelled bed. Saw a vase of deep pink and red geraniums.

Then, without another word, she left the room.

When Adi turned around, she was gone. Had she even been there? Had he simply imagined it? He heard her taking the stairs two at a time and looked down at the sharp angled pattern of deep reds and blues on the palette. It was all sadness and grief.

A sweat broke out on his forehead and top lip, and his hands began to shake as a bitter resentment flashed up the names of those he felt most angry towards. Not just Lisa and Mack, but all the others too that he would one day leave behind. He walked over to the grime-smudged window and rubbed at the glass, but all he saw was a train disappearing into the underground tunnel.

He imagined Lisa unlocking the yellow car door, dragging the seatbelt across her chest, revving the engine, letting go the handbrake. Her car made a chugging sound, it had no will to dominate. She was gone, and that was that. All he knew was that her rage and his had collided in an impossible intimacy.

As he turned back to his work, one of Marj's famous phrases came into his mind.

"I find it's best to always give people the benefit of the doubt," she often said, and he had memorised it when he first heard her say it.

He opened a sketchbook to a drawing of Lisa and, looking at her face, repeated over and over as if it were a mantra, "…the benefit of the doubt."

Chapter 19

Every year Pak Bambang invited Adi to join him and his family for community prayers at the end of the fasting month of Ramadan. This year the weather was fine, a brilliant spring morning, and so at 7.30 am they joined a large slice of Sydney's Indonesian community at an oval next to the Georges River in Tempe to pray. It was a real celebration, and they saw many friends before piling into Pak Bambang and Bu Wafa's van to drive to Bankstown for a family lunch. Adi had made a painting for the family and, as was the custom in his village, gave each of Pak Bambang's daughters a crisp new ten-dollar note. In return, they presented him with a book on contemporary Australian Aboriginal art.

The family lived in a seventies-style blonde-brick home in walking distance of Bankstown Station and he was enchanted with the place from the moment he encountered the suburb's shopping and pedestrian malls. On that first visit, Pak Bambang met him at the top of the stairs at the station and took him on a bit of a guided tour. First stop was a ground floor fruit and vegetable market in a rundown shopping centre to buy items for Bu Wafa, then on through a winding arcade and back onto a street where the pungent smell of spices announced themselves before they even set eyes on the rows of half-metre high cones of spice in rich hues of cream, orange, ochre, deep red, and brown.

While he was waiting for Pak Bambang to scoop different spices into cellophane bags, Adi took photos and enjoyed having his nose tickled by the mingle of aromas. Then they recrossed the railway line to a Lebanese sweets shop with a long glass counter that displayed dozens of varieties of biscuits sold by the kilo. Pak Bambang placed an order with a young man who disappeared behind a curtain of coloured plastic strips at the back, and returned with two plates of rubbery cheese strings topped with a sweet honey sauce and two small cups of thick black Lebanese coffee on a tray.

From that day, just hearing the word "Bankstown" made Adi's mouth water, and on subsequent trips he discovered even more scenes to delight him, such as the day when, at eight-thirty in the morning, he saw crowds of high school students converging on the street that led to the local high school.

"Where are they from?" he asked Bu Wafa, and she rattled off a list of countries, "Lebanon, Iraq, Sierra Leone, Somalia, Sudan, Egypt, Syria, Afghanistan, Ethiopia, China, Vietnam."

He had never seen so many people from different parts of the world and here they were, all in one place, ordering hot chips and milkshakes at the takeaway, and the young men greeting one another with their special handshake.

On a later visit, he discovered a second-hand shop that sold amber jewellery, and spent ages peering at the minuscule insects locked inside the honey-coloured rocks. In another arcade, where most of the shops were empty, there was a shop whose shelves were stacked high with the brightly coloured fabrics worn by African women. Again and again, he was drawn back to study their loud patterns and surprising colour combinations, for he discovered that the very finest of these were imported batik from the Netherlands.

From his very first visits to the family, he was warmly welcomed by the couple's three daughters – Fatima, Marwa and Miriam. At the time, Fatima was studying accountancy, Marwa was in her final year at school and would go on to study architecture, and Miriam was just thirteen and in her first year at high school. Bu Wafa was also studying a Master of Education part-time while working three days a week in a women's health centre, and Pak Bambang joked that he hardly saw her because she was so busy.

As he got to know them better, they invited him to join the family for important Indonesian Muslim holidays as well as Christmas Eve. All the girls addressed him in Indonesian as uncle, Om Adi, and he addressed them in turn as younger sister – Dik Fatima, Dik Marwa, Dik Miriam. At home the family spoke English, but Pak Bambang almost always spoke to his daughters individually in Indonesian, and they replied in Indonesian or English. When they felt like it, they also listened to or joined in the Indonesian conversations their father was having with Adi.

"I have always spoken to the children in Indonesian so they understand and speak it quite well. Miriam tends to speak Lebanese better than anyone – probably because she and her friends speak Lebanese at school. It's the cool thing to do apparently!" Pak Bambang told him.

Pak Bambang was a self-described "enthusiast" and the family had developed a growing passion for art after meeting Adi. This meant that over lunch they often asked for his opinion or, more commonly, for him to adjudicate disputes. One disagreement was about whether Sidney Nolan was a great artist or not, another time it was about Joy Hester – with Bu Wafa insisting she was the best of her generation. This was after seeing an exhibition at the National Art Gallery. Then there was an argument about Jackson Pollock's *Blue Poles*, and another time it was on who was the better Australian painter – Fred Williams or John Olsen.

Annual art events such as the Archibald Portrait Prize exhibition and the Art Express high school student exhibition invariably stimulated discussion. Every year Pak Bambang took a notebook and noted down the main issues and concerns of that year's exhibition of students, to be compared with the cohorts of previous years. He also insisted on counting up the number of students of "Asian" background who made it into the Art Express exhibition, based on their surnames and Artist Statements, and was always disappointed that there were many more Chinese or Vietnamese background students than Indonesian. It didn't seem to matter that, as Bu Wafa pointed out, they had bigger resident populations to draw upon.

Several times a year the family made the three-hour journey to Canberra to visit the National Gallery of Australia which, Pak Bambang discovered, had a collection of textiles – batik and weaving – from different parts of Indonesia. For Bu Wafa's sake, however, he became concerned that Middle Eastern or Central Asian textiles weren't a strong part of the collection.

He raised the matter with Adi. "Y'know, when we were in Lebanon we visited Amman in Jordan and saw the most intricate embroidered costumes made by Palestinians. Then in Damascus in Syria I met a textiles collector in the Old Souk whose tiny cramped shop was like an Aladdin's cave. It was chock-a-block with the most remarkable textiles – jackets, dresses, decorative pieces. Such knowledge this man had – he knew the provenance of them all, which city or tribal region they were from, when they were made. Wonderful, wonderful!"

The manner Pak Bambang adopted when telling such stories was transporting. "I visited the textile collector three times. He cast a spell over me with his erudition and spirit. Of course, the most tattered pieces were often the most expensive because they were so old or rare. He said a curator from a Tokyo museum visits him every year to acquire textiles for their collection. You see, they are building a collection of Central Asian textiles in Tokyo."

Pak Bambang stood up and retrieved the business card of the Damascus collector from the box of filing cards on his desk. He said, "Of course I'm happy that the National Gallery has Indonesian weaving and batik, but surely there's an opportunity for it to be looking to Central Asia and the Middle East as well."

As he handed the card to Adi, he asked, "Is there someone you could speak to about this?"

Adi didn't think so. "You could write to the Curator of Textiles at the National Gallery and send them a copy of the collector's card. Maybe they would like to contact him too?" Adi suggested.

Pak Bambang and Adi often pored over books as they discussed Pak Bambang's latest interest. Although most of the books were borrowed from the local public library or university library, Pak Bambang's own library lined the walls of the living room where they were organised by subject. Some were in Dutch, which Pak Bambang couldn't read, but they had belonged to his late father and he couldn't bear to part with them. He even had a single volume that documented President Soekarno's art collection. It was published in 1960 and included paintings by Indonesians as well as European artists who lived in Indonesia prior to, and after, independence.

On one visit – it was around the time of Pak Bambang's fiftieth birthday – Pak Bambang wanted to discuss the issue of identity with Adi, and he began by admitting to feeling less and less tolerant of the tiresome question, "Where are you from?"

Partly, he said, it was because he had begun to sense an edge to this question that he hadn't been conscious of before, particularly since the recent divisive politics around the issue of so-called "boat people," which was how some politicians referred to refugees, and the all too frequent ugly statements about Muslims and other minority groups in the media.

"When I'm asked this question, I always say I'm from Bankstown," he told Adi, "but I already know what will come next: 'But where are you from originally?'"

Pak Bambang sighed. "What can I say? I was born in Indonesia, lived there for ten plus two years and I've lived in Australia for thirty-eight years. You tell me where I'm from."

"Yes, many ask me the same question," Adi said.

"But it doesn't stop there," Pak Bambang continued, "Then they ask, 'So do you feel more Indonesian or more Australian?'"

The best thing about such conversations with Pak Bambang was that they were in Indonesian, and the ease and flow of them meant that Adi was often surprised by his own reflections.

"Sometimes I feel like I belong here, but other times there's a gap, and it's like I'm either invisible or too visible," Adi said. "Or that there's a perspex wall and I try to reach through it, but I can't. It's not just because of language, or the cultural differences, although that's part of it. Sometimes I think I know what I feel, but it only seems real when I meet someone who is Javanese and there's a shared communication."

Pak Bambang agreed. "Yes, I know what you mean. But if you look at us Javanese, we are all different to one another too. We may be from different villages or cities, or have very different lives and experiences in our families or communities. Perhaps we even practise a different religion."

He paused and looked around the room, taking in the framed family snapshots, the books, the roses on the coffee table, the lemons on the tree outside the window.

"Life! It's life that shapes identity!" Pak Bambang said. "You're an artist, your friend is a musician, the conversation you have together is different to the one you might have with another artist, or he might have with another musician. Isn't that true?"

Adi thought about the different relationships he had with the people he knew and was close to. "Yes, each person, each conversation brings a different kind of richness. It's as if a fresh part of me is linked to that person, and the understanding we create together enriches us both." He paused and then added, "It is real too, like the shadow in the *wayang kulit* is real."

"You don't think you might like to settle in Australia?" Pak Bambang asked.

"I can't. One day soon I will be asked to leave."

"You haven't found a nice Muslim girl here to settle down with then?"

They both laughed and Adi said, "Ah, is that what I should have been doing instead of messing around with paint all this time?"

On the train back to the city, Adi thought about how Pak Bambang and Bu Wafa were like family to him now. He felt privileged to be invited to their home but he had never seen such a family where every meal time was an arena for exchanging ideas, argument and discussion. Sometimes, if she couldn't remember the details of something she had read, Bu Wafa would get up from the table to fetch a book and read out a quote.

At first he'd felt intimidated, but they paid great attention to his opinions and so he gradually learned to feel less shy when they turned to him and asked, "So, what do you think Adi?"

Then when he did speak, they listened closely. This politeness lasted about a year, but after that it wasn't unusual for Wafa or one of the girls to challenge him in the same way they did each other, "Alright Adi, that's your opinion, but what's your source, where's your evidence?"

Being with the family was relaxing, but still there were matters he could not share with them or anyone, not even Akira. The conflict with Lisa, her anger and accusations had hurt him, and he still struggled with the memory of that morning.

"Are you alright?" Bu Wafa asked.

"Yes, it's just ... " He could feel tears. "I'm fine. It's nothing," he said and looked around to focus his attention on some other thing.

Bu Wafa looked at Pak Bambang as if to prompt him and he said, "Do you want to talk about it later?"

Adi nodded, but he didn't really want to. And anyway, where would he begin?

Chapter 20

Lisa felt humiliated as she drove away from Adi's studio after their argument. There was a barrier between them and she couldn't bridge it. Deep sobs pushed up into her throat and she was forced to pull over to the side of the road until they were spent. She felt bereft. Tired and emotional, she told herself, need to get a grip, need to talk to someone. She thought of Akira – maybe he could help her to make sense of it all.

At the Darlo Boarding House, Marj answered the door. "Hello love, how are you? You after Adi? He lives in Surry Hills now."

"Hello Marj. Actually I've come to see Akira."

"I'll call him. Come in love. I'll go up. He's probably got the earphones on, does that so he doesn't disturb the Boys. Y'know? Won't be a tick."

There was something about Marj that made Lisa want to fling herself into her arms for a hug. She fished in her bag for a tissue and blew her nose. The house was filled with the aroma of a still cooking Sunday roast lamb lunch and, by the time Akira joined her downstairs, Marj had settled her in the lounge room and brought her a cup of coffee.

Akira saw Lisa's red eyes and looked concerned. "Hi Lisa. Are you alright?"

"Yes, I'm fine, just a bit emotional." she said. "I had a bit of a scene with Adi. He left the party without saying goodbye and I went to his studio and, well, we didn't part on very good terms."

When Akira remained silent, Lisa began to feel it had not been a good idea to involve him after all. "Sorry, I'm not sure why I'm here."

He said, "You were upset about him leaving last night without saying goodbye?"

"Yes I was. I really like Adi ... but, well ... "

"Asian men ... we're impossible!" he said, laughing.

"Oh Akira, I didn't mean that. I'm sorry."

"Never mind, that was just my lame attempt to make a joke. I'm sorry you're upset Lisa, but how can I help?"

"Well, I just wanted to ask is he gay? One minute I think he might be interested in me, and then it's as if he doesn't even want to be friends."

While Akira waited to hear if there was more, she said, "And I don't get the religion thing either."

"Lisa, I can't answer for him but ... first of all, he's a Muslim. Maybe he's not practising at the moment, feels guilty about it? I dunno. Maybe he's attracted to you and feels guilty about that too."

"But why? What's wrong with that?"

"Well, there's nothing wrong with it. But let's just think about this from his perspective for a minute. You come from a rich first world country and in his country the economy is still recovering from a major financial crash, right? Your family is wealthy, his is poor. He's a Muslim, you're perhaps a Christian. He's also met your family and probably reckons they wouldn't regard him as a suitable partner. Yes?"

Lisa nodded.

"And later this year, his visa will end and he has to go back to Indonesia."

"Yes, but we could still be friends, couldn't we?"

"Well, yes, of course, but only if you don't put any pressure on him."

"But I don't … didn't … "

"Lisa, he's got a solo exhibition. He's working well and he's happy. So all his friends – and that includes me – have to let him focus on that. What's happened may not mean what you're thinking. If he wants to come to you, he will. I think you just have to cut him some slack."

"You think so?"

"Yes, a lot rides on the exhibition and who knows if it will be a success?"

**

Over the coming months Lisa tried to put Adi out of her thoughts, but as time went by she realised that the things she found attractive about him were rare. Of course he was very good looking and had a kind of rare beauty, but that wasn't so important. The qualities that drew her to him were related to his dedication to his art practice, as well as the originality of his work – she loved everything he did. His reserve attracted her, as did his low key gentleness and persona. In his company, she found him kind and thoughtful, but in a quiet way, as though he was not trying to impress her. His sense of humour was playful, understated. And when she saw how loyal Akira, Marj, Archie and Bert were to him, it suggested to her that he was someone who could be trusted.

Throughout the time of their split, she found herself returning to something Akira said that suggested the attraction between them was both real and mutual, and that was when he said, "He's met your family and probably reckons they wouldn't regard him as a suitable partner."

Chapter 21

Adi's exhibition at Grove Gallery featured eight large canvases and twelve smaller paintings. It was late March and a bar had been set up in the internal courtyard. Candles were in place and ready to be lit when the sun went down, and at six o'clock the place began to fill.

As well as Gerardo's regular collectors, media and critics, there were former teachers and students from the art school, Pak Bambang and Bu Wafa, some of Adi's Indonesian friends, and Marj, Archie, Bert, Akira and Lisbeth. Even before the opening, one large painting already had a red dot on it because Gerardo had made good on a promise of a private viewing for a collector.

Throughout the evening, Gerardo maintained an upbeat and reassuring presence.

"Don't worry darling, it's your first exhibition so people might hold off on the more expensive work, but I'm pretty sure of at least three or four sales. Try and enjoy yourself, that's the main thing. The art school has done a good job publicising it so there should be a good turn up."

People made their way to the courtyard to pick up a drink and then, catalogue in hand, began looking at the paintings.

Near the gallery entrance, Adi's Artist's Statement and some biographical details were displayed on the wall. One in English and the other in Indonesian. For the official part of the evening, Gerardo spoke and the Indonesian Consul General opened the exhibition.

In his speech in reply, Adi acknowledged Gerardo and thanked his art school teachers and fellow art students for their support. He also made special mention of Archie for inspiring him to pursue the theme of shipping and the shipbuilding industry that had once been so vital to the economy of the city. With Archie as a guide, Adi had made his way to Pyrmont, Glebe Island, Garden Island, Cockatoo Island, White Bay, and Woolloomooloo – sketching ships, wharves, slips, cranes and other maritime paraphernalia, relics of a previous era.

Painting them, being up close and experiencing their immense scale somehow reminded him of those other symbols of powerful and then fallen empire, Borobodur and Prambanan. Although built in the eighth and ninth century, they too had fallen into disrepair after the dynasties declined and the ordinary people had no further use for them.

For two hours Gerardo worked the room. Every time a painting was sold, he reported it to Adi. Pak Bambang and Bu Wafa had hoped to buy, and Marj too had discussed the possibility with Akira, but both parties felt discouraged when they saw the high prices. When he became aware of this, Gerardo gathered them up and led them to a shiny yellow metal cabinet in his office. He slid open the top drawer, and took out a folder of works on paper which he left for them to consider instead. If they found something they liked he could arrange the framing.

"Three large paintings have sold, two thinking about it," Gerardo told Adi before presenting a woman with vibrant red hair and blue framed glasses. "Isabel is the *Art Times'* critic and she's going to write a review of the exhibition, aren't you darling?"

As Isabel moved away with Gerardo, Adi looked across the gallery and saw Lisa with a group of people he didn't recognise. She looked up, saw him and smiled uncertainly. He raised a hand in a half salute and saw her smile broaden. Just then Gerardo was back with a young couple who were considering one of the smaller paintings. Two of his art school lecturers came up to shake his hand – they'd both bought paintings – and now Gerardo was with him again, excited because five paintings had sold. Then off he went again, to charm and cajole.

By eight o'clock Adi felt drained. People were leaving, the bar was packing up. Pak Bambang and Bu Wafa had arrived early and left after an hour and, soon after that, Marj, Archie and Bert had left by taxi. Marj had told him she was going to sleep on which painting to buy and this had upset him because she only had to say and he would give her any one she wanted.

In the past few weeks his greatest anxiety had been that nothing would sell and the world would know he was a fraud. So now there was relief, but his mind was blank. He remembered he'd not eaten since mid-day and began moving across the room to where he'd last glimpsed Lisa.

Just then she appeared in front of him. He looked at her, saw the way the cream coloured curls framed her face and noticed two small freckles on the tip of her nose. "Do you have to be anywhere?" he asked.

She'd already said goodbye to Gerardo and was just coming to congratulate him. "No, why?"

"C'mon then, let's go." He took her hand and collected a leather jacket and two motorbike helmets from the gallery office. They left the building and he led her around the corner to a shiny black motorbike. He helped her into the leather jacket, placed the helmet on her head, checked it was properly clipped, and then sat himself on the bike and waited for her to get on.

"I haven't been on a motorbike before," she said as she lifted a leg over and sat down behind him.

"It's nothing. If I lean, you lean the same, okay? Don't worry, we won't fall over."

He reached behind him and pulled each of her arms forward so that her upper body was pressed in safely behind him. Then, after turning on the motor and lights, he eased out onto the road and accelerated down the hill to William Street.

Chapter 22

At Bondi Beach Adi parked the motorbike and he and Lisa ordered fish and chips from a busy takeaway on Campbell Parade. The warm night had brought dozens of people onto the streets, but a salt breeze was beginning to bite through their clothes. With helmets in one hand and their white paper packages of fish and chips in the other, they made their way towards the headland at the southern end of the beach.

A path led around the edge of the sandstone escarpment, and on until they came to a sheltered overhang that faced out to sea. Adi pulled a sarong from his backpack, spread it on the rocky ground, and they sat down on it. There was no moon but somehow in the darkness they could sense the swell of the incoming tide as the waves fizzled out over the rocks, and made slurping, sucking noises before being dragged back to the ocean.

They unwrapped one of the parcels, and Adi squeezed quarters of lemon over the pieces of battered fish before making a little paper holder so Lisa could hold the fish without burning her fingers. From the cosy shelter they ate in silence, taking turns to pull the chips through a hole Adi had made in the second parcel. When they finished eating, they wiped the salt and grease from their fingers and lips and Adi retrieved a packet of cigarettes and a lighter from his backpack. He gestured to Lisa for permission to light up.

She nodded. "You don't talk when you're eating Adi. Why is that?" she asked.

He lit the cigarette, inhaled, and exhaled, "I don't know. Habit I suppose – food tastes better that way."

"I see. In my family, dinner time is when we come together as a family and talk. Or it used to be when my brothers still lived at home. It was when we talked about our day. Sometimes we had arguments as well. I remember feeling sorry for friends whose families ate dinner in front of the TV instead of around the dinner table. I was the youngest so my mother used to make my older brothers listen to me and not interrupt."

The slight breeze, the light spray that drifted up onto their faces, and the sound of the waves washing in and out were melting their bodies. They both felt it. As if they were being peeled back to some timeless part of themselves that was one with the rocks, ocean and stars. Seconds, minutes – perhaps lifetimes – passed by before they were returned to the present. Neither of them spoke but they now felt their bodies stiffening from the chill of the breeze and rock beneath them.

"Are you cold?" Adi asked.

"A little," she said, pulling up her knees and hugging them.

Adi pulled a sweater from his bag and wrapped it around her legs and ankles. "Better?"

Lisa nodded. "Do you think you'll stay in Australia, Adi?"

"Well, no. My visa runs out in October and the government says no more extensions."

It was almost midnight when they arrived back in the city, and Adi opened all the windows of the studio to let in the night air. As usual, the sea air had made him hungry and he set about making noodles for them both.

Lisa stretched out on the lounge. "So, what've you been doing since I last saw you?"

"Painting."

"Of course! The exhibition was amazing. Gerardo was thrilled. You sold five?"

"Six. Yes, Gerardo is very happy. He said we might sell two more."

As the studio filled with delicious food smells, Lisa picked up a book from the coffee table and began flicking through it, but when Adi crossed the room with two steaming bowls of noodles, he was surprised to find her fast asleep with the book face down on her chest.

For reasons he could not articulate he felt honoured that she was asleep on his lounge, and he was intrigued to see the limp vulnerability that had spread over her. Her face appeared soft and trusting like a small child's and, when he finished eating, he collected a sketchpad and charcoal sticks and began drawing. He worked quickly, urgently scratching marks onto the paper in case she woke. He moved around her to find the images he wanted – her face, the side of her head, the length of her body, hands, hair, feet, elbow. As he finished each drawing, he tore it from the pad, sprayed it with fixative, then put it on the long table at the centre of the studio.

He sketched all night, until there was nothing more to draw and his aching hand was black with charcoal.

When Lisa woke, the sun was streaming through the studio windows. Adi had showered and changed into a sarong and tee-shirt and the sketches, about thirty of them, lay scattered about the room. As he looked up from brewing a pot of coffee, he saw Lisa take a moment to register where she was. She looked at Adi, saw the blanket covering her, and took the mug he was holding out to her.

"Milk, no sugar. Right?"

"Thanks. I'm sorry, I seem to have slept all night. Thanks for the blanket too."

As Lisa sat up, she saw the drawings as well as the beginning of a large painting on the easel. She looked at Adi and smiled.

"I usually charge for this you know."

Adi held out his hands. "Sorry, I just wanted … Are you angry?"

Lisa laughed, "No, it's okay. Serves me right for falling asleep on your lounge."

Adi brought a plate of buttered toast to the coffee table.

Lisa took a piece and said, "Tell me about your family."

"Well, there's my father and stepmother and I have six brothers and sisters. My mother died when I was six …"

"Oh, I'm so sorry. That must have been terrible. What happened?"

"She had an accident," he said. "But I can't remember her face."

"You have no photos of her?"

"No."

"Have you tried drawing her?"

"No, no. I can't."

Adi looked down at his coffee. Black, sweet, just as he liked it.

Yanti, Budi and Ismoyo are asleep. Everyone, except Mama and Papa, and me. There is a lit candle and I can see Mama and Papa. They don't know I'm awake too.

Mama's hair is loose and hanging down and she is coining Papa's back. Her hand moves slowly, starting at the top and drawing down to the bottom, and I know Papa's eyes are closed even though I can't see them.

They are quiet. Mama is wearing her old brown sarong with the garuda wings – it's her favourite to wear to bed, and Papa's back is criss-crossed with angry red lines now.

Finally, Mama murmurs, "Uwis Mas," and then Papa turns around and I see him looking at Mama. He takes her hands and looks at them, and then he pushes the hair away from her face. He smiles at her, and then leans over and inhales – first on one side of her face and then on the other.

Adi looked up and saw Lisa looking at him.

"Adi, is something wrong?"

"Yes, yes … sorry. I was just thinking about my parents. Another coffee?"

"No thanks. I need a shower. Do you mind?"

"Go ahead. There are towels and sarongs in the bathroom cupboard. Help yourself."

Adi returned to his painting.

Eventually, the bathroom door opened and he could hear Lisa laughing. She was trying to secure the sarong but each time she tied the ends, the sarong refused to stay in place. Seeing her dilemma, Adi moved to retrieve the sarong which by now had fallen onto the floor.

He wrapped it around her and gently tied the ends in a tight knot above her breasts. The closeness of their bodies made him bold and he raised his hands and placed them on her shoulders. He drew her towards him and put first one cheek and then the other to each side of her face to inhale the perfume of her skin and hair. Desire flushed through his body.

"Mmmm … very sweet," he said.

"What are you doing?"

"Sniffing. It's the way we Javanese kiss."

Adi placed a flat hand on Lisa's chest and felt her heart pounding a beat that echoed his own. A joyful exhilaration, painful in its intensity, suffused his entire body as – laughing, crying, pushing and pressing against one another – they fell towards the bed.

When Lisa left the studio that evening, Adi took out Pak Harto's prayer rug and began to pray. After the success of the exhibition, a dream was taking shape – of a life as an artist, with Lisa, and the children they would have, in Australia. He felt a deep gratitude, excitement and joy for this new love, but slicing through it was a sense of guilt that he might be about to abandon his past, his family and his country. So, as always in moments of conflicted emotion, colours and patterns filled his body and mind – shades and variants of pink like the colours of certain bougainvillea, the flesh of a mangosteen, the fiery glow in a flooded rice field at sunrise, and certain artists' palettes.

Chapter 23

The year she and Adi began a relationship, Lisa was studying for the honours year of her Bachelor of Fine Arts. She had research to do and a thesis to write, and she was hoping for good results so she could enrol in a master's degree the following year. This meant her affair with Adi had to take a second place, but she spent any time she could spare with him. Other friends she neglected, including Mack who was now working as a graphic designer in an advertising agency.

After many rainchecks, Lisa and Mack had arranged to meet and, when she arrived at the coffee shop, he was already sitting at one of the tables. He stood up to greet her when she entered and, without being able to put her finger on it exactly, she thought he looked different.

"Wow, look at you. So cool and stylish. Who would've thought?" she said, looking him up and down.

"When was I not cool and stylish?"

"Well maybe you just have the look of a man with a real job," she said laughing.

"Like a grown up then," he suggested.

"That's it."

"So, howzit going with Adi?" he asked after they had ordered their coffees.

"Fine ... it's fine," she said.

He sensed there was more. "Fine? Is that all?"

Lisa was smiling. "Well, he wants to get married ... "

Mack was shocked. "Far out!"

"So ... as you know, I'm not really the marrying kind."

"Say that again!" Mack looked at her closely, "So what's changed?"

Lisa remembered that there was a conversation she'd been meaning to have with him, but she would put that off for another day.

"He feels guilty about making love when we're not married," she said.

"How quaint!"

"Mack, please don't be mean. I need you to listen."

"Sorry, please go on. Did you say yes or no?"

"Well, he needs to marry so he can stay in Australia. If he goes back to Indonesia now it will be the end of his career here."

"Whoa! Hang on a minute. Are we talking love and marriage, or career management?"

"Well they're connected obviously."

He was watching her. "You're fidgeting. That worries me. You don't usually fidget," he said. "Okay then, now tell me this: do you, as they say in the movies, love him?"

"Well, yes I do."

"Convincing? No, I sense a but."

"My family don't know yet ... Dad will go ballistic, Mum will be 'disappointed.' You know what they're like?"

"Yep, 'fraid so, but you're used to that aren't you? I mean, if you really love him and want to get married, then it'd be the first time you've actually got that reaction for something that wasn't pure rebellion. No offence ... but knowing Adi, I kinda think this is not part of your usual shock horror being dished up."

"So you approve?"

"Darling, you don't need my approval. You're my sister, best friend, soul mate. I don't know if you'll be happy with him, but you have to believe it's worth a crack. Put it this way, you have my blessing. I want you to be happy."

"Well thank you very much." Lisa was relieved.

"And if you're not happy, I want you to get a divorce." Mack planted a kiss on her forehead and put his arm around her shoulders.

She gave him a kiss on the cheek and said, "Well that's my news, how's your love life?"

As she turned back to her coffee, Lisa saw that Adi had been watching them from outside the café, and his face was distorted with rage and grief.

She stood up, rummaged in her bag, dropped some money on the table, and rushed to the door.

"Oh great … See you then," Mack called after her.

Lisa flew after Adi who was a good fifty metres ahead of her, and when she arrived at the warehouse, the lift was already groaning upwards. She turned and sprinted up the stairs and reached the fourth floor just as Adi was entering the studio.

"Adi …" she called.

Ignoring her, Adi went to his easel and began squirting tubes of colour onto a plate. She waited and then tiptoed over and touched him lightly on the shoulders. He began to shake.

"You were kissing Mack," he said hoarsely.

"I often kiss Mack, we're old friends."

"It looks like more … Not just friends."

"Mack and I could never be lovers or whatever it is you think you saw. You must understand – he is like a brother to me."

Lisa put her arms around him and pressed her body into his back.

"I was telling him about us getting married. He was happy for us, that's why he kissed me. Don't be jealous," she whispered.

He was jealous of Mack, always had been, jealous of their easy intimacy and physical demonstrativeness. In his country men were affectionate with other men, boys with boys – holding hands, arms around one another, sharing a bed even. But not women and men, not girls and boys. That was not acceptable. Seeing them sitting close – touching, hugging, kissing – it hurt and, even worse, it was in a public place.

"Adi, please turn around. Would I say I want to marry you if it was Mack I loved? You have to know how I feel about you and you have to trust that, no matter what."

The icicle of fear that had formed inside him at the window of the café had made his body set as rigid as a plank, but now, feeling the softening heat of her body, he turned to look at her. She was smiling at him with such luminosity that it filled him with relief.

"I'm sorry," he said. "I want to trust you but sometimes I fear that everything – this life, your love, my work – will be ripped away."

She took his face in both hands and said, "Be sure of this. I too want to trust you always."

Hours later Lisa felt for Adi in the bed beside her. He wasn't there and when she opened her eyes she saw him praying on a small rug on the floor. At first she was curious, but then, thinking she should give him some privacy, she went to take a shower. When she emerged he was sitting on the bed, with his back propped on the pillows against the wall.

"Do you want to hear a story?" he asked.

"Sure, I love stories." She sat on the bed and rubbed at her wet hair with a towel as he told her a brief version of the Ramayana. It was the only way he could think to express what his hopes were for their relationship.

"It's a story my mother always told me – the story of Rama and Sita. Rama was a prince, very handsome, strong, wise – the reincarnation of the god Vishnu. He married Princess Sita and it was known that one day they would become king and queen. But then, one of the old King's wives tricked the King and the King told Rama that another son would be king. So Rama had to leave the palace and go into the forest. Rama's brother Laksmana and Sita went with him. Sita gave up her jewels, fine clothes and life in the palace because of her love for Rama, but she was very beautiful and a wicked demon tricked Rama and Laksmana and kidnapped her. He took her far away, and there was a great war. Eventually Rama killed the demon and rescued Sita. This is the story of the Ramayana."

"I'm glad it has a happy ending," she said, as she got up to leave.

But Adi hadn't finished. "The Ramayana was performed in the shadow puppet show when I was a little boy. It is about a man and a woman, how they love and support one another, and stay together, even in the hard times, and how they forgive one another always."

Chapter 21

Lisa knew that Adi was a definite fail on her parents' marriage partner scorecard. He didn't go to the right school; he was not just a foreigner, he was a non-European foreigner and a Muslim; neither he nor his family were rich; his father was not a doctor or a judge; he had not one shred of noble ancestry; and he was from a place they still referred to as the "Third World".

When she arranged to meet Helen at the Art Gallery for lunch, Lisa's plan was to break the news to her mother first, and then take it from there. It was a sunny day, so they took their trays and sat in the courtyard outside.

As soon as they were seated, Lisa broke the news. "Adi and I have decided to get married," she said.

Her mother reacted as if she had been struck from behind, "Oh Lisa, look what you've made me do."

Helen had spilled her wine, and Lisa helped her to mop it up as her mother struggled to regain her composure. When she reached into her handbag for a handkerchief, Lisa saw that her top lip was trembling, "Mum, are you crying? What on earth ... "

"Well, it's a big shock … I, we, your father and I didn't even know you were seeing this man. And what do we know of him? Or his family?" Helen paused to catch her breath and take a sip of wine.

"You've met him a couple of times," Lisa said. She was still embarrassed by her parents' behaviour when she introduced Adi to them at the art school's graduate show.

"That's not the same thing. You didn't say you were seeing him or were serious about him."

This was not going as Lisa expected. At the very least she had expected curiosity from her mother – about Adi, about her love for him, about how they imagined their future together.

"Is it because he's Indonesian, Muslim or an artist?" Lisa asked. She was feeling frustrated and annoyed, and when no reply came, she said, "It's all three, isn't it?"

"Certainly not," Helen said. "I don't know why you have to spring this on us. Anyway, what's the rush? You know very well your father will be very put out when I tell him."

"Well, it's what Adi and I both want and I wanted to tell you first. It's important to both of us that we have your blessing."

Adi knew that Lisa's parents would not be in favour of them marrying, and this upset and hurt him. When he discussed it with Akira, his friend pointed out that they could not stop them from marrying. Even so, Adi insisted on asking for their blessing and both Pak Bambang and Marj agreed it was the right thing to do.

When he told them about the forthcoming lunch with Lisa's parents, Archie and Bert gave him some advice. It was something they had not done before and, far from reassuring him, their solemn care gave him a sense of foreboding.

First Bert explained that he had been at boarding school with people like Ian, and for the first time Adi noticed that he had the same polished accent as Lisa's father.

"It's important not to be afraid of him," Bert said. "He might try and intimidate you so the main thing is to maintain eye contact. Don't let him think you're weak and don't let him think you're scared of him."

Archie, practical as ever, said, "Just make sure you give 'im a good firm handshake."

He held out his hand, "Here, shake. This is what I reckon he'll do." Adi looked down at Archie's freckled and roughened hand that was almost twice the size of his own. He felt it envelop his hand and then squeeze like a python with its prey.

"Feel that," Archie said, "you've got to match it. Again … that's it, good lad."

Adi held out his hand again and, as Archie squeezed tighter and tighter, he imagined he was absorbing Archie's strength, returning it, and unblocking his paralysing grip.

Archie loosened his grip and was clearly pleased with his student. "So if he tries that on you, you watch the expression on his face. He'll get a shock."

"Now don't go getting him all worried," Marj said. "You'll be fine dear. Just be yourself. Lisa is very lucky to be marrying a nice young man like yourself. Isn't she, Boys?"

"Oh I dunno Marj … " Archie joked.

***

Lisa tried to explain to Adi what her father was like. "My father has no curiosity. Really! It's very difficult for him to let in any new information or different opinions. He loves me and I love him but difference unsettles him. He can be quite misogynistic and even racist at times. I think he has a fearful insecurity about his own superiority. It's part of his upbringing, the colonial mentality, private boys' school education, White Australia policy, but he'd never admit it."

As she spoke, Lisa became aware of how ignorant her father seemed and it saddened her.

"He's a barrister, well-educated, has travelled extensively. Been to every great museum in the world practically. He's seen so much but, in the end, it is his bank account and not his soul that has been touched. Travel is information to him, he might as well have stayed at home and read the travel book."

Adi didn't like hearing Lisa criticise her father. It seemed harsh.

"I used to be so embarrassed at the way he expected everyone to speak English, and when they didn't, or couldn't, he still spoke English to them, only louder. If he really felt out of his depth he'd get angry with the hotel staff. It was awful. That's why we stayed in five-star hotels. Oh god, how I hated the organised tours they made us go on! The best time was when Mummy and I went to Rome by ourselves for a month. Mummy was studying Italian and we stayed in a cool old apartment instead of a hotel. We pretended to be locals, going to the same bar for a pastry and coffee every morning, getting around on public transport. We even went to a nightclub to check out a famous female DJ."

"Rome – I'd like to go there one day," Adi said to change the subject.

"You'd love it. Anyway, don't worry about Dad, he'll come round."

Lisa was trying to reassure him, but he felt uncomfortable with the way Australians could be so negative about almost anyone – teachers or politicians, even their prime minister. He saw this in Pak Bambang's family too. For him, respect was important and he wondered how he would teach this to his own children if they grew up here. Could a child adjust to different ways of behaving in two or more cultures, he wondered.

Chapter 25

Ian and Helen Davidson lived to the north of the Harbour Bridge in a part of the city that was often referred to as the leafy north shore. Their house was on a large block with a sweeping circular driveway. The kitchen and family room opened onto a terrace and swimming pool at the back, and below that there was the tennis court. Beyond the tennis court, there was bush. On the inside of the house, floor to ceiling windows filled the rooms with daylight, and Adi was surprised to see many paintings by Australian artists throughout the house – Boyd, Olsen, Gascoigne, Olley, Whiteley, Nolan.

The Nolan, an oil on canvas, was a desert landscape, 1.5 x 1.5 metres, and he shivered when he saw the artist's signature in the bottom right-hand corner. In the mountain cliff on the right he saw rough downward brush strokes – pink browns, orange browns – that drew the eye down into a creamy orange valley which stretched all the way to the central horizon. In the valley, there were the faint curling bends of a river, a trace of trees and, in the far distance, orange, purple and grey-green ranges. The frame was completed by mesa like forms on the left, and a khaki smudge in the foreground. Half of the painting was given over to a wide expanse of blue sky – with soft clouds and then, higher up in the atmosphere, a bank of mauve and grey, and rub of yellow.

"Do you like it?" Lisa asked.

He gave a start and wondered how long she'd been standing beside him, "Nolan?"

"Yes, *Central Australia 1988*, I think. They bought it at auction in the early nineties on advice from their interior designer. It's a privilege to have grown up with it."

He would have liked to linger, to study each of the paintings – and the other objects he'd glimpsed as they walked through parts of the house – an exquisite wave-like Murano vase, some glass and marble sculptures by British and Australian artists, and a cream and soft grey porcelain assemblage by an Australian ceramicist he admired.

There was a baby grand piano as well. "You play?" he asked.

"No, not me. My mother, Helen."

When they sat down to lunch on the terrace, Ian poured chilled white wine into each of their glasses. Sensing that Lisa was about to tell her father he didn't drink alcohol, Adi gently touched her knee as he accepted the glass and, when she glanced at him, shook his head.

"How's Mack, dear, do you still see him?" Helen asked.

"Of course. He's fine, busy with the new job."

Ian said, "I saw James at golf. Said Mack's working for an advertising agency. He'll go far. He was a darned fine rower, you know?" He turned to Adi, "Do you row?"

"Dad! I totally don't believe you. Mum … " Lisa looked to her mother for support but Helen refused to be drawn in.

"Row? A boat? Yes, yes … I have – once or twice," Adi replied.

After lunch they moved back into the living room for coffee. The unaccustomed wine, a single glass, left Adi with such a sense of calm that he could almost have lain down on the pale green carpet and gone to sleep. But now was the time to speak, and when he looked across at Lisa he saw she was ready. He had rehearsed the words with her, so he knew that what he had to say was the correct grammar and pronunciation.

He looked up into the deep valley of the Nolan. By now Lisa was standing next to him and he could feel her presence and resolve igniting his courage.

Marj had advised him to keep it simple and so he looked first at Helen and then Ian, "Helen and Ian, Lisa and I would like to marry and we would like your blessing."

There, it was done. Now there was silence. He wanted to look back to the Nolan but knew he had to keep his eyes on Ian's face which had turned a deep and dangerous looking red.

Ian was opening and closing his mouth as if gasping for air, and Helen touched him lightly on the arm to release his voice, which sounded strangled and hostile, "If you're asking us the answer is no. If you're informing us, the answer is still no," he announced, and Adi had the feeling that he too had been rehearsing his words.

But Ian's words, far from being powerful, signified defeat. It was a tableau. They were puppets, waiting for the puppet master's next move. Time passed. Adi was still, silent, and when he didn't respond Ian began to sulk.

His face had returned to its normal tanned hue but now all he could say was, "We're not happy."

There was an impasse, and Lisa slid her arm through the crook of Adi's arm in a gesture of solidarity. They were as one.

"Darling, please," Helen appealed to Lisa. "Sweetheart, it's just that your father and I feel it's too sudden. We'd like you to wait, perhaps get engaged, but put off marriage while you finish your studies. This honours year is very demanding and I know you want to do well. It's best not to have any distractions, don't you think?"

Ian was angry and he wanted to wound. "Why do you want to marry an artist? There are no artists in my family, never have been. It's not a proper job," he said.

Hearing this, Adi permitted himself to look again at the Nolan. For the first time he saw scratchings in the paint just above the signature, vegetation. There were no human beings in the painting, they could only stand outside it, but what was it that Nolan was saying? It nagged at him but now he got it, he was showing them that the land was alive, living, immortal, infinite, a part of us, and we were a part of it.

Helen wanted to appease. "Sweetheart, Adi, it just seems too rushed."

"Mummy, we want to marry so Adi can stay in Australia – otherwise he'll have to return to Indonesia."

Ian looked at her hopefully. "And, really, I can't go to Indonesia, I've got too much on with finishing honours, plus I want to go on and do a master's. I suppose I could do it over there but I'd have to learn Indonesian and, anyway, we'd still have to marry to do that."

Adi looked at Ian and then at Helen. Akira had said to him, "Don't get side tracked. Stay on message."

He said, "Helen and Ian, we would like your blessing. This is very important to us."

Ian heard a string of racist slurs echo in his mind – terms heard in playgrounds or on shock jock radio. Now he feared they would apply to his grandchildren, and he saw for a second an image of a child being taunted by a gang of other children. He brushed his forehead with his hand as if to clear his thoughts, but it was too late – for, in a flash, they/them had merged with we/us, and this rare moment of empathic awareness caused him to emit an involuntary and audible expression of pain.

"Ian?" Helen said.

He looked up, "Alright but I expect you to support Lisa. I don't want you to think she has to support you. You have to support her, artist or no artist? Is that clear?"

"Yes sir, that is what I want also, and to have a family."

"Adi!" Lisa looked at him in surprise, "I'm twenty-three."

He looked at her and nodded. "One day," he said.

Chapter 26

Adi was studying the Javanese calendar and Lisa was curious. She held out her hand and Adi passed it over, but she soon saw that it was not in English. It was all written in black ink Javanese script on poor quality newsprint, and she could see it was laid out with the days of the month on each page, with some notes for each day. He told her he had borrowed it so he could choose the most auspicious date for their wedding.

"Will this tell you which is a good day or bad day to get married?"

"Yes, it tells you what each day is good for … "

"So, it's like astrology?"

"Sort of."

"Does everyone follow the calendar?"

"No, not everyone. Some people don't."

"But you do?" Adi nodded. "And what will happen if we don't choose the right day?"

Adi shrugged. "We may not have a good marriage."

"You really believe that?"

Adi had a sense of disquiet. He felt agitated. The impending marriage had reminded him of his family, of being Javanese, of responsibilities and obligations. He wanted to tell Lisa how important it was to have children, about the role of a wife and mother, the role of a husband and father. If she were Javanese he wouldn't have had to explain and he wouldn't have felt odd consulting the Javanese calendar.

Later, when Lisa told him the celebrant wasn't available on any of the dates he chose, his unease escalated.

"It will have to be the third or twenty-fourth of August if we want this celebrant. What do those days look like?"

"Well, the twenty-fourth maybe," he said.

"Okay, we'll have to go with that then because Mum and Dad are away for September, October."

Twice in the coming months Adi bought roses, and when it was still dark he rode his motorbike to the sprawling cliff-top cemetery at Waverley. There, on the headland overlooking the Pacific Ocean, he stripped off the petals and waited for the sun to rise, watching the sky colour from palest blue to pink before the glaring orange orb slid up over the rim of ocean. At that point he spoke to his mother, begged her forgiveness, begged her permission to marry in a foreign land, begged her blessing, and then scattered the rose petals to the ocean below. When it was done he was filled with a temporary deep calm.

Mama is making a batik for me. She has made a batik for the others, and now it is my turn. But sometimes she is busy and does not work on it for weeks, or even months.

She bought the finest cotton, drew the design and began applying the wax. Many times Mama has dyed it, doing everything herself. Papa's friend from the factory brought her the dyes and helped her as well.

"This is for when you are a grown man, Adi. In it I have waxed my dreams for you. Shall I tell you what I wish for you when you grow up?"

"Yes, Mama."

Mama points to the different symbols on the cloth.

"You will be a kind man. You will love your wife. You will have children."

Mama looks up at me. "You will have children, yes?"

"Oh yes, Mama."

"How many children, Adi?"

"Two, I'll have two."

"Only two, darling?"

"Three, I'll have three."

"Yes, that is what I thought. See here. You will go to school and learn many things. And you will be very clever. Maybe you will be a rich man. Would you like to be rich one day?"

"Maybe a little bit rich, Mama, so I can buy you a beautiful present."

"Really, how wonderful! What will you buy me?"

"I'll buy you a kite and a baby elephant and a new kebaya and ... "

"Thank you. I see you will be a very generous man as well. But also I hope you will be generous in love and forgiveness for that will make your marriage and your family strong."

"Can I have my batik now, Mama?"

"Not yet. You will have it when the time is right."

Chapter 21

On Observatory Hill there is a park with a rotunda, and from there a person can look across to the grey steel arch of the Sydney Harbour Bridge, see the trains and cars sliding back and forth. There is a line of climbers, like wee insects, inching up the outside of the arch to the summit and, immediately below, there is the area of the city known as The Rocks. It is where the first shiploads of English soldiers, convicts and settlers struggled to grow food on the harbour shores. All this, which they called Port Jackson, is First Nations' land, and its traditional owners are the Gadigal people of the Eora nation. There is no treaty, they did not cede sovereignty.

On this sunny warm Saturday in August, a crowd of about forty people have gathered in the rotunda to witness a marriage. The couple are wearing traditional Javanese wedding sarongs, the ceremonial part is over, and they and their guests are crowded around for the camera.

The photographer calls, "Smile." He looks up and sees that everyone is smiling except the groom, who has assumed a serious and dignified pose.

"Adi are you happy? Can you smile for the camera? Ready?"

Lisa lets out a shriek as Mack tickles her ribs and everyone turns to look at them.

"Look this way please. Smile."

In all the wedding photos, Adi looks like the adult who is waiting patiently for the children to stop mucking up.

***

Ian and Helen's wedding present for the couple is a paid deposit on a forties style two-bedroom apartment in Darlinghurst, not far from the art school. It is in one of four identical apartment blocks, two on one side of the street and two directly opposite. Each block has a low, dark brown brick wall at the front which contains six tiny mailboxes, and a wide, tiled path that leads to a pair of chrome-framed glass front doors. There are three storeys, with two two-bedroom apartments on each floor – each of which has French doors and its own Juliet balcony at the front.

Lisa, Adi, Ian and Helen meet in front of the building and Ian opens the door into the south-facing foyer with a key. An art deco stained glass window extends from the first floor to the ceiling of the third floor and draws light into the entry and stairwell. The foyer walls are lined with rich dark wood panelling and the floor is tiled with small hexagonal mosaics arranged in a green, black, white and orange pattern. Ian and Helen lead the way up the grey marble treads of the polished oak staircase to the third floor.

Ian tells them, "You're on the top floor. I've checked the contract and you could build in the airspace later if you want. The place is vacant so you can move in anytime."

At the rear of the apartment, a metal staircase zigzags down to a radiant sun-filled raggle taggle backyard. Two Hills Hoist clotheslines, one on each side of the block, are connected to a communal laundry by a concrete pathway. The lawn is overgrown, tangled, and shaded in patches by tall eucalypts. Bushy native shrubs screen the timber fences on three sides and provide a haven for birds and butterflies. There is a makeshift brick-paved barbecue area and a variety of salvaged benches, tables and chairs, arranged as if in conversation. Helen and Ian have put the apartment in Lisa's name and the couple will pay off the mortgage.

A week later there is a working bee to help Adi and Lisa move in. Cars are loaded up, a van hired, and wedding presents, books and furniture are carried up the stairs. Marj arrives and sets about washing out the cupboards and helping to unpack, and Archie and Bert mow the backyard, trim bushes, whipper snip, weed and rake. By five o'clock, everything is packed away, the removal van returned, pizzas ordered, and beers handed out.

When Gerardo arrives with champagne, the housewarming party is already in full swing.

Part Three

Sydney
2003–2008

Chapter 28

When they were first married, Adi and Lisa agreed they would visit Adi's family in Indonesia as soon as possible, but a fifth wedding anniversary had come and gone and still the plan was scuttled, partly because they were each balancing ambitious work and study programs. In preparation, Lisa had even attended Indonesian classes and pleaded with Adi to practise with her, but that lapsed too as other priorities absorbed their time.

Adi returned to art school for two years to do a Master of Fine Arts degree and Lisa completed hers too. When she first began the master's she thought she wanted to become a curator, but it became clear as her studies progressed that her real passion was art history and theory. After a two-year break, she began a doctorate in which her focus was on modernist women artists from the first half of the twentieth century.

On the first Sunday of each month after they were married, Adi and Lisa went to lunch with Helen and Ian. These monthly visits were a chore for Adi because, while Helen was friendly, Ian remained hostile. On every other Sunday they went to the Darlo Boarding House to have a roast lunch with Marj, Archie, Bert, Akira and Lisbeth, and this was a ritual they both enjoyed. On the previous weekend, Akira and Lisbeth had broken the news that Lisbeth was three-months pregnant.

Like Akira, Lisbeth was a musician, a jazz vocalist, and the couple had met when they were studying at the Conservatorium of Music. Lisbeth had grown up on a property down near Wagga Wagga and Marj warmed to her from the day they met. She was always joking with Archie or Bert, and the house seemed joyful and lively when she was around. It was part of her character, too, to be always ready to burst into song, often with comedic effect.

In the week following their announcement, Marj asked Akira to sit down and have a cup of tea with her, Archie and Bert, and she began by asking, "So now that Lisbeth is having a baby, what are your plans?"

It was early days and the couple had just found out themselves about the pregnancy, so they had only had the briefest of discussions with one another about where they would live after the baby was born.

"We've had a couple of goes at talking about it but we need somewhere where I can have the piano and still practise. Lisbeth's housemates said we could live there, but I'm not so sure."

Marj glanced at Archie and Bert. "Well, we had a bit of a talk and we thought Lisbeth could move in here. What d'you reckon about that idea? You could have Adi's old room for the baby."

Akira smiled. He'd been wondering about this, even discussed it with Lisbeth, but it had seemed too much to ask.

"We'd love that – I think I can speak for Lisbeth – but what about having a crying baby in the house, you don't think that would bother you?"

"Won't bother me because I'm half deaf," Bert replied, "Besides, I'm happy as long as Marj is happy."

"Archie?"

"Couldn't be worse than you bangin' away on the piano all day, could it?" he said, and Akira wondered if he was just covering his tracks. It might even have been his idea.

Akira looked at Marj who was smiling happily. "Marj?"

"Y'know what, love? Babies sleep most of the time and I reckon I haven't lost my touch after all this time."

And so Lisbeth moved in, and six months later they brought Eloise home to the Darlo Boarding House. As soon as they got the news that Eloise had arrived and mother and child were well, Adi and Lisa visited the hospital to welcome her. A month later when it came time for her christening, Akira and Lisbeth asked them to be godparents. There was some discussion about whether a Muslim could be a godparent to a child who was being christened in an Anglican church, but then they decided that since Akira's family was Buddhist, Lisbeth's was Anglican, Lisa was an atheist, and Adi was a Muslim, they probably had all bases covered.

The night after the christening Adi had a dream.

The rains have stopped and the water in the river is clear and clean. There is no one else about – just Mama and me.

I splash, and sing, and float, and swim down to the bottom with my eyes open. When I come up Mama's sarong has slipped to her waist and I can see her back. Her skin is wet and glowing. She is soaping her hair and her eyes are squeezed shut.

I want to play a trick so I sink down until the water is up to my shoulders and – slowly, very slowly – I move closer and closer. Now if I want I can reach out and touch Mama.

Mama is listening with her eyes closed, but I keep very still. She calls me, "Adi?"

I have a piece of grass and I tickle Mama's nose. Her eyes flick open and I start to laugh. I tickle her neck and breast.

"Don't – stop it!" Mama says and brushes my hand away. I fall backward.

The water goes into my nose and I start to cough. When I stop coughing, Mama is ducking her head into the water to rinse off the shampoo. I sneak around behind her, wait, and when she stands up again I push her hard on her back.

Mama falls down under the water. I think I know where she will come up. I see the bubbles spreading out, joining the ripples in the water.

I'm looking and looking but Mama doesn't come back up. Where is she?

"Mama," I cry. I'm so scared. "Mama … Mama."

When the sound of Adi thrashing about and emitting stifled, frightened grunts woke Lisa, she reached out and turned on the bedside light.

"Adi, what is it?" She patted him on the shoulder, "Darling, it's a dream. You're dreaming."

When Adi kept on with his anguished calling, "Bu, Bu," Lisa stroked his forehead, "Darling … It's okay, you can wake up now. It's just a bad dream."

Adi rolled onto his back and, although his eyes were wide open, Lisa was unsure if he was awake or not.

"What is it? What were you dreaming?" she asked as he struggled to sit up.

Adi gave her a blank look and then, recognising her at last, fell back and rested his head on the pillow. He closed his eyes and waited to feel calm enough to sit up again.

"I dreamt I pushed my mother and she fell in the river and disappeared."

"Oh, how awful," Lisa said. "But that is not how she died, is it? Your mother didn't drown?"

Mute with grief, Adi shook his head.

"Are you okay? Come, lie down." She lay back and put out her arms to him, and when they were lying arm in arm, she turned out the light and snuggled in close with her head resting on his shoulder. Within seconds she was asleep and Adi could hear her steady calm breathing.

After some minutes, in which parts of the dream replayed over and over in his mind and body, Adi realised he was wide awake.

"Lisa?" he called over and over until she responded. "Can you wake up? I can't get back to sleep."

Suddenly Lisa sat up. "What time is it?" she asked, looking at the illuminated numbers of her clock. "Oh god, it's only three o'clock. Adi, go to sleep. We have to sleep."

"I can't," he complained. "Will you come while I get something to eat?"

Lisa roused herself. "Sweetheart, I've got a big day – I'm giving a seminar paper. Remember?"

Resentment jabbed at him as he heard once more the slow even rhythm of her breathing.

"A good wife would," he muttered in Javanese and got out of bed. He pulled on jeans and tee-shirt, grabbed his jacket, and scuttled downstairs.

It was almost four o'clock when he made his way along Darlinghurst Road, across William Street, and on through Kings Cross. The usually busy streets were practically deserted. A solitary red-eyed youth offered him pills and he shook his head and stopped to buy a takeaway coffee.

At the El Alamein Fountain, Adi sat down to drink his coffee while the fine mist that drifted off the sputnik orb settled on his hair and shoulders. This square on Macleay Street was one of his favourite places, and at that hour there was only a trickle of cars cruising, some of which had deep revving engines and stereos that blasted a dull doof, doof onto the streets.

The dawn brought a drop in temperature and Adi zipped up his jacket, pulled up his collar, and set off towards the harbour. The streetlights were beginning to fade and a garbage truck began edging up the hill towards him – stopping here and there as the men in high-vis vests seized the red bins that were lined up outside the apartment blocks, and pushed them onto the back of the truck to be uplifted and emptied. Then they moved on, leaving a ragged trail of wheelie bins behind them. On the other side of the road, a council water tanker rolled past, spraying jets of water that swept the night's debris into the gutters and down to the nearest stormwater grate.

When he arrived at the waterfront, Adi found himself back on level ground and he strode past the ships at Garden Island and the restored Woolloomooloo Finger Wharf until he reached some metal stairs that led up a sandstone cliff. At the top he crossed a flat tree-studded park that was covered in a layer of morning dew. With each springy step he felt his canvas sandshoes become more and more soaked and stained with murky green streaks.

When he reached Art Gallery Road he paused by a stand of giant Moreton Bay Fig trees to consider which direction to go next. He could feel the tremble of traffic on the expressway below and the Botanical Gardens and harbour beckoned him to go north. He was tempted, but then changed his mind and walked briskly south to College Street, past St Mary's Cathedral, the indoor public swimming pool, and some billboards advertising animated dinosaurs at the museum.

He enjoyed seeing the city at this hour, as if with uncluttered eyes, and without the constant movement and noisy distraction of people and cars. Over in Hyde Park, solitary individuals slept rough, jogged or walked their dog as if it was their private garden. At Stanley Street he turned his back on the city and almost took flight on the steep descent into Darlinghurst where Italian coffee shops were already charging up their espresso machines, and where he stood at the counter to drink a macchiato before setting off on the steep uphill climb to their part of Darlinghurst.

He'd been gone hours and done a full circle, but a niggling irritation returned as soon as he entered the apartment building and began climbing the stairs. Inside the apartment he could hear Lisa moving around, and then she entered the kitchen in a rush.

She smiled at the sight of him. "Why didn't you wake me? I hope I'm not late for class."

Lisa spread butter and Vegemite on a slice of toast and, holding it in one hand, gathered up her bag and laptop, and went to plant her lips on his as she headed for the door.

When he turned his head to avert the kiss, she stepped back in surprise, "Ouch ... what's the matter?"

He shrugged, "Well, I had a bad dream."

"Oh, last night. I'm sorry, I've gotta go. We'll talk later, yeah?"

She tipped him on the nose with a spare finger and rushed for the door. He heard her skipping down the stairs, the front door closed after her, and he listened for the sound of her revving car.

Chapter 29

It had become a tradition for Adi to host a lunch after each exhibition at Grove Gallery, and this year had been his sixth solo exhibition. While the prices for his work had risen with each exhibition and he now had a track record that assured him some success with grant applications, he still did not feel secure enough to give up his part-time work as a gardener.

It was Gerardo's view that the global focus in visual arts was shifting away from China and India to South East Asia and, with this in mind, he had begun looking at other emerging artists from the Asia Pacific region. At the same time, the gallerist was making connections with other institutions in the region to promote Adi's work, and this led to him being invited as one of five contemporary Indonesian artists to exhibit at the Singapore Art Museum later in the year.

A year earlier, Adi had returned to Indonesia for his niece's wedding. Altogether he was away for two weeks, and this allowed him time with the family, and with Pak Harto and some of his old school friends who were now part of the artist communities of Yogyakarta and Solo. Everyone was thrilled to see him, but expressed disappointment that Lisa was not with him. She was, he told them, in the final stages of her doctorate and could not afford the time off.

It was his first visit since he left in 1997, prior to the Asian financial collapse that had so devastated the economy later that year, and prior to the end of the Suharto regime the following May. The country had been a democracy for over a decade now and he was relieved and surprised to note the signs of prosperity in nearby towns and villages. Quite a few of his own nieces and nephews were at, or planning to attend, university when they finished senior high school, and many people now owned mobile phones and television sets. Some of the young people even had motorbikes to get to and from school.

The most notable indicator of prosperity, though, was that many of the dark packed-earth floors of the houses in his village had been replaced with tiled concrete. This was a change he did not welcome for he missed the cool, gentle feel of the old floors. Another change in the village was electricity, and this opened the way for electrical sewing machines, fans, television, refrigerators, lights and computer equipment. But despite all the changes, most in his family still kept the *bak mandi* that they filled with water for bathing.

For his sisters and brothers – and there was no distinction between the children of his own mother and their stepmother in his mind – the priority was to educate their children in the hope that this would help them to get good jobs in the future. But while he appreciated their optimism, he believed that without the right connections it was unlikely they would find well-paid employment, even with university qualifications. Still, with Lisa's agreement, he had been allocating ten per cent of his income from exhibitions to fund family projects – a small restaurant for a younger brother, a batik enterprise for a nephew, electric sewing machines and overlocker for a brother-in-law's tailoring business, the purchase of ducks for breeding for Yanti, the payment of various school and university fees, and the purchase of computers.

It pleased him to see how helpful the small sums had been, and he was particularly impressed that his nieces and nephews were so intelligent, confident and entrepreneurial. So different from himself when he set out for Australia ten years earlier. Looking back he couldn't believe how innocent he had been. Such a village boy then. Perhaps still was. This new generation that had grown up in the post-Suharto era – known as *Reformasi* – seemed so much more self-assured than him or his peers at the same age.

***

With Akira and Lisa's help, by the time Adi's guests began arriving for the annual lunch, a table was laden with various Indonesian meat, fish and vegetable dishes. In preparation, Adi had gone early to the Sydney fish markets and had been chopping, grinding, marinating and cooking all morning, so that the aroma of cooking spices now filled the apartment and stairwell – garlic, chillies, ginger, turmeric, galangal, candle nuts, coriander seeds and shrimp paste. The meats were from the halal butcher in Surry Hills, a bike ride away and, in the garden below, Akira was overseeing the cooking of a large snapper wrapped in banana leaves and two dozen chicken satay sticks on the barbeque.

Gerardo was the first to arrive with his latest boyfriend, Joe, a fit young Greek man on a working holiday. Mack brought a young woman Ella from his advertising agency. There were Marj, Bert and Archie – and Marj was almost universally referred to now by the title of Bu, the shortened version of Ibu, the Indonesian word for mother, and the respectful form of address for an older woman. Lisa's parents had sent their apologies and Pak Bambang and Bu Wafa arrived with a dish of satay sauce. Lisbeth and Eloise were missing too, having gone to visit Lisbeth's family in the country.

Each person was given a plate with a precisely shaped mound of rice in the centre, and invited by Adi to help themselves to small serves from all the other dishes. When everyone was seated, Gerardo called on Adi, who was standing to the side like a conscientious waiter, to get a plate and join them, but Adi said he preferred to wait until later before eating.

"Please ... " he said, inviting them to start eating, but Mack got up and handed him a plate, and then they all waited until he had helped himself to some of the food and joined them.

Akira had responsibility for the drinks and was up and down, topping up their glasses with wine, water or fruit punch.

"Fabulous meal Adi. Come over to my house and cook sometime," Gerardo said. "Fish in banana leaves was great. Sambal too. Do all Javanese men cook as good as this?"

Adi looked at Lisa who was gathering up the empty plates from their guests and said, "Javanese men don't cook, they marry a good Javanese wife who will *macak, manak* and *masak.*"

"And, that means ... Adi dear?" Gerardo said.

Pak Bambang translated, "Makes herself beautiful, has children and is a good cook."

Mack jumped in, "Too bad, you fail, Lisa."

"Thanks Mack, I thought you were my friend," Lisa said.

"Well, you are blessed with beauty and brains so who cares if you can't cook, won't have babies and don't wear makeup."

Two red spots had formed on Lisa's cheeks and she turned on Adi, "Oh right ... and what does a good Javanese husband do?"

Adi was beginning to feel ashamed that the anger that had been swirling inside him for months had erupted at their lunch. His anger was directed at Lisa, but he knew the catalyst was his jealousy over the birth of Eloise. His emotions had been ignited again, two days earlier, when Akira had confided that Lisbeth was expecting their second child.

"Nothing, I knew it. Those attitudes are so passé," Lisa said.

"Well, I am from a third world country! What do you expect?" Adi replied.

Unable to resist, Mack weighed in again, "Ace serve Adi. Ball's in your court, Lisa … "

"Hey, you two, we are joking, aren't we?" Gerardo was looking concerned.

Marj said, "Now, now," and looked Mack, Adi and Lisa in the eye.

But Lisa was still glaring at Adi who began acting as if he and they were no longer in the room.

"Well, that's showbiz," Mack shrugged. "What's for pudding?"

It was almost eight when the last of the guests left and this gave them a couple of hours to tidy the apartment and get ready for work the following day. Other times they would have sat down with a cup of tea and shared bits of conversation and stories the other might have missed. But tonight they worked in silence, each immersed in their own thoughts, each unsure how to respond to what had taken place.

An argument over what makes a good Javanese wife? Where did that come from? And why? It was the first time Adi had expressed dissatisfaction with their relationship in public or private, and Lisa was puzzled. Of course the comments may have been perceived as critical, disloyal even, but Lisa refused to believe Adi really meant those things. It wasn't in his nature.

When Lisa entered the bedroom, Adi was already in bed asleep and so she turned out his bedside light and slid in beside him. He was curled up on his side with his back to her and she moulded her body to his by pressing her breasts and belly into the curve of his back. When he didn't respond, she placed her lips against his neck and let the tip of her tongue taste his skin as she ran her hand across his chest and down his belly. Under her touch his penis stirred but then, quite suddenly, he pulled away and, without a word or backward glance, got up from the bed and left the room.

At first she lay back in disbelief, but when the memory of what happened at lunch flooded back, she yelled at his departing back, "I suppose that's part of your culture too is it? What's wrong with you? Why are you doing this?"

The afternoon's comments she could forgive, but this was an attack on the sacred space of their intimacy. A line had been crossed and they found themselves wondering how they of all people had drifted into saying and doing things to needle and hurt. Lisa began to sob in angry gasps, but then her perspective shifted and it was as if she was looking down on herself, alone on the bed and shaking with pain. How pathetic, she thought, that is not who I am, that is not who I want to be. She got up from the bed, grabbed a carryall, and filled it with clothes, toiletries, her laptop, and walked out of the flat.

Adi was lying on the lounge with his eyes closed. He heard the sobbing, then the silence, then the bang of the front door and he felt calmly vindicated, even a little excited, that he could bring their relationship to the edge of a cliff that would force them to each see clearly what it would or would not bend to. For more than a year, whenever he had suggested putting aside the contraception, Lisa had said no. Month by month she kept putting him off and these constant and persistent refusals had been occupying him more and more. Now, and he was ashamed to admit it, he had even begun to resent his own god-daughter, Akira and Lisbeth's daughter, Eloise.

This was his guilty secret, and the news of a second pregnancy had ignited the old longing. It was as if the ancestors were urging him, and at times he was conscious of hearing a child speak, or he caught a glimpse of her, a little girl about four years of age with straight black hair, a fringe and dark, dark eyes.

All would be well, he thought, and drifted into a restful sleep.

Chapter 30

When Adi awoke he was certain Lisa had returned. The clock showed eleven o'clock and he wondered if she'd gone to work already. He went to take a shower and when he entered the bedroom he saw that her clothes had gone from the wardrobe and there were gaps in the line-up of her shoes on the floor. He pulled out her underwear drawer, then opened the other drawers. All were empty. Her laptop was gone as well.

This was not what he expected. Yes, he had wanted something from her, but not this. Not her absence. As the reality of her disappearance set in, his body began to shake, and his heart was pounding so hard he found it difficult to breathe. He reached for the phone, pushed a button and when Akira answered, he tried to control the gasping hoarse sounds that emerged. He felt like he was dying.

"Who is this?" Akira demanded.

He struggled to suck air into his lungs as he gasped his name into the receiver.

"Mate, you sound like shit. What's up?" Akira asked.

"Can't breathe. Lisa … " Fear and panic had weakened the muscles in his arms and legs and he felt as though he would melt onto the floor.

Akira spoke in a firm voice. "Mate, listen to me, take it easy. Sit down. Are you sitting down? Just breathe. Listen to me ... You're having a panic attack. It's alright. Happens to us musos all the time. Breathe ... Breathe in, breathe out. C'mon mate, big slow breaths."

It was as if Akira was standing by his side.

"Don't say anything, just keep breathing. Don't smoke. I'll be there in ten ... Are you at home? Focus on breathing. It's okay, you're okay. I'm going to hang up now. Just keep breathing, alright? I'll be right over."

When Akira arrived at the apartment, the door was wide open, and Adi was on the lounge with his head back and eyes closed.

"Hey mate, I'm here." Akira said, "Wait, I'll get you a drink." He poured Adi a glass of water and waited while he drank. "What happened? Where's Lisa? Is she alright? She hasn't had an accident has she?"

Adi put down the glass. "She's gone. I don't know where. All her clothes are gone, and her laptop."

Akira looked at him. "What happened?" he asked.

The colour in Adi's face deepened, "Um, I cannot say."

Akira could see he was embarrassed. "Okay, let me guess. Was it over what happened at lunch?"

"Kind of. I was still angry ... I did something. Lisa yelled at me. She was crying, and then she went out. I went to sleep, but when I woke up she was gone."

"Mate, you can't get angry with Lisa for not being a good Javanese wife, whatever the hell that means."

"But ... "

"Yeah, well, I think you'd better talk with her about what's going on. You can explain how you see things. Lisa is who she is. Maybe you're the one who has to change. I'm sorry, mate, but either you love her as she is or you have to get out of the way. Have you thought of taking her to Java to meet the family?"

"I think about it but she's too busy. Both of us are. I want children like you and Lisbeth, but Lisa says we have to wait."

"So that's what this is about? Listen mate, Lisa's still a young woman. How old is she? Twenty-nine?"

Adi nodded. "Soon she'll be thirty. That's very old for a woman to have a baby."

"Not here, mate. It used to be, but now some women have their first child at maybe thirty-five, forty."

"Old woman then," Adi said.

"Not these days. You think about it, how old was your mother when her last child was born?"

"Stepmother."

"Stepmother then. How old was she when she had her last child?"

"Maybe thirty-eight, thirty-nine."

"And how many children did she have before that?"

"Four."

"See. The main thing is that you're healthy and fit, and Lisa is. What does she say exactly?"

"She says wait until she has a proper job at the university."

"Well fair enough. She probably wants you to continue painting and you only do that as long as she earns a regular income. Yeah?"

"But I'm scared to wait. For me, there is pressure."

"Talk to her mate. You've got to talk to her."

"She says she will get the doctorate, and then a job, but maybe this is not so easy."

"Well you have to trust her. It's wonderful having kids when the time is right but it's not easy. It's full-on when it happens and sometimes it's even harder for a woman, especially if she's the main breadwinner like Lisa would be."

It was more than a week before Lisa would agree to speak to Adi on the phone. When she did, he apologised – both for his words at lunch and his actions that night. After that they met in a neutral place, at the Botanical Gardens, where they sat on the grass and talked for two hours. She listened as he described how on his return to Indonesia many people had wanted to know when they would have children, even asking if there was something the matter with him or Lisa. He explained how to him it was a sacred thing, not just for him and her, but for his ancestors, both their ancestors.

When it was her turn to speak, Lisa admitted to fearing a loss of identity if she had a child, that it might demand things of her that she lacked, and this surprised him because it hadn't occurred to him that Lisa might have such doubts about herself. She also reiterated her need to concentrate on finishing her doctorate, and positioning herself to be able to apply for a permanent job if a vacancy came up at the university. Realistically though, and even with two powerful mentors, it might take years for her dream of tenure to be realised.

It was not all new territory but as they took turns to speak and listen, they both gained a better understanding of the strains and stresses they had each been experiencing, and this led them to a deeper and stronger intimacy than before. When she asked whether, if they were to have a baby, Adi would be willing to let her be the main breadwinner while he cared for the baby, he said no, even though Akira did exactly that when Eloise arrived, and would care for both children when Lisbeth's next lot of maternity leave ended.

She was disappointed to hear this and told him she would like him to think some more about what he thought he could contribute when they did go ahead and have children.

Chapter 31

Lisa was first approached by the student, Mai Jansen, at the end of a lecture. The young woman introduced herself and asked if she could have Adi's contact details as she was planning to write her master's thesis on him and his work.

"I want to examine his art in the context of his being Javanese and explore how that shapes his worldview and artistic vision," Mai told her.

Lisa was surprised that the student knew her connection with Adi. "I see. And how can I help?"

"My supervisor suggested I approach you because she wants me to interview him as soon as possible. Are you able to please give me a number where I can contact him?"

Lisa wrote the number on a piece of paper and handed it to Mai.

"That's his landline. He doesn't have a mobile, but with a bit of luck a real person will pick up, and not the machine."

Mai took the piece of paper. "Thank you very much."

The next time Lisa saw Mai she was speaking to Adi at a Grove Gallery exhibition opening, and when Lisa joined them she was surprised to hear them speaking Indonesian. Mai greeted her, said goodbye to Adi, and went to join a group of her fellow students.

"What was that about?" Lisa asked.

"Oh, a student. She's been interviewing me," he said.

Lisa was curious about Mai's ability to speak Indonesian, and surprised that Adi had not mentioned the interviews.

"Yes, but what was she saying?"

"We were arranging another time to meet."

Lisa felt she was being excluded. "When?" she asked.

"On Friday."

Lisa persisted, "When on Friday?"

"Eleven o'clock. Why? Have we got something on?"

"How come she can speak Indonesian?"

"Her mother is Indonesian and the family lived in Yogya. She's quite fluent. That's not so unusual you know?"

"What's that supposed to mean?"

"Oh, I don't know. I'm ready to go home. You?"

This was the night it happened. Something about the shadow of the younger woman had caused a certain recklessness. No condoms in the packet. Alarm. Persuasion. And next morning: anxiety and regret on her part, apology on his. Remorse on hers, disguised hope on his.

"It'll be fine," Adi said. "Don't worry."

"Don't worry!" she scowled.

"We've missed before. It'll be okay."

When she returned from having a shower, Adi was sitting up in the bed. He smiled nervously and Lisa looked at him suspiciously. "Did you plan this?"

"No," he said. "Of course not."

She looked worried, "What if I get pregnant?"

While her anxiety gave him hope, he suppressed the thought and got up and gave her a hug.

The following Friday, Lisa arrived at Adi's studio as Mai was leaving. Adi had had to give up Madrill's studio, but then the apartment next to theirs had come onto the market and so, with the help of Lisa's father, they had bought it and converted it into a studio for Adi.

Once again, Lisa found Adi and Mai speaking Indonesian.

"I've got eight weeks to go before I hand in the thesis so I may need to check a few things before I do if that's alright."

"Of course. Any time. It's interesting," Adi said.

Mai held out her hand and Adi shook it. "Great, I'll be in touch," she said.

Lisa stood in the doorway watching their exchange. She didn't understand what they were saying and she felt invisible.

"For heaven's sake, would you mind using English seeing we can all speak that perfectly well?"

Mai looked surprised, "Lisa, I'm sorry. I thought you spoke Indonesian. Goodbye then."

For a while after she left, a dark cloud settled between them.

When Lisa missed her period, she waited before making the appointment with the doctor. By that time, she was sure she might be pregnant.

"Well, you were right. You are six-weeks pregnant," the doctor said.

Despite being fairly certain, the doctor's bald statement came as a shock and Lisa took a moment to absorb the reality of it, "Oh damn. Oh well, it may be what we need."

The doctor looked up from her note taking and placed the pen down on the desk. "Why? Are you having relationship problems?"

Lisa thought about the past couple of months and the unexamined strain that had reappeared between Adi and her. While she sensed his unspoken demands, she was afraid to admit or acknowledge them because, at some level, it was as if he was asking her to give up her autonomy.

Now the thoughts she'd kept hidden from herself came spilling out, "Things have been a bit rugged lately ... mainly because Adi has been wanting to start a family and I've wanted to wait. And I've been getting annoyed with him for pressuring me and he's been getting annoyed with me for refusing to talk about it." She smiled ruefully. "He'll be very happy about this turn of events."

After leaving the surgery, Lisa crossed the road to a park. It was a clear sunny day and the wattle at the entrance to the park was alive with the murmur of bees, a sign that winter was in retreat. She wanted a moment in the sun to consider the effect the pregnancy would have on both their lives.

The park contained a fenced-off area with colourful hard plastic play equipment. It was soft underfoot so that a child would be less likely to break a limb if it fell. Lisa watched a young man playing with a little boy, and saw how he used words of encouragement and kept his hands to the ready as he let him slide down the slippery dip or make his way on unsteady feet to the rocking horse seat that sat on a wobbling coiled metal spring. The man was so focused on the child's safety and delight that he was unaware he was being watched, and she couldn't help wondering what kind of a dad Adi would be.

A baby's cries reached her even before she saw the tall red-haired woman pushing the pram. There were two small girls with her, both about three or four years old. The woman released the childproof lock on the playground gate, and watched the girls race to the swings. Then, closing the gate, she wheeled the pram over to where Lisa was sitting and leaned into the pram to pick up the screaming infant.

By now the two girls had captured a swing each and were walking backwards, pushing their bottoms up in the air until, standing on tiptoe, they swooshed their legs forward, then back, then forward, riding gravity and competing to make the swings go higher and higher.

The woman undid her blouse and with one hand cupping the baby's head and the other holding her full breast, she pressed the two together until the whole of her nipple disappeared into the baby's open mouth. In the sweet silence, the baby let out breathy snorts as it suckled. Now the woman relaxed and settled into a more comfortable position. She looked up, checked the girls were safe, then glanced at Lisa and smiled.

Lisa returned the smile. "Are those your girls?" she asked.

"One is – the redhead. The other one is her friend," she said, while looking down and caressing the baby's forehead with her hand.

The hair on the baby's head was so fair it was as if it was bald, and Lisa could not tell if it was a girl or boy. "Does it hurt?" she asked.

The woman looked at her blankly, and then followed her gaze to the breastfeeding baby. "Not at all. I had a few problems with my first – cracked nipples, that was no fun – but it's been smooth sailing with this little chap. Touch wood. It's very pleasant actually and so convenient not to have to mess with bottles." She looked at Lisa questioningly.

"I just found out I'm pregnant," Lisa said. She sounded excited and even felt some tears tip out onto her eyelashes.

"Oh, congratulations! Pregnancy is wonderful. I didn't think it would be but it was. Well, for me anyway. Everyone's different."

"What about the birth? Doesn't it hurt?" Lisa asked.

"Well yes, a bit. But I'm a marathon runner … used to pain I guess, though both my labours only lasted a couple of hours."

Lisa decided not to go to work that day. She had no face-to-face classes and she wanted to break the news of the pregnancy to Adi. She began to laugh as she imagined his response and when she reached her car, she saw a pair of blue wrens flying in and out of some bushes by the footpath – the male in all his iridescent royal blue glory, the female plain and brown – and she smiled as she remembered that they mated for life.

She'd suggest a picnic at Watsons Bay, or the beach. They had to be outdoors on this beautiful day that was so alive, so bursting with colour and life. She wanted to sit on the headland, look out to sea, perhaps see some whales on their annual voyage north to give birth in warmer waters.

Me a mother, how hilarious! Now she and Adi really would have to go and visit his family.

Chapter 32

Mai arrived for the fourth and final interview with Adi and, as on the previous three visits, they sat opposite one another with the microphone resting on the coffee table between them. She was wearing a low-cut top and short skirt, and she tucked her long brown legs to one side. Her black hair was fixed into a loose bun at the nape of her neck.

Before starting on her master's, Mai had worked for a community arts organisation in Jakarta for a year, and then for the same organisation in Yogyakarta for another year. With a Dutch father and Javanese mother, she had spent her childhood in Indonesia, part of her adolescence in the Netherlands, and completed the final years of high school and university in Sydney. Her father, she told Adi, studied at the Institute of the Arts in Yogyakarta.

She checked the microphone was on and, looking at her notes, began by asking about the influence of batik making on his development as an artist. It was a question they had not really considered before and he was conscious of her deep interest in what he had to say. In all their conversations, he had felt like he was being led into unfamiliar territory, and at first he had found the questions intrusive and confronting.

In time, as the rapport between them grew, he was often surprised by what he had to say because, up until then, he had mostly avoided speaking about his work, or articulating why he did what he did. Now, with her prodding, he found himself being drawn back to the village to consider the things there that might have shaped his art practice.

Regarding batik-making, he said, "There are many stages – preparing the cloth, making the design, applying the wax, dyeing, applying more wax, adding more colour, and so on. The final product is so completely itself that only a skilled practitioner can guess the stages that have contributed to it. The finished batik is both different to and more than the sum of all the stages. That's the magic."

"But why is that important to you as a painter?"

"It's important because I can choose to make the stages and elements of my painting visible or invisible to the viewer."

"And which do you choose?"

Adi smiled. "Sometimes one, sometimes the other. It depends."

"Some people would say that batik is no longer a big thing in Indonesia, that it's a stereotype. Do you agree?"

"If it is, then my family and whole village are a stereotype. My aunts and cousins still make batik. They certainly wear it, just as I'm wearing these right now."

He was wearing a batik shirt over a black tee-shirt, and a batik sarong.

She took note of the sarong's fine quality and recognised its characteristic creamy orange background and rich brown, indigo, and black coloured symbols and patterns. "Is the sarong from your village?" she asked.

Adi nodded, "Yes, my sister-in-law sent it to me for Lebaran last year. She probably bought it from one of the local factories."

Mai had been to Solo many times and was aware that his family was from a village at the centre of a batik producing area.

"Have you been influenced by batik in your painting? For example, do you think the layering of images, text, colour, and your use of symbolism – which are such strong elements in your painting – are linked to, or a reflection of the batik process?"

Adi looked down at the sarong's floral and wing-like motifs, "Possibly. I was always very interested in the symbols and designs as a child, so you could say I've been influenced, but it's not something I've been particularly conscious of. Of course I've always liked it that the traditional symbols and motifs have particular meanings for different occasions such as marriage, fertility etc."

Adi spread the sarong out with his fingers for her to see the design. "Like this *Semen Gendong*. Do you know it?" He laughed, "It's a gentle nudge from my sister that I should be starting a family!"

She ticked the question off her list and he waited for her to ask the next one.

"You mentioned that you loved the *wayang* stories – the Ramayana and the Mahabharata. What did you take from them?"

"Many things. My mother and I loved the Ramayana, but my friends and I mostly talked about the Mahabharata, who our favourite characters were, what they did, if it was the right thing or not. What also interested us was the power of storytelling in relation to morality and truth. I remember once we decided to try and write a version of the Mahabharata where Arjuna refuses to listen to the Lord Krishna, and refuses to kill his cousins. We couldn't do it."

"And is this kind of storytelling – the kind that embraces ambiguity and avoids closure – also important to you in your work as an artist?"

"Yes, very much so."

"There have been many changes in the years since you left Indonesia in 1997. To what extent have you been able to find out about and keep track of those?"

"Well, I've been back once. That was in 2008. I was only there for two weeks but it was a surprise to see so much change. More democracy, more freedom of speech, but more corruption too."

Mai nodded. "And what do you think about that?"

"I guess I'm at a distance so maybe I see things a little differently."

"In what way?" Mai was eager to pursue this because until now he had refused to engage whenever any of her questions had a political edge.

Now he took his time to answer. "Well, I think we're all responsible, responsible for the good and the bad."

"So what is to be done?" Mai asked. She would consider later how this conversation, one they had not had before, might or might not affect her reading of his work and how it had developed over time.

Adi reached for his cigarettes and held up the packet to ask her permission to smoke. She nodded and waited for him to light up. "I don't think blaming or punishing people for past wrongs is going to solve anything," he said.

"But what of the people who have been active in hurting others – perhaps killing or torturing or enslaving people – shouldn't they be brought to justice?"

This was an opinion he'd heard others make and it sometimes led to heated arguments.

"I think the most important thing right now is for the truth to be told about what happened in 1965, but also before that, during the 1950s. There's a lot of history we don't know about."

"But what about the people who were put in gaol and who suffered from a loss of citizenship? People treated them very badly, even in their own families."

"Yes, I know people like this, and in a way this is what I've been exploring in my last exhibition."

"Would you say then that your work has become more political?"

"I'm not sure about that. By the time I came of age, Suharto was gone, and then for a while there was instability, economic hardship and, in some places, violence. And then democracy. But I was in Australia during this time, and I had a very different experience to my friends, say, who were becoming artists in Yogyakarta. I was living in a different culture, speaking a different language. Being so far away, my grip on what was happening in Indonesia was weak. I felt guilty too."

"Why guilty?"

"Because I escaped, because I wasn't part of the suffering or what was being built. Does that make sense? I suspect or fear that I'm not part of that world any more – even though that is where my roots are. Soon I will have lived here as long as I lived there."

"Is that a good thing or a bad thing?"

"Well, it's both good and bad. It gives me the freedom to see the big picture in terms of my own place as an artist, but it's painful too, difficult in that I sometimes feel like an outsider – both here and there. But maybe that's a good place for an artist to be? I don't know."

"Can you imagine this changing at all?"

"In relation to Indonesia, or living here?"

"Both."

"I think my sense of belonging here or there could change if Lisa and I were to have children, but I don't know for sure. Thanks to Gerardo promoting my work and supporting my career I feel more confident about my future here, but in Indonesia I don't come up on the radar at all. I'm told there have been changes in the art market and many artists are making a lot of money, even younger artists, but there's a concern they're not getting the opportunity to develop as they would have previously."

"How do you mean?"

"Well, they're being asked to produce work for group shows, work the curators know will sell. The work sells but I'm told that the lack of solo shows constrains their creative development. That's just what I've heard. Of course, I've had one solo show a year with Gerardo and I'm very grateful because it's kept me in work, and also kept me developing. I still do a couple of days gardening a week but I don't mind that. There aren't too many artists who can live solely off their art and I'm certainly not one of them."

"Not yet! Do you have plans to return to Indonesia to live and work?"

"I dream of this but it's not practical. My wife has a job here and I couldn't ask her to give that up, but I'm sure we'll visit one day soon."

"What about overseas travel, scholarships?"

"We talk about it but, again, we've been too busy. Lisa's been many times to Europe and the United States. I've not been at all and I'd very much like to go to China and Japan – perhaps I'll get a residency at some time."

Mai thanked him for his time, closed her notebook and bent forward to turn off the tape recorder. As she did so, Adi felt he could almost see to her waist. She looked up, smiled broadly at him, and he realised she'd done it deliberately. She had been flirtatious with him at their other meetings and he'd been very careful not to encourage her. Now he felt a strong temptation to touch her, to feel the texture of her skin.

He stood up quickly with the aim of backing away from the smell of her perfume, but Mai stood at the same time. She looked up at him and he took her hands and looked at the black bracelets she was wearing on each wrist. He touched them and was surprised that, although they were made of rubber, they felt spiky to touch.

"What are these?" he asked. "They look like barbed wire?"

"Yes, that's the idea. I work for Amnesty International as a volunteer. I wear them to start conversations. Like this one."

"You work for free? What do you do there?"

"Oh anything they want – filing, stuff envelopes, produce the newsletter, put things on Facebook. I just go in one day a week."

He let go her wrists and she reached out both hands and slid her left hand under his tee-shirt and around his ribs until he felt it circling his back, the bracelet scratching his skin. His heart was pounding as she pushed her breasts against his chest and he was driven with a desire to feel them bare against his skin. He reached under her top to release her bra and then lightly ran his fingertips over her nipples before drawing her to him. He felt her mouth opening against his as they began pulling at each other's clothes, and when he felt her hand pushing down over the front of his sarong, a soft moan escaped his lips.

Just then he heard the studio door open and, looking up, saw Lisa standing in the doorway. She had a hand over her mouth and was so pale he thought perhaps she was a ghost. His body buckled with shame and he pushed Mai away. This shouldn't have happened.

He began to retch as Mai turned around, saw Lisa, gathered up her things and ran from the room. Lisa's body sagged and fell against the wall. Her mouth was opening and closing, and she was turning her head from side to side as if to wake from a nightmare.

"My god, Adi … "

Adi saw her pain, felt it flooding into him, and felt powerless to offer comfort or words of remorse.

"Nothing happened," he protested.

Lisa reached her hands to her belly and rested them there awhile. Her skin had turned a ghastly pale grey and when she looked up her lips were moving and he strained his body towards her to hear what she was saying.

"How long has this been going on?"

He wanted to rewind everything, he wanted her to forgive him, he wanted to forgive himself.

"Well, it's your duty to win me back … "

He saw her body buckle and the distorting look of hatred and disgust on her face.

"What? My duty?" she screamed at him. "You! You must be mad!"

Rage propelled her to look about the room and then she crossed over to the wall and ripped down the Tree of Life and began tearing at it.

"No, not that, not that," he thought or said, he wasn't sure which. He tried to take it from her but she held it up high and moved over to the open window and threw it outside. Unspent, she began flailing at him with her fists and feet, landing blows wherever she could.

Then, suddenly, as if in answer to another call, she stopped and raised both hands high above her head in a gesture of helplessness.

She went to the door, and then turned to him and said, "I don't know who you are or who we are anymore. You have no idea … "

And she walked out.

When Lisa left, Adi packed a bag and headed for Central Station. He needed to put what he had just done behind him, along with the guilt and shame of being caught doing it. He did not know where he was going, but when he got to the station, he boarded a Blue Mountains train that was ready to depart, and as it made its way out of the city, he decided to get off at Lawson and spend time in the bush. He had friends whose holiday house there was empty most of the time and he was sure it would be fine for him to camp there.

All he knew was that he had to find a way to make things right and he would not return until he knew what that was.

Chapter 33

Two and a half weeks went by and, when she did not hear from Adi, Lisa was sure he was with Mai. She had gone to stay with Mack and each time she tried to call Adi the phone cut to the answering machine and she heard her own voice asking her to leave a message. He had never owned a mobile and time was running out. All attempts to find him had failed and she had even had a friend ask Mai if he was with her, and the reply came back that he was not.

Lisa knew she had only a few weeks before she had to act, one way or the other. She was certain too that she didn't want to go ahead with the pregnancy on her own, but each time she raised the matter with Mack, he begged her to give it more time. Finally, she made a booking at a clinic and, on the day of her appointment, she and Mack caught a taxi into the city. The clinic was close to Central Station and when they arrived there was a gaggle of right-to-lifers holding up placards and half-heartedly chanting, "Abortion is a sin" and "God will punish." Their comments weren't directed at anyone in particular because they couldn't tell who was arriving for an abortion and who wasn't, but Lisa still found their aggression harrying.

As instructed over the phone, they found the front door locked and entered the four-number pin she had been given to get in. A lift took them to the sixth floor where it opened onto a waiting area.

"Phew, I needed that like a hole in the head!" Lisa said as the lift door closed behind them.

A woman wearing faded grey jeans, a loose white cotton shirt and red canvas shoes got up from a computer and stepped forward to greet them.

"Good morning. Sorry about that. Terrible, isn't it? And, you are ... "

"Lisa Davidson."

"Hi Lisa, my name's Sheree and I'm a clinic sister here."

She gave her a pen and asked her to fill out some forms while she let Caro, her assigned counsellor, know she'd arrived.

"I'd like to skip the counselling if you don't mind," Lisa said. She couldn't imagine what good counselling would do at this stage.

"Lise?" Mack pleaded.

She was sorry to drag him into this but who else could she turn to? He was almost grey under the tan and she tried to smile, but then her mouth began to wobble.

"Yes, I will see the counsellor. Thank you."

The waiting area had four orange leather two-seater lounges, embroidered cushions, and several large paintings on the walls. On the coffee table a flowering orchid gave off a faint smell of the Australian bush.

There were no other clients in the room and they sat down to wait for the counsellor.

Mack said, "Please Lise, are you sure about this? We can leave, go home? It's not too late."

"Mack, I've thought about nothing else for the last month and I know I'm not cut out to be a single parent. I can't do it, and it's not what I want."

"I support you … It's just that … Don't you think it might be a good idea to talk to Adi first?"

"No. I won't bring up a child on my own. I just can't. Anyway, I haven't heard from him. Not at all. He hasn't answered any of my calls and I don't even know where he is. No one does. It's been almost a month now and he's only called Akira to say he's alive and alright. That's all."

A woman came through the door and held out her hand to Lisa, "Hello Lisa, my name's Caro, would you like to come in? Bring the form with you and I'll get your Medicare details when we get inside."

To Mack, she said, "Lisa will be ready to go home in about three hours so, if you like, you can go and we'll give you a call when she's ready."

"I'll stay," Mack said. "I brought my laptop and I want to be here in case she needs me."

A light rain was falling when Mack and Lisa arrived back at Mack's place, and when he led her into her bedroom, there were floating love heart balloons on the ceiling and a vase of yellow roses on the mantelpiece.

How lonely and lost and afraid she would have felt if he hadn't been with her. "You're my best best friend, you know that?" she said.

"What about a cup of tea? Or would you rather a stiff scotch or brandy?" he said.

"Cup of tea would be lovely, thank you."

Lisa put on her pyjamas and got into bed and, just as a cloud of sadness and grief loomed over her, Mack was back again.

"Are you decent?" he said.

"Yes, you can come in."

He put the tray down on the bed. On it there was cup of weak tea with milk – the way she liked it – and a plate of buttered oatmeal biscuits. That made her smile – where on earth did he get those?

"Here you are then, ducks. Drink it up … Want anything else? Some honey for your tea or on the biscuits?"

She shook her head. She wanted to ask when he'd put the roses and balloons in the bedroom, but the words wouldn't come.

"I'll leave you in peace then," he said, and gave her a light kiss on the forehead.

Mack was in his room checking his email when the phone rang. When he picked it up, it was Adi.

"Hello, this is Adi. Is Lisa there?"

"Oh g'day Adi. Sorry mate, she's having a rest right now."

"What's the matter? Is Lisa ill?" Lie, ya bugger, lie, Mack told himself. Oh shit, oh fuck. Let the cat out of the bag, stupid stupid.

"She's fine. Just sleeping."

"What's the matter?"

"Look mate, I'd rather not say. How about you leave it with me and I'll get her to give you a ring later?" Mack hung up the phone. He would have to tell Lisa Adi called but not now, not while she was resting.

Lisa slept for two hours and then got up to help Mack prepare dinner. When the doorbell rang Mack went to the door, opened it and saw Adi standing on the doorstep. He tried to block him but Adi was insistent and, if he didn't know better, he might even have thought he was drunk or on drugs.

"I want to see Lisa," Adi demanded.

Mack felt so angry with the man he could have punched him. "Trouble is mate, she really doesn't want to see you. I said I'd ask her to call you, and now I'd like you to just clear out."

Mack tried to close the door, but Adi pushed past him and headed down the hallway.

"Great bloody timing," he muttered to himself before calling out to Lisa, "A visitor, it's Adi."

Lisa was chopping vegetables into small piles on the kitchen bench when she heard Adi call her name. She looked up in shock, "Adi, what are you doing here?"

"I rang, Mack said you were resting. I thought maybe you were sick. I miss you and I want to talk," he said.

She felt strangely detached as if her body and mind had separated. Chop chop – the dismembered vegetables lay on the board and the onion fumes were making her eyes water. She wiped them with her sleeve, "You've got your girlfriend, I'm sure she's happy to have you all to herself."

'She's not my girlfriend, and I'm very sorry. I was very stupid and I want you to come home. I promise this will not happen again. Never."

"Adi, that was weeks ago, and I haven't heard from you." She put down the knife and went to the sink to wash the onion juice from her hands. "You would not take my calls, you did not return my calls when I left messages, or even when I told Akira to tell you to call me. Can you imagine how much that hurt? Can you imagine what that meant to me? How cruel that felt?"

"I was confused. I ran away – from the house, from Sydney. I went to the mountains. I didn't know if I could live. I was so afraid, but I'm back now. Mack said you were sleeping. Is something the matter?"

She stood still at the sink, with her back to him. "I'm not sick," she said, "I just had an abortion. I was coming to tell you I was pregnant when I saw you with that woman."

Now she turned and faced him. "The really sad thing is that I was feeling so excited about being pregnant because I knew how happy it would make you. Then ... " She began to sob, "I saw you ... her. I couldn't go ahead with it on my own. But I wanted to have that baby and I waited four whole weeks to hear from you and nothing. And now you show up. I tried so hard to find you … "

Adi felt himself drifting as if he had been flung backwards off a cliff. He raised his arms to protect his eyes from the birds of prey that were circling above him, and were diving and pecking at his head and face. He seized hold of the knife on the bench and began moving towards Lisa.

At first she said nothing. Then she spoke quietly and firmly, "No, stop it Adi. Put it down."

But he kept coming. She stepped back, two steps, three steps, behind a chair. He pushed it out of the way. Now he was holding the knife high above his shoulder, and she moved again and again to get away from him. Finally, there was nowhere else to go.

Then she heard a roar of anguish and pain – a scream so loud and piercing she felt her eardrums would burst – and it went on and on. And it was only when she saw Adi snap back into the room and look with terror at the knife in his raised hand, that she realised she was the one who was screaming.

Adi's face was filled with horror as he watched his fingers open and the knife clatter onto the floor. He turned and pushed past Mack who was coming to investigate.

"What's going on?" Mack yelled at Adi as he charged down the hallway and out the front door.

Lisa remained pressed into the corner of the room. Her eyes were closed and her face was a ghostly grey. She was beginning to sink to the floor and Mack rushed to catch her and levered her limp body into an armchair. As he did so, he caught sight of the knife and then, in panic, began checking her all over for stab wounds. When he was reassured there were none, he picked up the knife and put it in the sink. He went to the bathroom to fetch a damp face cloth and when he returned he saw that Lisa's mouth was skewed with grief and tears were streaming down her cheeks.

It was the silent tears that stung him the most.

***

It was mid-afternoon and Adi was lying in semi-darkness on the lounge, staring at the mute television screen. When he heard Lisa's voice he thought perhaps he was imagining it, and with that he felt the pain return that had been with him since she told him about the abortion. The pain that crushed his chest, gripped his scalp and made his head ache.

"Adi?"

He looked up and saw her standing next to the television.

"May I?" she said and, without waiting for an answer, she reached for the remote and turned the television off. "Please … we must talk."

He could not move or speak. The colour and images faded from the screen and a blank darkness took the place of light, life and movement. Lisa crossed the room and raised a blind to let in the daylight, and the screen came alive once more with the play of light and the unbearable image of himself lying on the lounge. This he just couldn't bear and so he rolled over onto his back and looked up at the ceiling.

"Adi, I beg you … "

He did not know if he could talk, and his voice stumbled on the word, "B-b-broken."

"Adi, please? We have to talk."

He wanted her but he could not look into her eyes. It hurt. He hurt.

"Well, if you won't try and talk I'll just leave."

"But … " It was all he could say for he feared he would disintegrate if he tried to say more.

"Please, Adi, we don't have to talk right now. We can make some other time, we can go to a marriage counsellor. I just want you to agree that you will do that."

The faint perfume of her presence caused the weight on his chest to press even harder so that even breathing became a struggle. He wanted to reach out to her but he felt as if he were paralysed.

Even when he heard the door close after her, he still could not raise himself up.

Mama is climbing the giant mango trees and us kids are so excited. We've picked all the low down mangoes but there are still lots up high. I think Mama loves climbing trees because she's laughing, and she looks so shining among the branches and leaves.

One by one she calls our names and when she throws a mango we run to catch it and put it in a basket. We've filled one basket already.

Mama is a laughing butterfly, a singing bird, a quacking duck, a chee chak gecko, a moo moo cow, a buzz buzz mosquito. There's light all around. I'm happy when it's my turn and I catch the mango, but the little ones cry if they miss.

I call, "Look Mama, there's one. Over there!"

There's a loud crack. Mama tries to find another branch to hold onto, but there's another crack, and Mama is falling.

Mama is lying on the ground. Mama is crumbled and twisted. I think she is dead. Her head is turned, eyes closed. She doesn't move, but then she groans.

Bude makes us move away but I want to put my arms around Mama. Yanti fetches Papa and he tells Yanti to take me away but I don't want to leave Mama.

So Papa yells at Yanti and Yanti and I both start crying, and Yanti lets me sit on her knee and she puts her arms around me. It's hot sitting on Yanti's knee and I put my hand up to her face and she lets me feel her wet cheeks.

Papa and Lik Dul carry Mama inside. They are very gentle, they carry her like she might break. Mama is very still and quiet.

It's as if the sound's gone off. I'm afraid, I can't hear, my mouth is open but I can't talk. I'm like Mama, I can't talk.

Yanti is crying and then I can talk, "Is Mama hurt? Is Mama going to die?"

Yanti says, "Mama will be alright. Come, let's walk to the river – we can see Mama when we get back."

But Mama lies in bed for a long time and every day I go and see her and she smiles at me, but the stars in her eyes aren't there anymore.

I ask Yanti, "When will the stars in Mama's eyes come back?" And she begins to cry and I cry too, because of the stars and because of Yanti crying.

Chapter 34

Painting was the only way Adi had of anaesthetising the pain – that and the music he played over and over while he worked, original recordings by local jazz musicians whose performances he'd seen and whose CDs he'd listened to many times over. The familiar, raw intensity of the music formed a tunnel through which he directed all that he was feeling onto the canvas.

Some months earlier, Pak Bambang had lent him a book about the violent events in Indonesia during 1965 that told a different history to the one they'd learned about in school. Now he felt driven, in canvas after canvas, to bear witness to the inflicted violence, the haunting silence, the empty ruined houses, the mass graves, the missing persons. These were the wounds passed on to later generations and, for those who managed to somehow survive the torture, enslavement and cruelty, there was the ongoing persecution and discrimination. Year after year, decade after decade, generation after generation, a reign of terror had endured that was based on a fabricated history they were made to watch on television every 30 September.

When Pak Bambang visited Adi, he found several canvases in various stages of completion which depicted scenes of rape, torture and murder, or their aftermath. Bodies piled one on top of the other in an open grave or on the back of trucks. Bodies floating in rivers, or snagged by their clothes on fallen tree branches. A person being beaten with sticks and machetes in front of a mosque and, at the side of the road, three vehicles – a United States military jeep and two sleek black cars, one with British flags and one with Australian flags. Pale ghost faces look on through the darkened car windows.

It was hard to look at the paintings and Pak Bambang said, "This work is confronting. It fills me with terror."

"It's something I've been thinking about but I didn't know how to approach it until I saw Botero's work on Abu Ghraib," Adi told him. "It's been said that he described the work as 'painting out the poison'. Have a look at his paintings – I think you might understand."

Adi indicated the coffee table where a book titled *Botero: Abu Ghraib* had a painting of an oversized hand hung by a rope on the cover. Next to it another book was opened at Picasso's *Guernica*.

When Pak Bambang opened the Botero catalogue, he had the immediate strong reaction of wanting to close it again, but one by one he willed himself to look at the painted abject images of the ritual torture of prisoners by United States army prison guards in Iraq. It was not just the inhumanity that appalled, but the political systems that nurtured such cruel disregard for human dignity and life.

"How did the paintings help?" Pak Bambang asked.

"Not just Botero, Picasso as well. Their paintings record and reveal pain, injustice, cruelty. For me, I just wanted to try and feel in my mind and body how a million or more of our people suffered in 1965 and after."

Adi's voice was wavering, "Maybe it's easier when you can see and know the enemy as other, but in 1965 the enemy was our own, and that hurts, doesn't it? I can't feel how the victims and their families suffered. I can't feel what it is like for the perpetrators to know what they did and not be punished and, I ask myself, how would I feel if I knew my father or grandfather or uncles had done those things? I don't think they did, but I have never asked. I wasn't born until ten years later but everything the regime told us was lies. We know this now."

"Yes, yes," Pak Bambang said, and nodded for him to continue.

Adi recounted a story from childhood that he could only now begin to really understand, and for which, even though he was only a child, he still felt complicit.

"In my cousin's house, his uncle returned home one day after a long absence. They said he had been on Buru Island and us kids thought he must've been working there, or on holiday. We liked his uncle, but it was like he was a ghost. No one took any notice of him and they made him do all the dirty jobs like collecting rubbish. We knew he was a scientist at the university before and that he wasn't a bad man, but the adults told us not to ask questions and I think we sensed their fear."

Pak Bambang knew of similar stories. "Yes, and people had good reason to be afraid. Another part of this tragedy is the talent that was lost for a whole generation. All the teachers, doctors, nurses, writers and community leaders who were killed or sent to prison, or scientists like your uncle. Such a waste and no one questions whether this was too high a price to pay for the West to have its way with our cheap labour, and resources."

Adi went to the kitchen to make coffee and when he returned Pak Bambang said, "I've been speaking with Lisa, Adi. She asked me how you are."

Adi was still. It was unusual for Pak Bambang to visit, especially without calling first.

"She doesn't want to be married any more," Adi said.

"Perhaps she thinks you've found someone else."

"She had a …."

"An abortion. Yes, I know and I'm so very sorry to hear that, but she said you were kissing another woman. That you didn't contact her for a whole month and she couldn't find you. That she left messages but you didn't reply. Isn't it understandable that she thought the marriage was over?"

"She's living with another man."

"She's staying with Mack and he's been caring for her. That's true. But I'm not here to judge her or you. I came to see how you are," Pak Bambang said. He gathered his jacket and stood up, "Shall we go out for something to eat?"

Budi never lets me play with his shanghai but one day I find it on the bench at the front of the house. I put a stone in it like he does and aim it at a bird that is pecking the flowers in the tree. I let the rubber go, the stone flies up, and the bird falls down on the ground like Mama did.

I run and touch the bird but it doesn't move. Its eyes are closed and it just lays there.

I know I killed it, but I was just playing. I didn't mean to.

What if Mama should die too now because of this thing that I did?

I drop the shanghai and run into the house.

"Mama," I cry. "Mama."

Mama is lying in her bed and she opens her eyes and smiles. Papa is sitting beside her and he stays there all day now.

"Mama," I ask, "where are your stars?"

"Dear boy," Mama says, and falls back asleep.

Then Yanti comes and takes my hand, and that's when Mama opens her eyes and says to Papa, "Be kind to the boy."

I wait every day for Mama to come back. I know she wants to.

Chapter 35

Adi was having nightmares almost every time he closed his eyes to sleep now. In all of them, he was with his mother and they were doing things together, joyful things – making a kite, planting rice seedlings, feeling the soft down of a duckling. And always, as he sunk into the comfort of her love and attention, he would look up to her loving face and see only the shining white light that was where her face should have been.

Day and night, the ghostly images of the faceless mother began to haunt him, causing him to become more and more fearful of sleep. In desperation, he began adding the image to his paintings, first one, and then another, and another, until every canvas was painted over with the haunting witnessing faceless mother. He worked day and night, stopping only to eat some hastily made noodles, or fall asleep on the lounge. He rarely went out, and piles of dirty dishes and ashtrays full of cigarette butts littered the studio and apartment.

As the weeks passed, the earlier painted scenes of torture and violence lay like traces under the dominating images of the faceless mother nursing a child, making batik, squatting to grind spices, feeding ducks, winnowing grain, in prayer.

Gerardo had tried phoning Adi, but when there was no reply he decided to drop in. The studio door was wide open and when he entered he saw Adi lying on the daybed with his eyes closed. He barely stirred when Gerardo spoke to him and for a moment Gerardo wondered whether he was asleep or unconscious.

"Hey, Adi, you okay?" Gerardo called out as he opened windows and doors. "My god, this place smells."

Failing to arouse Adi and reluctant to leave him on his own, Gerardo called Marj and Akira. They said they would come immediately and, while he waited for them to arrive, Gerardo began looking over the work. He was thrilled at the quality and complexity of it – it was a new direction and he was keen to discuss it with Adi. There were clearly enough paintings here for the entire February exhibition.

In less than an hour Akira was at the door with bundles of shopping bags he'd carried upstairs for Marj, who had brought everything she thought she might need to restore some sort of hygiene and order. Although Gerardo had forewarned them, neither Marj nor Akira was prepared for the state in which they found Adi, or the apartment. When Akira failed to wake him, Marj told the two men to leave her to look after him and they agreed, but only after she promised she would call one or both of them if she was at all worried or needed help. Neither man wanted to admit the gravity of their fears about Adi's state of mind, and these snapped at their heels as they made their way downstairs.

Marj began by cleaning out the fridge so she could pack away the food she'd brought. Her next step was to clean the bathroom, and when that was done she went to wake Adi. She got him to stand and held him steady as she steered him across the hallway and into the apartment. He only weighed a pocketful of pennies at the best of times but she'd never seen him this poor. The bones in his cheeks and his collar bones were so prominent it was as if he'd been starving himself. There was more than a week's beard on his face and he smelled of stale sweat and cigarettes. His hair was greasy, knotted and dank, and the flesh under his eyes was almost black, as if he'd been in a fight.

"I'm afraid you look like a bloody scarecrow, dear," she said as she manoeuvred him into the bathroom. "Now we'll just get you showered and fed and you'll be right as rain, won't you? There's shampoo there so you can give your hair a good wash. I'll go and get you a bite to eat."

Marj had removed all the used razors from the bathroom cabinet, but something told her not to hand over the one she had just purchased. Instead, she put it in the bottom of her handbag.

When he emerged from the bathroom, Adi found a steaming mug of tea and sandwiches waiting, and began to wolf them down. Marj was moving about the apartment and collecting up every skerrick of rubbish in a green plastic bag. When it was full, she sealed it and left it on the landing for Akira to take downstairs later.

Adi had still not spoken a word and when she returned to the living room she found him fast asleep on the lounge. She covered him with a doona and set to work in earnest, only stopping at intervals to have a cup of tea. Archie and Bert had offered to accompany her but she thought she'd get more done by herself. In the past year or so they had been trying to get her to slow down, to leave more for Lisbeth and Akira to do, but no matter what they said she seemed to stretch time to do more than ever – clean house, cook, mind children, read them stories and take them to the park.

In another dream, Adi watched as Suriani applied another layer of wax to a batik. How excited they were to press the cloth down into the tub of dye and then remove it, rinse it, and hang it up to dry. But when he looked up, all he saw was the shimmering white ghost face and it terrified him. He began thrashing about and struggled to untangle himself from the doona. His body was covered in sweat, he tried to stand, but his legs gave way under him and he crashed to the floor. Marj looked up from her crossword just in time to see him fall. The tears were streaming down his face when she went to help him up, and as soon as she had him settled back down on the lounge, she rang the doctor who agreed to a home visit.

When Akira and Gerardo returned, Marj informed them of the doctor's diagnosis. Nervous exhaustion and malnourishment.

"Doctor Joseph wants him to stay in bed and have complete rest," Marj said. "He said he could put him in hospital, but I told him that wouldn't be necessary because we can look after him. He said it was very important that he not be left on his own."

Marj said she would stay with Adi that first night and Akira called in the next morning to see how he was, and inform her that Pak Bambang was on his way. Adi had woken up several times in great distress during the night, and Marj didn't know if he recognised her when she went to calm him.

When Pak Bambang knocked, Akira opened the door. "Hey Pak, thanks for coming, Adi's having lunch so you can go in. As I said on the phone, the doctor thinks he's had a nervous breakdown."

Pak Bambang stayed with Adi the whole afternoon. Gerardo arrived after lunch and he and Akira worked on their laptops while Marj took a nap. When Marj re-emerged they had afternoon tea and, soon after, Pak Bambang joined them. Like the doctor, he believed Adi needed bed rest and good nourishing food in the first instance, and someone to be with him at all times.

"Adi and I have agreed I'll come to see him later in the week." Pak Bambang said. "He also wanted me to tell you that he's very grateful for all your care."

For ten days, Marj, Akira, Archie and Bert took turns to stay with Adi, and Gerardo called in every other day with Indonesian meals from a nearby restaurant. As Adi grew stronger, the idea of returning to Java took shape in his mind.

"I want to go home," he told Pak Bambang.

***

On the day of his departure, Gerardo and Akira drove Adi to the airport.

"You know I've got you booked for an exhibition in February," Gerardo said. "The work's finished I know, but you will be back for the opening, won't you? You've got the dates." He glanced across at Adi who did not reply. "I hope you're back by then."

Adi was looking out the car window. He saw so much colour – the vast clear blue of the sky, the freckled patterns of blue-grey green in the roadside bush, the sun-split muddy yellows and subtle hints of red and pink in the leaves, and then, in the industrial area near the airport, the assault of advertising billboards and road signs.

Mama is taking the kettle off the fire and pouring the hot water into a deep tin dish. She puts my batik butterfly into the hot water to remove the wax. Then we wash it with soapy water, and then clean water. She holds it up out for me to see.

"See darling, now it's finished. What a clever boy you are. Do you like it?"

"No Mama, it's very bad, not like Mama's batik."

"Don't worry, little one, one day you will be even better than Mama."

"I will?"

"Yes, of course. But I think it's a beautiful butterfly. Do you want it or shall I look after it for you?"

"It's for you, Mama."

"Really, a present for me? What does it mean this beautiful butterfly?"

"It means … everything will be alright."

Mama laughs. "Is that what butterflies mean?"

"Yes Mama. When I see a butterfly, this is what I think."

"You do? What a clever boy. Dear Adi, do you know how much I love you?"

Mama hugs me close and I breathe the smell of her.

"Yes, Mama."

"And you know what else?" Mama says. "Not just me. Many people love you and you will always be looked after. Always."

Chapter 36

Lisa was marking papers in her office when she heard a knock, and then a voice she didn't recognise, "Hi Lisa."

When she looked up, she saw Mai standing not one metre from her desk.

"You!"

Mai spoke quickly, "I've brought you a copy of my thesis on Adi. I've also written a piece for an international art journal which they've accepted so I've included that as well. It's called 'How being Javanese informs the artist Adi Nugroho'. I believe he's returned to Java so maybe you could forward them to him. Or I could send you PDFs if you prefer?"

Lisa couldn't move. The pain of all that had gone on was reignited. Now here she was, so brazen and in her office. Wasn't she ashamed to even show her face?

Mai continued, "I just wanted to say I'm sorry for what happened. It was my fault. And you should know that I've not heard one word from Adi or seen him again since that afternoon."

"Get out of my office! Now!" Lisa's eyes blazed and her reddening face was contorted with disbelief. She felt the hairs of her arms prickle as heat, and then a chill, suffused her body.

Mai did not move and it became clear that she had a speech prepared. "But I think you have to take responsibility as well. What do you really know about Adi, his family and culture? You've never learned Indonesian, you've never visited his family. And since he's been with you he's stayed away as well. Anyway, here are the essays."

Mai dropped the envelope on the corner of the desk and retreated, pulling the door shut behind her, and leaving Lisa feeling violated and vulnerable. Had she really been there, really said those things?

An object on her desk caught Lisa's eye and she stared at it. It was a little red truck, a pencil sharpener, and she remembered that Adi had given it to her for her birthday the year they first got together. She wondered where it came from. She must have found it and put it there herself but she had no memory of doing so.

Raw grief spluttered from her body as she got up from the desk and stepped over the envelope that had flopped onto the floor. She locked the door and went to sit on the sandstone window ledge with her legs pulled up and chin resting on her knees. Arrows of rain were striking the leadlight window panes with such ferocity she could barely see across the quadrangle and, once again, she could not stop the flow of tears.

When Mack arrived home that evening, Lisa had almost finished reading Mai's paper. She looked up when he entered.

"I'm reading a paper about Adi."

"Not the one by the evil temptress?"

"Not funny. It's made me think about all the things that shape us as we grow up ... how indelible that all is."

But he wasn't listening. "I've got something to tell you," he said. "I've met someone."

She looked up and waited for him to speak. He looked so boyish and excited she could barely help smiling.

"I think I'm in love," he said.

"Really? You think? Man or woman?" They never did get round to having that conversation and he was looking at her so lovingly she felt she might cry.

"Man of course and he's coming to dinner to meet you. Tonight!"

He saw her raise an eyebrow and said softly, "I think you knew before I did, didn't you?"

"Yes, we knew or thought we did, Gerardo and I. But we weren't sure and we knew you needed time to work it out – one way or the other. Were we wrong to do that?"

"No, I honestly didn't know. I know that might seem strange to you. I mean I knew I wasn't happy, or things weren't right, but I suppose I didn't know who I was, let alone what to do about it."

Lisa stood up and put out both arms for a hug. "I'm so happy for you," she said, kissing him warmly on both cheeks. "Now I'd better get ready. I want to make a good impression."

Lisa showered and dressed and they began preparing the dinner. As Mack passed her the lettuce she said, "I've decided to enrol in an Indonesian class again."

"What for?"

"Well I might go there one day … meet Adi's family."

"Oh god, I forgot to tell you. Sorry, sorry. Adi's gone back to Indonesia – did you know?"

"No, what? When?"

"Apparently he was in a really bad way. They even had a twenty-four hour roster going to look after him."

"But why didn't anyone tell me?" Lisa said. "Aren't I his wife?"

"Look hon', I'm sorry about this. I first heard about it when I saw Gerardo last night at an opening. He said they took Adi to the airport yesterday and that it was Adi's decision to go back to his family in Indonesia. Gerardo said it might take a good while for him to recover."

Lisa was livid that neither Akira nor Gerardo had told her about Adi's illness or departure. She wondered how Mai had known he had returned to Java, but she hadn't.

All of a sudden she felt like she was going to faint or throw up, and she went to her room to lay down. Her heart was pounding, and when she closed her eyes all she could hear was the buzzing of a fly at the window pane.

Part Four

Sydney and Central Java
2011–2012

Chapter 31

It was September in Yogyakarta and the rainy season was months away but Adi sensed that sometime soon there would be a downpour. His skin, which was dried out by the Sydney winter, sucked in the hot steamy air and he felt pinpricks of sweat gathering in beads on his forehead, and then running in trickles down the middle of his back and chest. His underarms felt clammy, his feet tight and damp inside his trainers.

On the long journey from Sydney, thoughts of Lisa caused his body to recoil as if he'd been landed a kick by an angry water buffalo, and now he asked the taxi driver to take him to a Wartel so he could phone Gerardo to let him know he'd arrived, and to ask him to tell Lisa she could move back into the apartment.

"No worries," Gerardo said, "I think she's already planning to do that. It's become a bit crowded at Mack's now that he's in love."

"What?"

"Mack's head over heels. First big love and all that."

Adi was puzzled. "Oh? Not Lisa."

"No, he's fallen for a stockbroker. Met him in a bar. It's all wine and roses."

"A man?" Adi could not believe what he was hearing.

"Yeah! Quite sweet really," Gerardo said.

"Mack is *gay*?"

"Yeah, he's come out of the closet at last."

Adi was confused. "But he has many girlfriends?"

"Yes, well, friends who were girls. He seemed like a bloke's bloke, all that surfing and rowing, but really he just liked hanging out with a crowd."

"Did Lisa know?"

Gerardo laughed, "I think she knew before he did!"

"And his family?"

"I guess it's only a matter of time before they find out. Oh, and by the way, Lisa was really upset that no one told her you were unwell or that you were leaving. She's very cross with all of us."

When Adi thought back over the years there was nothing about Mack that told him he was gay. It just didn't seem possible. Gerardo said Lisa always thought so but she never mentioned it to him. She said they were just friends, even though it seemed to him that Mack was always competing with just about everyone for her attention and affection.

He tried to call Lisa and listened to the same message they had always had on the answering machine. "Hi, it's Lisa and Adi. Please leave a message."

"Lisa, it's me. I'm in Yogyakarta. I'm going to see my family. I'm sorry – for everything." He wanted to tell her he loved her but the machine cut him off. He put down the receiver.

Lisa heard Adi's voice as she was opening the door and hurried to pick up the receiver, but it was too late. She'd visited the day before and found the place clean and tidy, with a note from Marj that she'd been in to "give it a good going over". The simple message brought tears to her eyes, "Ah Bu," she cried.

In the bedroom, she opened Adi's side of the wardrobe. All that remained were some pairs of pants, a few shirts and, on the floor, a pair of boots and shoes that held the character of his foot. In the top drawer there were two brown, cream and ochre sarongs, side by side, neatly folded. It was the pair they'd worn when they married. She put out her hands to touch them both.

When he first showed her the sarongs she was disappointed. She thought the earthy browns ugly and didn't want to wear them. But then he explained that the colours were a feature of the batik produced in Central Java and that his sister and aunts and the generations before them all made batik. He brought books to show her the batik process and invited her to smell the wax that lingered in the fabric. Finally, he told her that his sister Yanti had done the waxing on the cloth and he pointed out the symbols and described the meanings and good fortune that wearing them would bring. It was hearing that Yanti had made them that really convinced her.

Lisa lifted the sarongs out of the drawer and lay down beside them on the bed, examining them closely, trying to work out the processes, the layers of wax, the repeat dyeing. She tried to recall what made them so auspicious but all she knew was that they were imbued with a sister's love and best wishes. As she traced the symbols with her finger a calmness settled over her and she drifted into a deep and restful sleep.

***

Lisa did not hear from Adi again and nor did anyone else. Neither Akira, Marj, Gerardo, nor Bambang. It was as if he had disappeared. He had always refused to own a mobile phone, but even when they emailed there was no response. Thinking he would stay in touch, they had not thought to obtain a postal address for him.

At times Lisa felt frantic with worry, that maybe Adi was very ill or dying, and she began to dream violent vivid dreams of Java, recurring dreams of dark uniformed figures appearing in the darkness to take people away, the sounds of women and children crying, of being pursued in the dark, stumbling and falling over.

A friend persuaded her to take up yoga and the concentration and body work helped ease the feeling she had of constantly bracing herself against some future calamity. In the quiet final moments of the yoga class, she would ask the question and listen with her being, and in this way she came to know that Adi was still alive. With this insight, she convinced herself that no matter how weak the thread between them, it was up to her to find ways of strengthening it. And so, after reading Mai's essay, she went to see Pak Bambang.

When she mentioned to Pak Bambang that she was thinking of studying Indonesian again he encouraged her, saying he thought it might help heal the grief and loss that kept tripping her up without warning. The three-hour classes were on a Saturday and she enjoyed meeting and studying with other students who were linked to Indonesia in some way – through family, friends, work or travel. Rosida, their Indonesian teacher, who was from Central Java, had a sense of humour and made learning the language enjoyable and stimulating.

Lisa studied, read, and practised Indonesian whenever she could spare the time, but then her attention shifted to Indonesian history, and then art and craft, and finally, contemporary art. Mostly, she was both surprised and excited by what she found, but at other times she felt taken over by a form of culture shock which caused her to feel stripped bare, as if her identity could not quite absorb the new knowledge. And at such times, far from bringing her closer to Adi, he grew more distant.

Was this how he had felt – always having to adapt, bend, compromise, give up or give in – unable to explain desires that were so culturally and religiously integral to who he was?

The more she studied, the more it seemed that the cultural differences – Australian and Indonesian – were thrown into sharp relief.

"But our cultures are so different. How can Australians and Indonesians ever even communicate, let alone get on?" she complained to Rosida in class. "In Australia, if you're extroverted you're popular, in Java it's crass. In Australia people think they have a right to complain, in Java you apologise if the bath plug in your hotel is missing. In Indonesia you smile when you're giving sad news so the other person doesn't feel so upset, here they'd think you a cold hearted monster if you did that. In Australia people in power give orders and dominate, in Java they're quiet, reserved, humble …"

Throughout this litany, Rosida's face was lit with a warm, amused smile. The rest of the class listened; some were nodding, some had wondered the same thing. Then, as one, they looked at each other and at Rosida and burst out laughing, Lisa included. They were doing it, getting on, communicating. Between the class and Rosida there was dialogue, respect, appreciation, and now, at this moment, a shared sense of irony. It was the intercultural differences that made dialogue possible, and those who continued in the class found themselves expanding, while those who found it all too difficult stopped coming.

Several times Lisa had recurring dreams in which Adi appeared as a demon with blood red eyes, wild yellow straw hair that reached to his knees, long orange tongue lolloping from a fang lined mouth. His foot long razor sharp fingernails threatened to rip apart her body and face. Adi or this creature wanted her to have his baby and, when she awoke, she would find herself in a lather of perspiration and, once or twice, filled with an aching lust.

Chapter 38

When the taxi stopped in front of his father's house in the village, a niece Adi no longer recognised began spreading word of his arrival. He paid the driver and, picking up his luggage, turned to see his stepmother emerging from the house. She seemed to have shrunk since he'd last seen her but now she was hurrying towards him and murmuring his name. He took her hand, bowed and lifted it to his forehead, and when he released it she clasped him on both shoulders and put her face to one side of his face, and then the other.

The next to arrive was Yanti who now lived in the new house next door. She stood, head on one side, looking him up and down and smiling broadly. Then, without touching him, she led him into the house with her shoulder dropped submissively and her hand extended to guide him up onto the verandah and through the open doorway. One by one, other members of the family began arriving – on foot and by motorbike – his brothers and their wives, neighbours, Yanti's husband Goenawan and, finally, his father Totot who hurried back from the rice fields when he heard the news.

The house bubbled with voices, laughter, curiosity. Glasses of hot tea were brought by the trayful. Snacks were placed on a table. Adi's suitcase and other bags stood like orphans on the verandah, and the visitors made their way around them while the children pulled at the zippers and fingered the small brass padlocks. For a time, Adi remained standing so as to greet wave after wave of visitors as aunts, uncles and cousins began turning up from other villages.

Totot slipped away to bathe and reappeared in clean clothes. He sat across from Adi and drew a cigarette from a crumpled pack. It was the same brand as always. By the time Adi finished drinking his tea, the crowd had thinned and his father asked, "Your wife – is she joining you?"

Suddenly the emotional and physical weakness Adi had been keeping at bay threatened to overwhelm him. As the panic attack took hold, he tried to stand. Gasping for breath, he staggered and put out a hand to stop himself from falling. Goenawan responded quickly to break his fall and was soon joined by Budi and Ismoyo who, on Yanti's instruction, moved Adi's now unconscious body out of their parent's house and across the yard to her house.

They laid him on his side on a bed and Yanti brought water to bathe his forehead. A doctor visited and prescribed complete rest, plenty of rice porridge and vegetables, and no spices or fried food until he said so.

Adi spent six weeks sleeping and being cared for by Yanti and the rest of the family. The relapse left him in a weakened state but it seemed that, whenever he opened his eyes, Yanti was always there – ready to bathe him morning and evening, or getting him to eat the small portions of food she prepared but which he complained he could barely taste. Often she was sitting nearby, preparing ingredients for a meal, picking small stones from the rice, or applying wax to a cloth. They rarely spoke and, when she saw him looking at her, she smiled gently and let him fade back into sleep.

Only once did he manage to say, "So Mbak, you're looking after me again?"

"It's nothing," she replied. She was so happy to have him back after such a long time and it brought back memories of how it had been for her, for them all, when he left. His absence had been a continuing ache and now, God willing, even though he was so ill, she knew she could make him well again.

But what happened? Why was he so ill? Where was his wife and why wasn't she taking care of him? Why was he alone? These and other questions remained unanswered as the various households went on with their daily lives. On most days Totot looked in on Adi two or three times and, if he saw Yanti, he would chat quietly with her awhile, or just sit on the verandah as though keeping vigil. Children came and went to school, adults attended meetings to discuss water allocations, and there was work to do in the rice fields, crops to be harvested, small businesses to run. For the women there was also the weekly Koran study session at the mosque.

By the end of the second month, Adi had begun to recover physically but it was a slow process of building up his muscle strength and energy to do the simplest of things – like sitting up, standing, and then walking without support. Step-by-step he became more aware of the life around him, both inside and outside the house. The call to prayer marked the passing hours of the day and he sensed the household's response: Yanti getting up to bathe and pray at 4.30 in the morning, other members of the family taking their turn, the noisy squabble of Yanti's ducks feeding in the morning, the echoing croak of a *têkèk* at night.

The flow of village life began to penetrate too: roosters at dawn, the bellow of a neighbour's cows being scrubbed clean of parasites, motorbikes passing, the put-put of a motorised plough heading out to the rice fields. Raucous children trudged to school, their excited voices fading as they entered the schoolyard. Sometimes Yanti's grandchildren came to watch television and the melody of *Shaun the Sheep* filled the house. Twice now he'd heard Yanti humming the tune as she did her chores. Some days he got up and joined the family as they watched comedic talk shows in the evening or, if it was too hot or the mosquitoes were too bad inside, they lit mosquito coils and put down woven cane mats on the small patch of grass at the front of the house and sat outside.

Despite these physical milestones, Adi's emotional and psychological state was proving less resilient and, several times a day, tears streamed down his face without warning. At such times, or when the panic attacks made it difficult for him to breathe, Yanti brought ginger tea. The days when he was unable to get out of bed gradually became less frequent and, as soon as he was strong enough to bathe and dress without Yanti's help, they booked a masseur to come every second day to give him a massage. And then – as the masseur dug his fingers into the painful points and knotted muscles of his body – if Adi cried out, Yanti would appear and warn the man to be gentle.

By the fourth month the return of his sense of taste meant he could enjoy Yanti's cooking and he began to put on weight and feel more energetic. He relished the signature sounds of the passing food vendors – the tink tink of spoon on plate of the *bakso* man, the melody of the *es camcao* vendor ... (da da da, dadadada da), and the bell ring of the *jamu* lady who came daily to mix him a tonic drink. At first he couldn't drink too much of the grey-green liquid, the effort tired him, but as his strength returned he began to gulp it down. He even began sketching in the mornings and, bit by bit, ideas for some new art work began to take shape. By then he knew it was time to find a studio and his own place to live.

Everyday Adi thought of Lisa and wondered how she was. Scenes of their marriage came to him time and time again, and sometimes the loss was too great and he withdrew from the family for days at a time. It was a relief when they no longer asked about her, but it also caused him to feel sad. The thoughts of what might have been haunted him, and he worked hard to banish them from his mind. It wasn't easy, and he wondered if he would ever mend. There had been no contact with anyone from his Sydney life and he was pleased about that because, although he missed them, he felt too unworthy.

One morning on Yanti's verandah, Adi found Totot sitting and enjoying a smoke. As he sat down next to him, Yanti came with bowls of rice, topped with an egg, and glasses of tea for them both. They nodded to one another but did not speak. Finally, when he'd finished eating, Adi spoke up, answering the question his father had asked on the day of his arrival.

"Lisa, that is my wife … We're separated. It was my fault, I wanted her to be a good Javanese wife but she's not Javanese, she's Australian. We argued a lot because of this and I think I've lost her now."

Totot was silent for a while, lost in a struggle with some long ago memories of his own. Over the next hour or so, he told Adi the story of his mother Suriani, and it was the first time he had ever spoken of her to him that Adi could remember.

"Your mother was called Suriani. When she was born she was called Wagiyem, but even when she was a child she was called Suriani because it suited her so well. She was like sunlight – she shone so brightly that when her flame went out there was darkness. Everywhere darkness. For me, perhaps also for you and your brothers and sister, and for everyone who knew her."

"As you know, the village where I was born is across the river and, after my father died, I came here to work for my uncle. He was a blacksmith with no sons so he asked for me to come and help him. Before that I was working in the batik factory."

"The first time I saw Suriani I thought she was very beautiful and graceful. One day I even followed her to the river and watched her playing with some children in the water. As soon as they saw her they started shouting at her and teasing her and straightaway she started playing wildly, chasing and ducking them in the water, splashing. It was such a contrast. First she was so quiet and refined, and then she was so lively like a naughty boy. It made me laugh and I had to creep away before anyone saw me spying on her."

"The matchmaker arranged our marriage and I moved into your grandparents' house. For one year I did not see her. Yes, that's right. She hid from me. Every morning I got up and Mbah Tini, your grandmother, brought breakfast for me to eat with your grandfather. I went to work every day and in the evenings your grandmother brought me my dinner and again I ate with your grandfather. I slept alone for the whole year. Sometimes I saw her sarong or kebaya drying on the clothes line, that is all."

"Always there were clean clothes for me, a glass of tea on a tray, but I was never sure if they were prepared by Suriani or Mbah Tini. Every day Mbah Tini said to me, 'Your wife cooked these. Your wife washed these.' Every day was the same. I only ever saw her in the distance. But I waited. For a whole year I hoped something would change but it didn't, and so I divorced her and went back to my uncle's."

"Mbah Tini and Pak Daliman were unhappy when I left but I think Suriani must have been pleased. Perhaps she was too young – only seventeen – but eventually the matchmaker came to them with another offer of marriage to a man who was quite a lot older and whose previous wife had died. Suriani wasn't happy about this marriage either but her parents insisted."

"After the new husband took her to his house, Suriani was having tea with her new mother-in-law and sister-in-law when the man came in and handed her some dirty clothes to wash. She was so angry he treated her like this, and she told him that he should get a servant if he just wanted someone to cook and clean and wash his clothes. Then she left the same day and returned home to the village."

"The whole village was talking about it. They said she was spoiled and no one would marry her now, which was exactly what she wanted. Well, about a year later the matchmaker came to see my uncle again. She said that Suriani left her husband because she realised she liked me. Of course, she told Suriani that I hadn't married because I still liked her. The matchmaker said Suriani had changed, grown up, matured and so, eventually, I agreed to marry her again."

"This time her parents were strict with her but even though we shared the bed she wouldn't talk to me or look at me. She put a bolster down the bed between us and every night we lay side by side in the dark. No matter what time I woke in the morning she would be up already, and when it was time to eat she would bring me some rice and an egg. Sometimes our hands would touch briefly, but still she refused to look at me. Despite that I loved her more and more each day."

"Every night the bolster lay between us in the bed. And every night I'd say good night and blow out the candle. Then we'd lie in the dark, and soon I'd hear her breathing and know she was asleep. I longed to hold her of course but I decided to be patient. I simply believed she had some feelings for me."

"One day I saw her returning from the river with some other women from the village. They were carrying bundles of washed clothing and I watched from a distance as they joked and talked. Then she saw me watching and that was the first time she smiled at me. The other women saw it too and started to tease her."

"Not long after that Suriani was making the bed in the morning and I couldn't stop myself. I walked up behind her and touched her arms and she stood very still, then she turned around and we were so close, and face to face. She stood very still and I leaned forward and inhaled the perfume of her skin and hair. She stepped back then, but as I walked down the road to my uncle's I looked back and saw her watching me go. I waved to her. I was so happy that day."

"Things went on as usual but one day something happened that changed everything. Suriani was cooking in the kitchen and there was a snake sliding towards her. She was very frightened of snakes and at first she didn't see it, but then the chickens and goat became agitated and she became aware of its presence. She froze. I was outside when she screamed and I came running. I killed the snake but she was crying and trembling in fear so I went up to her and she let me hold her and comfort her."

"That night when I went to bed the bolster was gone, and step-by-step we began to touch one another for the first time. Soon after that we became husband and wife."

The two men remained sitting on the verandah and then Totot handed Adi a parcel wrapped in thick plain paper and tied with a thin ribbon of cloth. Adi untied the ribbon and opened the leaves of paper to see the batik sarong his mother had made for him all those years ago.

Totot said, "Your mother wanted you to have this when you were married but I wouldn't let Yanti send it. I thought it might get lost. Maybe I was wrong, maybe this is why your marriage wasn't successful."

Shuddering pent up grief and sadness shook Adi's body as he pushed his face into the cloth in search of any lingering scent of wax. His father waited calmly for his throaty gasps and tears to subside before getting up and touching his fingertips gently to his shoulder.

When he opened out the kain, Adi found tucked at its centre the batik butterfly he made as a child. For the first time in months a warm golden brightness began suffusing his body, bringing with it a new sensitivity to everything around him – the damp air in contact with his skin, the fresh familiar smell of the soil, the flowers and fruits on the trees, the maturing rice crops.

There was life all around and he was a part of it. There were things to do.

Chapter 39

Adi's curiosity about the myriad changes that had occurred since his departure in 1997, and also since his brief visit in 2008, deepened with his emotional and physical recovery. Through Pak Harto he was drawn into the artist communities of Solo and Yogyakarta. In the south of Yogyakarta he made new friends and soon had offers of places to stay when he attended exhibition openings. In time he got to know the artists he'd read about in art journals or known only briefly before.

As well as offering greater freedom for artists, the current democratic era – *Reformasi* – had also opened the way for some previously suppressed voices to assert themselves. For those whose arts practice was shaped by resistance, the past decade had been a time of reassessment and renewal and, for Adi, these artists remained an inspiration because of the way their work was intertwined with familiar cultural practices, beliefs and struggles.

While his own development as an artist had brought him to European, American and Australian contemporary art and, more recently, Chinese artists, he was discovering his fellow Indonesian artists were more likely to be inspired by each other or other artists from the region. Something intangible was happening – something diverse, unpredictable and exciting – and it was even inviting some artists to play once more with the old cultural forms. In this milieu, he felt like an outsider, but when he spoke of feeling like this to Pak Harto, his old teacher merely assured him that he did have a place in the Indonesian art world.

"Don't worry. Whether you recognise it or not, your work is grounded in Central Java. If anything, this exile of yours has sharpened your sensibility. Perhaps you don't recognise it yet. An artist never arrives … they are always on the way. Of course they may have stops along the way, but they are just that. Stops."

Adi's perspective was that of a kite flying high – over the politics, the history, the chatter of the becak drivers, the powerful and prolific art world of the cities. In the foreground, however, were the village, river, surrounding rice fields, and nearby villages where the various branches of his family lived. He saw the river snaking its way towards the coast; motorbikes, bicycles, pedestrians waiting their turn to cross a plank bridge; ten metre long rows of screen-printed fabrics stretched out on the ground to dry. He saw clusters of red ceramic roof-tiled houses tied to one another by brown earth tracks or bitumen grey roads, the glint of fish ponds, the texture of lines drawn by rows of tomatoes, cassava or beans, and rice fields in all their seasonal variations.

He sensed the ghosts of the powerful empires that rose and fell in the 1600 years before the Europeans brought their particular brand of oppression and hardship. His was an ancient culture and an ancient land, ground and spiced in cosmopolitan encounter. The victory over the colonising Europeans, that proud struggle, was linked by a strong thread to the overthrow of the Suharto regime and the ongoing call for an end to corruption. The chorus of voices in support of the rule of law was growing, he was sure of it.

Surely no country could be better placed, or be more experienced, in dealing with globalisation than the archipelago? Every day he saw rich and poor, young and old, sending text messages and talking on mobiles. A stroll through the village revealed that most houses had televisions. Children played computer games, and at least one becak driver he knew had an iPad. In Sydney he had refused to use a mobile but now he found it a necessity – to call a taxi, to learn of exhibition openings and other art events, to see if Yanti or his stepmother required anything from the markets.

Many of the younger artists were incorporating multimedia into their arts practice – working collectively or alone. They were active on social media. At exhibitions he saw people photographing the artworks with their smart phones and wondered why. Were they posting them on social media, sharing them with friends? He met foreign artists who were living in the city or visiting as artists-in-residence. It amused him that the younger artists addressed him as "Pak". He was thirty-five and yet they saw him as an old man, someone to look up to.

Where should he live? Should he remain in Indonesia and make it his base? Should he remarry? Should he move to Yogyakarta to be part of the artists' community there? Or Solo? Or Jakarta? Or should he build on land that he owned, opposite Yanti's house, where there was once a school and the foundations remained hidden under a swathe of weeds.

In the end he decided to build a studio with timber doors that opened onto a garden of fruit trees and, beyond that, to rice fields on two sides. He re-discovered how much cheaper everything was in Java – not just building materials, but artist supplies as well, and he began painting again. As Pak Harto predicted, his work began to absorb and reflect the colour, light and images of the village. Lighter and brighter than the paintings he'd done in Sydney, they reflected a kite's eye view of the world that preoccupied him now.

On the days he felt stuck or restless, he borrowed a bicycle and went cycling in the late afternoon or early morning. Sometimes he rode all the way to the morning markets in Masaran where he loaded up the saddle bags with fruit and vegetables. He saw broccoli and cauliflower for sale in the market, something he didn't remember seeing before. A bunch of fresh watercress reminded him of Lisa making a salad and he wondered where he might find olive oil and balsamic vinegar. Then he remembered the supermarkets that had sprung up in his absence and stocked all kinds of things he associated with his Sydney life, like pasta, baguettes, and even jam. Who bought them? Was it people like him who had lived overseas? It bothered him to even consider that the local growers' markets might one day disappear, but he hoped they would survive, and go on selling what was fresh, locally grown, and in season.

And this was how it went. He would think of Lisa – something would remind him of her. Then another thought would come, and another, and he would be thinking of something else entirely. His artist friends assumed his marriage was over. Cross-cultural relationships were difficult and everyone had a story to tell – their own or someone else's. Of those that endured – usually in cases where an American, Australian, Japanese, European or Canadian woman was married to a Javanese – it was discussed as being down to the woman's behaviour to make or break the relationship. One success story according to two of his friends, Nuranto and Yusuf, was where the English wife was seen as being "more Javanese than the Javanese".

"In what way?" Adi asked.

"Well, she serves drinks to her husband and friends."

"Is that it?" he asked.

Yusuf nodded, "Even the sultan's wife serves her husband drinks. She might not make the drinks, but she serves them."

The two men were well-known artists in their late thirties. They did exciting work and were highly regarded but, it seemed to him, they had very traditional marriages and you rarely saw their wives at exhibition openings. Would such a relationship satisfy him? Was it really that easy? Their wives took care of the daily practicalities of life, looking after the children, shopping and cooking meals, clothing everyone, keeping track of expenses, dealing with the bureaucracy.

"So, your wives serve you drinks?"

The men laughed. "No," said Yusuf. Adi looked at Nuranto, "No. Well maybe, sometimes, if we have guests."

"So you're just talking about Western women serving drinks then?"

In his own family Adi observed his father and brothers sitting and waiting for their drinks and meals to be served. His stepmother, sisters-in-law, and sister Yanti were still traditional in that respect but the men often cared for the children, worked hard in the rice fields, participated in village and mosque activities. He asked his niece Yuni, who was studying anthropology at university in Yogyakarta and whose fiancé Dedy was studying to be a doctor, whether she thought this was an important custom.

"If I have time I will. But I expect Dedy and I will both be working so we'll have to share all the tasks. It's different now, a different age."

"So, they say a good Javanese wife should make herself beautiful, have children and be a good cook. What do you think of that saying?" Adi asked.

"Well, I think *men* say that. It dates from a time when women were seen as possessions. You know the old saying,

"In order to be happy a Javanese man needs five things: a house, a vehicle, a kris, a wife, and singing birds." Dedy doesn't think like that. In fact, his mother and father both cook but if Ibu Titik has cooked she'll sit and chat with guests while Dedy or his father serve drinks."

"So it's changing then?"

"Well, maybe not for us in the village so much, but in Dedy's family – his grandparents and parents studied abroad – the women have professional jobs."

"I see," said Adi. "So, what do you think the role of the wife is now? Like, in the Ramayana, would a good wife give up her life of luxury and follow her husband into the jungle like Sita did for Rama?"

"The Ramayana? Oh uncle, it isn't so simple is it? Look at Rama's treatment of Sita?"

"How was she treated?" he asked.

"Well Rama fought the battle with Ravana and then he made Sita enter the fire to prove she was pure. Three times. Then, after all that he banished her into the forest, pregnant, with nowhere to go. What a jerk!"

"You don't think Rama did the right thing?"

"You know what Uncle, I think most of us just work out what's fair. It's not like the wife will do this, the husband will do that. Lots of people get divorced these days but maybe it's because they can't work out how to care for and listen to one another. Is that why you split up from your wife, Uncle, because you couldn't work it out?"

Adi was taken aback. "Perhaps you're right. Perhaps that was the problem."

"Well, can't you make it up, start again? Are you just going to walk away? You could easily get another wife, couldn't you? You could get a Javanese wife if that's what you want. But maybe you wouldn't be happy with her either? Maybe you would just want your old wife back? Maybe you'd make the same mistakes." She stopped. She'd gone too far, again.

"I'm sorry, Uncle. Please forgive me?"

Adi smiled, "I'm not sure she would have me back."

"Have you asked her?"

"Well, no."

"What's to lose then, Uncle?"

"Come on," he said, "let me buy you ice cream." He could sense she was worried that she had been too outspoken.

"Okay," she said, "but only if you'll promise not to give up yet."

"My dear Yuni, how did you get to be so wise?"

As they waited to cross the busy road to the ice cream shop, Yuni turned to him, "It's easy to be wise Uncle, it's putting it into practice that's so difficult."

As one, they turned and looked at one another and burst out laughing. She had crossed that line again.

Chapter 15

Lisa arrived in Yogyakarta in early May and for the first four weeks she boarded with Mas Firdaus and Mbak Mifta and their three children aged two, six and nine. She had enrolled in an Indonesian language course recommended by Rosida, her Indonesian teacher in Sydney, and for four hours a day, six days a week, she had been attending individual lessons with two teachers, and for the rest of each day she revised and did homework.

She'd been lucky with her homestay family. She and Mbak Mifta were the same age and, with her help, and that of her teachers, her knowledge about Indonesian life burgeoned. With Mbak Mifta available to take her across the city on her motorbike, she had been able to set up her mobile phone and the modem for her laptop by the evening of her second day, and it was while staying with the family that she soon learned about local dishes and specialities, how to eat with her right hand, and the intricacies of text message abbreviations. She even got used to squat toilets and using a dipper to splash cold water over herself for her twice daily shower.

Adi had been gone for eight months and there had been little contact with him in that time. With a sense of foreboding,

Gerardo, Akira and Marj had called a meeting with Lisa to discuss what was to be done. Lisa still had access to his bank account so she could at least provide some assurance that he, or someone, had been withdrawing money. In fact, some fairly hefty amounts had been withdrawn in the past two months and, if he continued spending at that rate, he might run out altogether. The only deposits to the account were the proceeds from his February exhibition which had gone ahead in his absence.

Marj asked Lisa if she would consider going to Indonesia to see if he was alright and Lisa said she wanted time to think about it. By the end of the meeting, however, she had promised to go. She applied to the university for leave and was given the go ahead to use the time to conduct preliminary research into contemporary Indonesian women artists.

Before her departure, Pak Bambang sent her the name of Adi's village which she located on Google Maps in the regency of Sragen, some thirty kilometres northeast of the city of Solo. A further online search confirmed it was in the batik producing area and this gelled with what she knew already. She even found advertisements for batik factory tours to the area. That was all they had so she'd just have to go to the village and see if she could find someone who knew the family. She had brought some family group snapshots and photos of Adi in the hope they would be of some help in locating either him or his family.

Thinking it would be impossible to remain committed to the research if she met Adi and he rejected her, she decided to dig herself deeply into the work first. On the advice of colleagues, her first stop was the Indonesian Visual Arts Archive which housed an extensive collection of books and exhibition catalogues from the past decade or longer. She found the staff, Ina and Rohmat, so helpful that by the end of her fifth week her initial long list of possible artists had grown, shrunk, grown again. Now she had to whittle the list down to just five artists. When that was done, she would visit their studios if they were local, and interview them and, possibly, their gallerists or curators as well. In the article she was writing, the focus would be on three artists only, but she had plans to write about all five at a later date. On her return to Sydney, she would seek funding to hold an exhibition of their work.

Raindrops began striking the road as Lisa strode towards Jalan Parangtritis, the main road south to the beach. She was in the tourist area in the south of Yogyakarta and heading back to her hotel. Motorbikes sped past, going faster than usual to beat the rain. Several *becak* were parked at intervals in the hope of pickings from the tourist trade that frequented the string of restaurants and hotels along the street. Now the drivers were draping hooded plastic cloaks over themselves and plastic sheets over the roofs of their *becak*. If the rain became too heavy they would crawl inside to wait it out.

As she passed by, the drivers called, "*Becak* Miss?" but Lisa shook her head or waved no with her hand. One wiry fellow with grizzled grey hair, and a rascally tooth-gapped grin that spread all the way up his face to his eyes, had driven her to her hotel during a downpour a few days earlier. He offered to repeat the service for the same price, but still she declined. She had just spent the equivalent, probably, of a driver's fortnightly or monthly income on lunch and was feeling slightly ashamed – ten Australian dollars was a lot of money here and most days she ate for only one or two dollars at nearby *warungs*. Today, however, when she arrived at the cafe favoured by resident expats, the manager had tempted her with the day's special of rack of lamb served with couscous, chickpeas, stuffed baby eggplant, and a mild tomato sambal. Then she had a café latté and read the English language newspaper *The Jakarta Post*.

In Yogyakarta, she was an observer of life, watching, trying to understand, wondering. As well as introducing her to local Yogyakarta dishes at home and welcoming her help in preparing the ingredients, Mbak Mifta had taken her on a tour of the growers' market where she insisted she photograph and write down the names of all the fruits and vegetables she'd never seen before. She was astounded at the variety and abundance – thirty-four varieties of banana alone.

Living with the family was novel and fun for a while but by the fourth week she was beginning to feel the strain of the unfamiliar as well as the lack of privacy. The heat and humidity taxed her, but then there was the sheer necessary concentration it took to understand and be understood. Everyday life was no longer ordinary and the encounter with so much stimulation and strangeness often caused her to feel so intensely alive that she felt she might burst like an over ripe tomato. At such times, a wave of homesickness would roll over her, usually when she was tired or hadn't eaten, or a situation seemed particularly difficult. These weren't life and death issues, for more often it was the ordinary mundane things that got under her defences – like arriving at the post office and finding it closed, or realising she'd paid too much for a hand of bananas. Sometimes she longed to do her own washing and hang it in the sun to dry, or she craved some food or other, like poached eggs on sourdough toast.

Other times she could become suspicious and irritable, and these were the most shameful, for that was when she reacted in a disproportionate way, such as when she grew annoyed that the call to prayer seemed too loud, the price of a taxi or meal seemed too high, or when she felt pestered with the constant inquiry of "Where are you from?" An honest answer to this question, she found, was invariably followed by an invitation to buy a ticket to a play or dance performance, or visit someone's shop. What dismayed her was when these really quite minor irritants made her feel like bursting into tears.

So, in a bid for more privacy, she informed her hosts that she needed to be closer to the major art galleries and arts community, and moved to a hotel in the south of Yogyakarta. This gave her more time alone to write and manage what could only be spiralling culture shock. The hotel had a pool, air conditioning, clean sheets, flush toilet, wifi access in her room and hot water for a bath or shower. She loved it there but there was no avoiding the feeling that she was just a spoiled tourist after all.

The south, which was closer to the sea, was hotter and more humid than the north and on some days, when she was out, she found it difficult to even take a breath. She tried walking more slowly like the locals, but it was as if she was wired to power walk. She was working full time on her research now and meeting more and more people. This led to more and more invitations she found hard to resist, like the opening of a massive group art show, a twenty-four-hour dance festival in Solo, or a public weekend viewing of a private art collection that meant a two-hour journey into the mountains on the back of a motorbike.

In the short space of time she also attended presentations by visiting artists-in-residence at local galleries, an all-night *wayang kulit* performance in the artists' village, various performances at the Sultan's palace, and an evening of mask dances by a visiting troupe from Cirebon on the north coast. There was so much still to learn, such as why there were no obvious price lists for the artworks at exhibitions. Why was that? Were they not for sale? How did it work here? She was yet to find out.

As the frequency of the rain blobs amplified to a spattering rhythm, Lisa breathed in the aroma of the damp earth – like freshly cut ripe pears – that was different to how it smelled at home but just as refreshing. She tucked her book under the shawl Mbak Mifta had insisted she wear at all times to protect her skin from the sun, and pulled her umbrella close to the top of her head. Looking back on the past seven weeks she had more understanding of how it must have been for Adi fitting-in to life in Sydney.

Now that she was in the last week of her second month, life seemed so much easier to Lisa. Things that were strange in the beginning had become familiar, even homely. She had routines. She had befriended an Indonesian journalist, Eko, at an exhibition and he invited her to meet his wife, Tata, a visual artist and graffitist. The three had become friends and Tata introduced her to some women artists and several prominent curators. Both Eko and Tata were from Central Java originally – Eko from Yogyakarta and Tata from Solo – but they met when completing postgraduate studies in the United States. They spoke English fluently and Tata had been helping Lisa with interpreting and translation.

The three of them usually met at a vegetarian organic restaurant that was a short walk from her hotel. It opened in the mid-afternoon and had small octagonal gazebos scattered throughout the tropical garden in which they could sit on cushions on the floor and order food to fuel their conversation. The couple had a passion for debating politics, art and culture and often disagreed with one another. While Eko was the more vocal of the pair, when Tata spoke he leaned in to give her his full attention. Lisa found them generous with their time and hospitality and, every time they met, she brought along a list of things she was curious about.

On most days Lisa read the English language daily newspaper which gave her a sense of local breaking news, and for international and Australian news she went online. It was odd observing Australian politics and society from another place, and at a distance she saw how others in the region might find the comments of their politicians ill-informed, and even crass at times. Fortunately, though, not too much notice was taken of their southern neighbour.

One question nagged at Lisa though and it lead her to ask them, "Australia and Indonesia are part of the same geographical region yet they barely see each other, why is that? It's like the other doesn't exist."

Eko who had spent several years working as a journalist in Melbourne in the early 1990s had his own theories on this topic, "We have very different colonial histories. That's one thing. Also in Australia the Indigenous people were outnumbered and outclassed with modern weapons after white settlement. In our country, however, the population became a cheap source of labour for the colonial power, and when we finally gained independence, global capital combined with the dictatorship to deny us the kind of justice the union movement fought for in Australia – the living wage."

"Yes, but it's as if the two countries don't really see each other, isn't it?" Lisa asked.

Tata said, "They both think they're superior to the other, that's why."

"In what way?" Lisa asked.

"Well, Indonesians think Australians are rude and uncouth as well as quite stupid. And Australians think whites are superior to non-whites, but they're not quite sure, and so that worries them."

Eko disagreed, "It's more than that. Australians are focused on the land, they fear the sea and what it might bring, so borders and the whole issue of border protection is an over-reaction. But for Indonesians the sea has been a source of wealth, empire and greatness."

"Yes, our borders are porous and we have a population of 240 million to be worried about. An entirely different issue," Tata said. "But isn't Lisa really asking how the two countries could begin to know one another better?"

Lisa nodded. Being in Indonesia for the two months had made her wonder why, despite being married to an Indonesian, she hadn't been more curious about the place before now. It was as if she had been hard wired to the idea that the priority art centres in the world were in the United States, Europe and, more recently, China. But Mai's paper had challenged all that, and even forced her to reconsider her interpretation of Adi's work in regard to culture.

"We need – I need – a new way of seeing Indonesian art, but what would that look like, I wonder? Where would I start?" she said.

"Well, you could start by looking at the various aesthetic themes, cultural outlooks, materials used, and communitarian spirit, and the way these impact on artistic practice here and across the region," said Eko. "But I think you're onto that already, aren't you? Or you could consider how the region's artists have responded to living with political repression. That's been a common thread."

Tata said, "Also, many of our artists have gone overseas to live and work since the 1980s and they're in touch with what artists are doing around the world, but particularly across the region. I think you'll find this current generation is developing contemporary art on their own terms, which is exciting."

"Well, that's what you would say because you support that," Eko argued, "but quite frankly, there are a few curators, who I won't name, who don't have this broad picture of what is happening the way you do."

When these conversations were taking place, Lisa often found herself reaching for her notebook. Although rambling, and often inconclusive, they stimulated her to consider new ways of seeing the world, and the artist's role within it.

Chapter 41

Lisa loved the Yogyakarta accent, the way it dropped a loud emphasis on the last syllable: *JogjA, BeringharjO, ayO*. Sometimes this was used to great effect as with a cross-dressing comedy duo who emceed a dance festival she attended. While her lack of language fluency was often frustrating, she found herself absorbing so much by paying attention to what was going on around her. This became clear when she borrowed a friend's bicycle and, just ten minutes from the main road, found herself in a sea of rice fields with space, nature, sky, and fresh air all around.

On her daily rides, she witnessed small day-to-day scenes such as the women throwing the rice up in flat cane baskets to let the chaff fly away, or men making thin grey bricks by the edge of the track. Further along, she came upon batches of the bricks that had been fired to all shades of red. On her first forays off the beaten track she'd been fearful, and even projected that the places she visited and people she met were hostile. But, with time, the anxiety diminished, and she began to feel more at ease. And then she realised she was actually becoming more competent. More adult, like she was in her other life, and it pleased her to note her accomplishments. She could serve herself in the Padang restaurant now, post mail, extend her mobile phone coverage – *pulsa* – without help, bargain in the fresh food market or with the *becak* drivers, eat in the temporary streetside *warungs*.

Once on her bike ride, she came to a village that was so tidy, as if an official entry in a tidiest village competition. Clean swept streets. Flowering pot plants lined up along the front fence of each of the houses to beautify the street. Not a cigarette butt or scrap of paper or plastic anywhere. On another day, on an early morning walk to catch a view of Mt Merapi before it was screened by cloud for the day, she arrived in a small square she'd not been in before. At the centre of the square, a woman had placed a woven mat on the bare ground, and was arranging some large metal containers on top of it. These contained meat and vegetable dishes, and another was filled with steaming rice. She had a low wooden stool which she sat on to serve the customers who began streaming into the square from all directions. Some she served on the plates they brought with them, and others she served on brown waxed paper that she folded into a pyramid parcel and stitched at the top with a fine stick.

Next morning, Lisa returned to the square with some money so she could sample the dishes of the makeshift chef. She was practically the first to arrive, but competition was fierce and within ten minutes the food was all gone and she'd missed out. She felt teary and dejected as she turned to leave, and behind her she heard a lively discussion break out in Javanese among the remaining customers. As the day wore on, she resolved to try again. This time, she told herself, she'd push and shove with the best of them.

When she arrived back in the square the next morning, the same woman was setting up and once again customers were flowing out of the adjoining laneways. When they came together they were animated, and one man in particular was gesticulating excitedly. She couldn't understand, they seemed to be talking about her, voices were raised. Were they angry? Did they not like her being here? Slowly it dawned on her that they were standing back, waiting, inviting her to place her order first so she didn't miss out again.

In all these small ways she was absorbing the city. It was becoming a part of her, imprinted in her, and with this realisation she knew it was time to try and find Adi.

***

Eko navigated the car through the narrow streets of the part of the city known as the artists' village until they came to a large white cube of a building that was bordered on two sides by flooded rice fields. It was Lisa's first visit to the gallery which was built and owned by an artist whose work had been selling for high prices in Singapore and Hong Kong over more than a decade. By the time they got out of the car in the makeshift car park across the road, the sun had slipped away and dispensed a shimmering blue and pink light in its wake.

On first entering the ground floor exhibition Lisa was taken aback by the massive proportions of the space that seemed to almost dwarf the very large abstract paintings hanging on the walls. They were by a single artist and each of the paintings was textured in different tones of a single colour – one in blues, the next in greens, then reds, pinks and oranges. The oil paint had been applied in thick slabs, as if with a trowel, and each painting was sealed with a gloss finish that somehow cheapened the effect.

The works overall were strangely lifeless and flat, garish even, but one painting caught her eye – here the artist had departed from the formula and achieved a three-dimensional effect in which blue marks strained forward as if trying to escape the shades of brown and beige that formed a receding background. There's something interesting happening here, she thought. This is nothing like these other works.

The man standing in front of her began turning, as if to respond to her thoughts, but when he set eyes on her he became transfixed, as if digging deep into his memory for a link between them. And she too was captured, first by his face and then by the details of what he was wearing, and how he held his body.

It was a delayed reaction. "Adi?"

Adi was shaking his head as if trying to wake from a dream. He turned away and she stepped forward and put a hand on his shoulder. He flinched and turned back to her.

"Lisa, is it you?"

"Yes, it's me," she said laughing. "I was imagining you'd been listening to my thoughts about this painting and were about to reply."

"I think it cannot be you, that it must be a ghost. So often I think I see you in places. In Jakarta, in the market, even on a visit to Candi Sukuh. What are you doing here?"

"I'm here for different things, but I mainly came to see how you are. I was going to come to the village to try and find you there. I didn't expect we'd meet like this."

Adi led her out of the gallery and through a courtyard where a band was beginning to play. At the back of the complex, they came to a low wall that ran alongside a rice field and was just the right height to sit on. It was bathed in light from the gallery and a surround sound broadcast of frog and cricket song floated up from the rice fields.

It was strange after all that had happened between them to be face-to-face, exchanging news, and her first question was about his health. He said he was well and asked for news of everyone in Sydney, and she gave a brief rundown and said that they all sent their love and were hoping to hear from him soon.

"You are coming home sometime, aren't you?" she asked.

When he didn't respond, she tried for a more neutral topic.

"How is your family? Are they well? What about the art scene here, how do you find it? Are you painting?"

As the questions rolled out of her he laughed, "So many questions?"

"Yes, truly."

"Alright, but first, tell me, how long have you been here?" He was unused to speaking English and the words faltered in his mouth. "Why you come?"

She described her research project, the artists she was meeting, the friends she had made, and her Indonesian language studies.

"You study Indonesian?"

"Yes, I began studying just after you left. It was Pak Bambang's suggestion. He thought it might help me through a difficult time."

"And did it?"

"I don't know. Maybe. It was wonderful to get to know our teacher Rosida. She said she knows you, that you've been going to Friday prayers with her husband for many years."

"What's his name?"

"Abdullah?"

"Ah yes. A lecturer at university – Sydney I think."

"That's him. I learned so much in her classes. It's frustrating not being able to speak the language better but I manage simple conversations, and luckily there are many people here who speak English."

"I didn't know," Adi said. He took out a cigarette and, after looking to her for permission, went ahead and lit it.

It seemed entirely fantastic to be sitting there with him on a wall in Nitiprayan. "Look. Fireflies," she said, as a tiny cloud of yellow green lights hovered barely a metre away, and then faded into the darkness. There was a splash, probably a fish or bird, or perhaps a frog leaping into the water. In the courtyard, the music had stopped and someone was making a speech. After a while they heard clapping, and then another speech.

"Have you been painting?" she asked.

"Yes, I have an exhibition in Jakarta next month and I'm working on that now. I just finished making a studio."

"Oh, that explains the withdrawals in your bank account."

"Yes, I needed a place to work. I already had the land. Remember?" Lisa nodded. "So I have a studio and I can live there as well. Simple. It overlooks the rice fields."

"It must be great to have your own place?"

"Yes, I'm happy … "

Lisa looked up and saw that his chin had fallen onto his chest and his body and shoulders were sagging forward, as if he was being drawn into the dark watery surface in front of them.

"Adi?" He straightened up and looked across the rice fields to the flickering lights of a village. Then, without looking at her, he began the story of his mother, Suriani, as told to him by his father when he was recuperating.

The world around them receded as he brought her to his mother, and to the light and nurturance of her presence. In the days to come she would look back and know that no matter what happened after this, whatever they could become or not become together, they had sat side by side next to this rice field and felt Suriani's love and blessing.

When he stopped speaking, she said, "It seems we are not too different, your mother and I. I think we would've gotten on well together."

Chapter 12

When the train pulled into the station in Solo, Adi was waiting for Lisa on the platform. He'd been relieved to get her text message to say she was on the way, and his plan was to show her around the parts of the city that meant something to him. His nephew had told him about a batik museum that housed a large private collection, and when he mentioned it as a possibility she had leapt at the suggestion.

The batik museum was new, air-conditioned, and the entry fee included a guided tour by a young woman who spoke English with an American accent. There was a series of rooms and, in each one, she described where, when and by whom the pieces were produced, and what was significant about them. With barely a pause, she ushered them through a history of the art form, from the time before 1912 when natural dyes were used, and then on to exquisite examples by the most famous twentieth century regional producers, including those of Central Java, Yogyakarta and the north coast.

It opened Adi's eyes to see the collection in its entirety, and he was impressed by Lisa's interest in the mystical and cultural significance of the traditional textiles, and her sensitivity to the ambiguity of meaning of the symbols depicted in them.

He could tell she was frustrated with their guide, who hardly allowed them time to pause and really study the pieces before drawing them on to yet more fine examples from the different eras and regions.

He was surprised to find that the styles of Central Java attracted Lisa's interest the most and, as she explained, that was partly because of their abstract and highly stylised designs, but also for their use of shapes and signs to hide complex information. She had questions, like wanting to know why some designs could only be worn by royalty, but the guide resisted her attempts to stray from the set narrative, and they realised later that this was because she had so much to get through. As it was, by the time they reached the reception area and shop they were overwhelmed by the sheer quantity of information provided.

As well as the batik museum, Adi took her on a walk to his old high schools, showed her the house where he lived as a student, and they visited some of his favourite *warungs*, including one that was run by three women and served local dishes. At the antiques market, he explained how to tell if a piece that was being sold as a batik was a real batik or just a print, whether it was hand drawn or stamped, or a combination of both. Lisa bought several old sarongs, an old brass instrument called a *cap* that was used to stamp a water lily design on the cloth, and a wooden puppet of a woman that was attached to bone sticks that moved her arms. The puppet was dressed in a batik sarong and kebaya and, even though the shop owner couldn't tell them what character she represented, Lisa liked the way her maker had given her a strong proud face.

Just as they were leaving the market, heavy drops of rain began striking the footpath and drove them into a nearby hotel. By the time the waiter showed them to a table in its open air pavilion, a curtain of water was drenching the surrounding pavement and garden and forcing those who were seated around its perimeter to relocate. Once it had cooled the air, the rain departed as abruptly as it had arrived.

After the emotional highs and lows of the past eight months, it was as if Lisa and Adi were now on neutral territory, and this allowed their words, insights and stories to flow. He questioned her more closely about the artists she was researching, the families at the Darlo Boarding House and in Bankstown, and her roiling feelings of culture shock during the two months of learning the language and doing her research.

When it was her turn, she returned to the questions she'd blurted out that night at the gallery, and so he told her about his weekly visits to Yogyakarta for exhibition openings, and how impressed he was with the work of some of the artists of his generation and older. A number had international reputations and some had even relocated to other countries while still holding regular exhibitions in Indonesia.

"Do you want to be a part of the art world here?" she asked.

He smiled, "Perhaps eventually, but at the moment I feel more like an Australian artist than Indonesian. Do you think that strange?"

"No. Of course not. You've lived much of your adult life there, fifteen years. It's where you've trained and exhibited. Do you feel divided?"

"Not really, but I think being here has connected me more with what is happening in art in the region, and I like that."

"Do you think you were feeling cut off there?"

"Perhaps, although there is the Asia Pacific Triennial in Brisbane of course."

Lisa was curious about how he had adjusted to being back in the village and the country, "What about all the social change that's happened since you left? Has that been difficult to adjust to?"

"A little, but I'm still learning about that. Somehow, being in the village has been a screen. Solo and Yogyakarta look more or less the same, but Jakarta was a big surprise. Very modern. Many tall buildings. Shopping malls. So many cars, so much traffic. Traffic jams. I hadn't been there before, you see."

He was trying to understand what it was about her that was different. "You're, calmer?" he said.

"Perhaps from being on holidays?"

"No, it is something else."

"You seem different as well, on your own soil. It's strange that here I'm the one who stands out."

"Does it bother you?"

"Sometimes. When I look in the mirror, I often get a shock. It's strange, like I'm believing I look like everyone else – black hair, brown eyes. I guess the main thing that bothers me is the feeling of being cut off by language, when I can't communicate easily. You must have felt that too?"

He shrugged, "You get used to it."

After hearing all the news about friends and family in Sydney, he wanted to ask her about Mack.

"Gerardo said Mack is gay. Is it true?"

"Oh yes, he's met a lovely man. They're very happy, very much in love."

"I didn't know. I thought he loved you."

"Well he does, of course, but not in a girlfriend-boyfriend way."

"Even after all this time, this is something I'm still not used to. If men and women are friends like that here, they get married."

"Even if they're gay?"

He considered this, "Maybe."

"But why?"

"Well it's important to marry, have children. It's what makes you human, Javanese, an adult."

"What if someone doesn't marry?"

"That's unusual."

It was time to go and he signalled to the waiter to bring the bill.

"Adi, we need to talk about what happened to us. I'm sorry I didn't really understand about the pressure you felt to have children."

"I think you did understand but you were not ready. I was too impatient."

"Well no, I don't think I understood it in the way you felt it. The sense of urgency. People rush into marriage much younger here, they used to in my parents' generation too. So, at thirty-two I'm still a chicken in Australia, but here I'm an old chook."

Chook was a swear word in Indonesian but this was not why he laughed. The image she painted made him feel happy.

"I still can't think about this thing that happened, y'know? But when my father told me the story of my mother I was so impressed that his love for her was so great. He forgave. I feel much respect for my father now and I feel I must learn to forgive too."

"And Mai?"

"I'm very sorry. When it happened I wanted to blame you, punish you. Why? I don't know, but it wasn't right or fair."

"She came and saw me."

"Who?"

"Mai. She brought a copy of her thesis and an article she wrote to my office. First she said that what happened was her fault, and that you didn't see her again, which I didn't know. Then she told me that what happened was my fault, or words to that effect. As you can see, no mention of you."

Lisa paused to take stock of the emotion that had been rekindled, and realised she could make a joke about it now. "So I threw her out, probably would've punched her too if she hadn't got out the door so fast."

He waited for her to continue.

"I read the thesis and it pains me to say it, but she has really opened up my thinking about art history, particularly in relation to the region. She also reveals aspects of your work I hadn't known about or considered, just by coming to it from the angle of your Javanese heritage. I think you'll find it interesting. I brought a copy with me – it's at the hotel."

Back at the hotel, they had a swim and ordered drinks by the pool.

"So, Adi, have you taken another wife?"

He laughed and shook his head. He'd forgotten how direct she could be.

"No, not yet. Too busy."

The fear that she might have met someone else was niggling him as well.

"And you? Is there anyone else?"

"I still love you Adi. There is no one else."

She said it in such a matter-of-fact way that, not knowing how to respond, he simply looked on as she gathered up her things to go and shower and dress for dinner.

That night they were going to have dinner with Pak Harto and his wife.

Chapter 13

On their way to the village, Adi asked the taxi driver to stop at a market where they bought baskets of fruit for the family households they would be visiting. Their first stop was the house of his eldest brother Budi in Masaran but, when they arrived, the neighbours told them Budi and Nur had gone to Solo for the day. So they left a fruit basket for them and, from there, Adi directed the driver to take a route that approached the village via a straight tree-lined road that sliced through a grid of silver sky mirrors, all with even spiky rows of newly planted rice seedlings.

Each plot appeared to be a regular-sized rectangle lined with narrow trimmed banks. "How does everyone know who owns the plots? Are they owned by all different people?" Lisa asked.

"Yes, all different."

"Are there deeds of ownership?"

"Sometimes. If someone wants to sell."

As the vehicle slowed at the entrance to the village, Adi pointed out key buildings and the houses of different family members. On the right, a high school, then his niece's house, then Ismoyo's house, which had a tiny mixed business at the front. Then a batik factory and showroom, followed by a string of houses and the primary school on the left. At the crossroads, he pointed to the dark timber building on the corner that was his studio. Then they turned right and after several houses and a side street he asked the driver to pull up outside his father and stepmother's house.

Adi had sent a text message to Yanti to say they were on the way and Pak Totot, who was wearing a clean white singlet and sarong, was waiting on the verandah when they got out of the taxi. He shook hands with Lisa and then Ibu Yuni joined them, followed by Yanti. Both were wearing a *jilbab*, signifying that the welcome for Lisa was to be a formal occasion. Pak Totot and Ibu Yuni sat down and gestured to Lisa to sit on one of four cane armchairs arranged around a low coffee table. Adi sat next to her, but bobbed up from time to time to greet visitors and introduce them to Lisa. Glasses of tea were soon placed on the table, followed by a plate of snacks and a small hand of stubby bananas.

They'd entered the living room through two wooden doors that were slid wide open. On the left side of the room there were two sewing machines, a wall unit containing fabrics, and a wide wooden bench on which someone was part way through cutting a piece of cloth to a paper pattern. Three pairs of open shutters drew air and light into the room and thin shafts of sunlight slipped through strategically placed perspex tiles in the tiled roof to light the work area. The underside of the roof tiles formed the ceiling, and timber beams supported the roof. Woven mats were spread out on the floor in the centre of the room.

As individual women arrived they were introduced, and then disappeared through a door at the back where Yanti had gone earlier to prepare the food. Soon Lisa was invited to move to the mats on the floor, at the centre of which was a stack of clean plates and cutlery. An array of food dishes was brought in. Rice, jackfruit curry, gado-gado, a platter of fried fish, and a dark green vegetable which Lisa correctly guessed was cooked papaya leaf. Pak Totot asked Adi to inform her that the fish were from Yanti's pond.

At Adi's suggestion, Yanti had provided a fork and spoon for Lisa but she washed her hands and ate with her right hand like everyone else, something she'd learned to do while staying with Mbak Mifta and Mas Firdaus. He was worried that she might feel uncomfortable being surrounded by everyone speaking Javanese but she told him to relax, and so he let her eat in peace. When they finished eating, the plates were whisked away and replaced with glasses of black coffee and a platter of papaya slices.

When Adi suggested they move on, they collected their belongings and walked next door to Yanti's house.

Yanti's house was constructed out of thin red bricks like the ones Lisa had seen the farmers making out of mud in the rice fields in Yogyakarta. The floors were formed of rough concrete and the brick walls were exposed, with a thick even line of grey mortar between each row. The internal walls were also brick and reached only as high as the wooden triangular beams that supported the pitched tile roof; the spaces left for windows were boarded up with thick raw planks of wood. Presumably tiles and windows would be installed when there was more money. In the sitting room there were four woven cane armchairs, a coffee table, daybed and television. A souvenir tea towel of Australian native birds hung on the wall.

Yanti's husband Goenawan joined them and Yanti brought glasses of tea. When they finished their tea she opened a door to a bedroom next to the living room and invited Lisa in. A small four-poster bed took up much of the space and was veiled on four sides by a pale green embroidered mosquito net that reached almost to the floor. The mattress was covered in a floral patterned cotton sheet and there were thin pillows at one end. A child's school uniform hung from a hook on the wall next to a chest of drawers. Adi handed Lisa's backpack to Yanti and she put it on top of the chest of drawers. Then Yanti took her down the hallway, past a tiny bedroom on each side, to show her where the bathroom was at the end of a kitchen.

Yanti's kitchen was a large room that stretched across the entire back of the house. It had a knee-high low shelf that served as the food preparation area and an empty wok sat on a gas hob. At the far end, outside the bathroom, two tubs of clean water stood ready for washing glasses, dishes and vegetables. In the bathroom a double-sized smooth grey concrete *bak mandi* was filled to the brim with crystal clear water and there was a squat toilet next to it. The only ornament was a white plastic holder on the wall for soap, toothbrushes and toothpaste. Single taps, one in the kitchen and one in the bathroom, provided running water, presumably from a well.

Yanti left her to use the bathroom, and when she returned to the living room, Adi was sending a text message. He looked up, "All okay?" he said.

She nodded. She was touched by how solicitous he was, as if he had concerns about how she would manage in the village, with cold water for bathing and the lack of flush toilets. This was confirmed later that afternoon when Yanti offered to heat some water for her to bathe.

"We have to go to Ismoyo's house now, they're expecting us," he said.

It was three in the afternoon and the heat pressed down on her as they walked through the village to Ismoyo's house. She saw now that there were several streets parallel to the main road in the village. Many of the houses had their front doors open, with a timber batik stand at the front that looked to her like a Victorian towel rack. Next to it was a low wooden stool no more than a foot high. A few people were on their verandahs or standing chatting in the street, and they called out to enquire who the visitor was. Lisa could feel the sweat coating her face and skin, her bra was soaking wet and she felt streams of fluid trickling down her ribs. She hoped she wasn't getting sick.

At Ismoyo's house they were greeted by Ismoyo and Dewi, his wife, and once again they sat on mats while tea, then snacks, then more food were brought and Lisa again felt suspended in a tumble of Javanese language. But then Adi's nephew, Jaya, who majored in English at university, arrived from Solo and Ismoyo directed him to sit next to Lisa. He began by asking about her trip – the research, where she was staying, how she found living there, and she learned that he was designing and making batik silk scarves for stores in New York and San Francisco. At Adi's prompting, Jaya invited Lisa to visit the batik studio which operated in another part of the family home.

**

In the batik studio, a group of five women sat sideways in a circle on low wooden stools around a gas-heated dish of simmering wax. Each one faced the back of the one in front and they were positioned so they could comfortably reach out to dip the *canting* into the creamy orange liquid. All but one wore colourful hijabs over long-sleeved blouses that covered their pants or jeans to the knee. She watched closely to see how they held the wooden handle of the *canting* with their right thumb, middle and ring fingers, while using the little finger and index fingers of the left hand under the cloth to guide the flow of wax onto it.

She was told that the women worked from seven in the morning until twelve, and then returned to work for another two hours later in the afternoon when it was cooler. They were at the front of the building and the doors were pushed wide open to let in the air. Through Jaya they asked Lisa a tally of questions. When did she arrive? (This morning) How long was she staying? (Just one night) Why not longer? (I have to return to Yogyakarta to work) How old was she? (Very young) Why didn't they have children yet? (She was too young). She had learned from Mifta that such questions were asked out of politeness and an answer that made people laugh was as good as any.

Jaya showed Lisa pieces of white cloth that had intricate pale gold wax patterns already applied to them. In some parts there were solid areas of wax, in others finely drawn leaves and flowers and shapes that contained repeat geometric patterns. He took one piece and explained that it was for a man's shirt and that the design ensured that, when the shirt was made up, the patterns on the sleeves, back and front would match up at the seams. While the men's shirts and the sarongs were all worked on high-grade cotton, most of the scarves were of various grades of silk, some of which were sourced from other countries.

Jaya's batik was nothing like the work they'd seen in the batik museum, but she could see that the quality was fine and intricate. One woman was working on fresh white cotton, setting down the first fine even trace of wax over the pencilled outlines of the design, and the others were working on pieces that had been dyed already in bright orange, purple or dark green. Some pieces had already been through two lots of dying and had a bright orange or green background where they had once been white, and others had dark grey or black parts added to bring up the design. After finishing each stage of the waxing the women got up and hung the cloth on bamboo poles strung in parallel rows from the ceiling. Then they took another piece to work on.

Lisa wanted to understand the process better and asked Jaya if he would write out the stages of making the batik for her to study. She wouldn't allow herself to take photos until she felt she had really seen and smelled and listened, and now she closed her eyes lightly and listened to the "phew phew" outbreaths as the women blew away the air bubbles in the spout of the *canting*. Beyond the rhythm of breath she heard other village sounds – a cow mooing, a woman's voice raised in complaint, children laughing, the splutter of a motorbike that wouldn't start – but above all she felt comforted by the soothing smell of the wax.

Jaya had disappeared into the house and came back carrying a suitcase. He opened it up to show her a pile of exquisite finished scarves and sarongs while explaining that the problem he had selling them in the United States was that there was little or no understanding of the detailed handiwork that went into their making.

Lisa said, "This is very fine work and your designs and sense of colour are wonderful. I hope you're very successful."

"Thank you." Jaya bowed modestly.

Just then Adi returned pushing two bicycles. "I thought we could take a bike ride and see the studio on the way," he said.

The studio was in an L-shape on a corner block at the crossroads and had rice fields on two sides. It was built of recycled timber and was the only house on that side of the road. They entered via a courtyard that contained the remnants of a mature fruit orchard and, on the side facing into the garden, there was a verandah and two large wooden doors that were padlocked. Adi undid the lock and slid back the doors, one on each side, and they stepped up into a long room that looked out through the garden to the rice fields. The timber floor was covered with a thick plastic sheet where Adi had been painting, and in the base of the L there was a kitchen and bathroom. A collection of very large paintings leaned against the walls ready to be sent to the exhibition in Jakarta.

The studio had little furniture – four cane chairs around a marble-topped table on the verandah, and some improvised plank and brick shelves for paints and art materials. In the bedroom a large glass window framed a view of the rice fields and there was a thin single bed mattress on a raised platform. Opposite the bed there was a fine antique chest of drawers with a marble top like the ones she'd seen in the antique shops in Yogya.

"It's very elegant," Lisa said. "The timber is beautiful and it seems as if the building has always been here. I also like the way it opens onto the rice fields."

"There was a school here before. It fell down a long time ago but we could still use the foundations. We got the timber from an old Javanese house that was being pulled down in my aunts' village."

"How long did the build take?" she asked.

"Several months, but I asked my brother to supervise it so I could focus on painting."

"Do you mind if I ask how much it cost?"

"Well I owned the land already. In Australian dollars, perhaps fifteen thousand all up."

Lisa turned her attention to the paintings. From a distance they appeared to be aerial shots of the countryside, similar to what she'd observed on Google Earth, but up close she saw images floating beneath the surface of flooded rice fields. As with the layering process that went into the making of the batik, so too it seemed that Adi's latest paintings brought together fragments of meaning from ancient times to the present – lines from letters, snatches of poetry from classical manuscripts, details from ancient monuments, the struggle for independence, and many of the symbols that fused the country's hundreds of small islands and cultural and linguistic groups into a nation.

Floating like shadows in the water, they insisted the viewer pause, move close, and consider the web of meaning in the present that was being woven from their past and future histories.

All of it, he seemed to be saying, was part of a mapping and a reminder that responsibility for the future depended on the recovery of real true stories from the past. And these could provide a new base for compassion and forgiveness going forward. This is what she saw and it pleased her that this deeper insight into his work was due to her time spent in the artists' community and the city.

That night she slept at Yanti's house, and on her second day in the village another niece showed up. Her name was Umi and she worked in Jakarta for one of the big banks. For the past two years Umi had worked with the same bank in London so, while Jaya had an American accent, it amused Lisa that Umi spoke with an English accent and often injected cockney expressions into their conversation.

Another bike was found so Umi could join Adi and Lisa on a ride around the villages and, on the way, she explained to Lisa the correct forms of address to use with Adi's family. She was preparing her, she said, to find her place in the family, as a daughter-in-law, sister-in-law, aunt and even a granny.

"Granny? How can I be someone's granny?" Lisa asked.

"Well, you're not really a granny, it's just that they have to address you as Granny."

Lisa said, "Let's write this all down when we get back. It's doing my head in."

Umi laughed. "Okay. We'll do a family tree."

Lisa's teachers at the language school had wanted to teach her the forms of address but she really couldn't see the necessity. Now she realised it was about behaving respectfully with those she met. When they got back to the village it was time to revisit each family to say goodbye and, as with when they first arrived, this was not to be rushed.

Before they left Yanti's house, Yanti called for her to sit on the bench beside her and asked Umi to interpret. Then she looked at Lisa affectionately and spoke to her in Indonesian.

"Lisa, maaf ya... rumah kami sangat sederhana jadi mungkin kamu gak betah lama-lama tinggal disini. Makanannya juga gak mewah kayak di Australi, maklum di kampung jadi cuma gini-gini aja, seadanya. Kapan-kapan kalau berkenan, main dan mampir ke sini lagi, jangan kapok dan gak usah malu, kami semua masih keluargamu. O ya, walaupun kamu sebentar di sini, semoga berkesan."

Even before Umi translated, Lisa felt touched by Yanti's words, "Lisa, I'm sorry, our house is very humble, so perhaps you didn't feel comfortable to stay here longer. Our food is not as good as the food you have in Australia but, please understand, we live in the village where everything is modest. Next time when you have time, please come to visit us again. Don't be shy, we're still your family, after all. Oh, and although you just made a short visit, I hope you enjoyed it."

Lisa was filled with love for this gentle affectionate woman and felt blessed by the ritual. She wanted to respond appropriately, so she said to Umi, "What do I say?"

Umi said, "You can say thank you very much for having me here, and I'm sorry if I've been a burden on you."

"Okay, how do I say that?"

"Terima kasih banyak atas segalanya ... dan maaf kalau saya sudah merepotkan."

Lisa turned to Yanti and, with as much heartfelt sincerity as she could muster, repeated the words.

Chapter 44

It was about an hour's ride by motorbike to the station in Solo, and when Lisa and Adi arrived the parking attendants directed them where to park. They bought her ticket to Yogyakarta and Adi led her to the women-only carriage of the waiting train. When it came time to say goodbye she stepped forward to hug him, but then recoiled. Remembering where she was, she turned and stepped up into the train.

"When will I see you again?" she asked from the doorway.

"I'm coming to Yogyakarta on Wednesday. Lunch maybe?"

"Great. Send me a text. Oh, and by the way, Akira and Gerardo have both SMS-ed me to get your phone number. Can I send it to them?"

"Oh yes, please."

Lisa waved to Adi for as long as she could see him and then settled down for the hour-long journey. Unlike the other carriages in which many were forced to stand, the women-only carriage was half empty. At each station whole families crammed into the carriage, only to be told by the guards that the men had to go to another carriage. More often than not, the women and children went with them, which left spare seats in the carriage all the way to Yogyakarta.

As the train faded into the distance, Adi was possessed by the thought that he might not see Lisa again, that she would slip out of his life forever. But did he want to go back to that old life in Sydney? Was that even possible after all that had happened?

There was no doubt that the country's contemporary artists were receiving international recognition and many wealthy collectors were buying up their work – not just in Indonesia, but in Singapore, Malaysia, Thailand and Hong Kong as well. He had met several artists who were living entirely off their art practice, in part because living here was more affordable, but also because they were getting good prices for their work.

Lisa must have sent his phone number to Akira, Gerardo and Pak Bambang because there was a phone call from Gerardo before he even reached his motorbike. This was quickly followed by text messages from Akira and Pak Bambang. Then there was a second message from Akira that had clearly been dictated by Marj.

"Dear Eddie, I am very happy to hear that Lisa has been able to find you and that you are well. We miss you and hope you will return soon. Archie and Bert are well though Bert's right knee has been playing up again. The children are growing up. Akira is a very good father. Please give our best regards to your parents and family. Yours, Marj."

The message brought his former Sydney life into focus. He found himself trying to picture how much Eloise and Frank had grown since he left, and he imagined them working in the garden with Archie, or sitting next to Bert on the lounge to hear a story. He saw Marj carrying Frank up to bed and taking the wrapper off a chocolate Paddle Pop for Eloise. He realised he was missing them too, and that they were and always would be a part of his life in Sydney. And the same could be said for Gerardo, Bu Wafa and Pak Bambang, and their girls.

He'd been surprised at how well Lisa's visit to the village had gone. She seemed relaxed and comfortable with everyone in the family, sometimes playing with the children and making craft things with them. Sitting with the women making batik. Showing an interest in Jaya's batik business, and even going with Yanti to pick beans for dinner. Riding around on bikes with Umi, and insisting they take tracks he'd not been down before, or which led to dead ends. Happily eating whatever Yanti cooked and wanting to help.

When a motorbike laden with two large baskets of cakes stopped in front of Ismoyo's shop, she bought enough to feed three households. He'd thought the family would find her unrefined because of her Australian ways but, oddly, it seemed to him that her demeanour was quieter and more still, more Javanese. Perhaps it was his imagination, or because of the time spent in Yogyakarta, or maybe it was due to the language barrier that prevented her from joining in.

Could he forgive her for what happened? He believed he had. Could he love her again as he'd once done? He didn't know. While the connection between them had been burned by grief and anger, he still wanted to go on seeing her, even though he knew they would make no plans. Not yet.

Lisa's train pulled into the station in Yogyakarta at five o'clock and by then the overload of impressions and emotion of the past few days had begun to catch up with her. Her frayed feelings were further compounded when she was accosted by a wall of hopeful taxi drivers who began pestering her with offers of a fare at twice the usual meter rate. In a blind rage, she stormed out of the station and was almost run over by a motorbike as she crossed the road.

In Jalan Malioboro she hailed a taxi, got in and gave the driver the address. I will not be unhappy to leave Indonesia, she thought.

The day after she returned from the village, Lisa began writing her paper on the three Indonesian women artists. She was keen to make a start while she was still in the country, but also because she often didn't know what she thought or felt until she began writing. One of the artists who lived in Belgium had recently had an exhibition in Yogyakarta and, while the artist did not make it to the exhibition, Lisa was able to interview her twice on Skype. The other two artists lived in or near Yogyakarta so she'd been able to visit their studios in the previous week to interview them once again. She still needed an overall theme to link the three, but she was hoping that would emerge in the process of getting down the first draft.

At about eleven o'clock that night there was a loud knocking and when she went to open the door, she saw Adi standing on the doorstep. "Adi, what is it? Come in. What's happened?"

"Akira just called. He said Bu died." His face was swollen with grief and haunting growling sobs shook his body from the belly up. At first Lisa was confused, but then it sunk in that "Bu" was what they all called Marj. It took a moment to register the shocking news before she moved to wrap her arms around him. She led him to her room where they sat side by side on the bed and then, try as she might, she found that her imagination could not stretch to the possibility that Marj was dead.

She located a box of tissues and put it next to Adi on the bed, "You stay here. I'll go and make us a cup of tea."

When she returned she found him curled up on the bed. He was quiet now and he sat up to drink the tea.

Lisa waited for him to speak, "Akira … It happened tonight when Bu was cooking dinner. She was peeling potatoes and she fell down on the floor. They called the ambulance but it was no good."

"Marj … Who found her?" she asked, wondering why such details were important.

"I think Archie found her in the kitchen, but she was already dead. Akira, Lisbeth and the children were out. Akira says Eloise keeps asking, 'Where's Nanna Bu?' She keeps on crying for her, like she knows. But no one can believe it."

Adi began to cry again and Lisa put a hand on his shoulder. "It's okay, darling, take your time."

When he had finally calmed himself, Adi continued, "Archie is very upset. He thinks he should have saved Bu but the paramedic said maybe she died before she fell. I wanted to call Archie but Akira said the ambulance took him to hospital. The doctor wants him to stay in overnight. For the shock. Bert is staying at the hospital with Archie."

"What do they think caused it?"

"Not sure. They have to wait for the report. Akira says Bu was taking tablets. Maybe for blood pressure, or heart."

Adi finished his cup of tea and looked at Lisa. "I have to go to the funeral for Bu," he said, "Will you come?"

"Yes, of course. I'll book the tickets."

"What about your research?"

"I've done a lot already. If necessary I can come back, or finish it in Sydney. What about the Jakarta exhibition?"

"It's packed already. My brother will meet the courier at the studio in the morning. The driver will deliver it to the gallery in Jakarta. I just have the titles to do."

"When is the funeral? Do you know?"

"Not yet. Akira said he will call tomorrow."

Lisa took Adi's empty tea cup and put it on the desk. She went to him and they lay down on the bed, face to face, just looking and breathing. The loss was too much to bear alone, and they took off their clothes and, skin on skin, felt the exquisite joining of their bodies. Deep down, in body and soul, the layers of their grief and loss at the news of Marj's death set alight the accumulated pain of their months of separation, and fuelled a reconnection.

The news of Marj's death triggered the return of Adi's nightmares and he didn't want to be alone. Whenever he was by himself, and even when he wasn't, the tears would suddenly stream down his face. His family was worried he was becoming ill again but Lisa reassured them he would be alright. They had become inseparable.

"Let the tears come," Lisa said, "It's okay to feel sad about Marj going. You loved her. And she loved you."

"She was so kind when I came," he said. "And Akira and the Boys. She gave us a home, a place to live and work. Safe, with no pressure, only love."

Lisa held him and let him speak.

"I didn't tell Bu I loved her. I didn't say thank you for all she did for me."

"She knew you loved her by the way you included her in your life, and the way you brought the rest of us to her – me, Gerardo, even Bambang and Wafa. We knew it and so did she."

"I can't imagine what it will be like without her around. What about Archie and Bert? What will happen to them? Where will they live?"

"Marj would have made provision for them, I'm sure. But I think Bert has money of his own anyway, doesn't he? Marj told me he had a farm which he leased to his brother."

"What will Akira and Lisbeth do? I'm sure they'll want to stay with Bert and Archie."

"They'll be so very sad, but at least they've had this time together so the children will remember her."

An email came from Akira to say the funeral was being organised and it would be a celebration of Marj's life. He and Bert and Archie were collecting photos and other bits and pieces for a slide show, and he asked if they had photos too that they had taken over the years. There was also talk about whether Adi could donate a painting for auction so they could create a scholarship in Marj's name for an overseas student at the art school.

Something about Marj's can-do attitude and energy, her earthy commonsense and welcoming inclusiveness, had inspired a desire to do something constructive around the event of her death. For Adi, this other life – the community of friends, colleagues and fellow artists – was drawing him back, reminding him that he still had responsibilities there.

In the village, Lisa left Adi in his studio to finish packing and went over to the batik studio. When Jaya showed up, he handed her the notes she had requested about the stages of batik making.

"Here I explain the stages of the batik process, Auntie. I am sorry if the English is not understandable but, hopefully, you get the meaning."

Lisa looked at the notes and tried to match what the five women were doing as they worked on their different pieces. Seeing her sister-in-law, Mbak Dewi, covering the pencilled lines on some fresh white cloth with a thin line of wax, she said, "*Nglowongi?*"

Mbak Dewi pronounced the word for her and she repeated it back, "*Nglowongi?*"

"*Betul,*" she agreed.

Another woman was adding dots to the inside of leaves so she said, "*Ngiseni?*" She wanted to imprint the process in her mind and uttering the words like this, and linking the word to the waxing action, helped with that.

She sat watching the women for over an hour, looking at what they were doing, and looking back to the notes Jaya had given her. It was a gentle, skilled process that required calm patience and faith. The parts could only be seen in the whole if you knew and understood each stage, and how it related to every other stage. And that included the dyeing, which was integral with the waxing for the final effect. She had wanted to see that too, but that wouldn't be happening on this trip.

Chapter 45

Adi asked her to go to a local factory with him to buy batik for friends in Australia and, as the manager took the piles of batik out of the glass-fronted cabinets, she wondered whether their friends would really appreciate the traditional local designs and colours of brown and indigo on a cream background. How far removed from these was Jaya's use of purple, bottle green, orange and soft shades of silver grey, in designs that seemed, to Lisa's eyes, Japanese-influenced. And yet, despite this, they were still of the place, of Central Java and of the village. She didn't know how his creations were received locally, but she found them utterly beautiful and original.

When they returned to Adi's studio, Lisa began typing the titles for Adi to email to the gallery. All the paintings had been shipped already and he had spread out large prints of each painting on the floor of the verandah. He pointed to the first in the line and stated the title – *The Ship of Unity*.

"What's that?" Lisa wanted to know.

"Ah, it's from a speech by Bung Soekarno 1926 about the movement for independence." Adi pointed to a detail of the painting and Lisa saw a ship with three sails labelled "Nationalist, Islamic, Marxist".

"Bung Soekarno said the Ship of Unity would unite people in a movement for freedom, and bring a 'single, gigantic and irresistible tidal wave'."

"I get that Islam and Nationalism were seen as important aspects of the struggle, but Marxism?" Lisa was puzzled.

"Even in Holland many people criticised the exploitation of our people, and so the struggle for social justice and equality became linked to the idea of a nation."

"Are you saying the nationalists were socialists?"

"Some, not all. Different groups put forward their own ways of achieving the same goals. Some saw an opportunity when the Japanese drove the Dutch away, and after the Japanese were defeated they joined together to stop the Dutch from coming back."

"You must be proud of what was achieved?"

"I take it for granted. But now I see that this time also shaped who we are today."

"What do you think though? Does Indonesia still need the Ship of Unity?"

Adi would not be drawn. "I don't have answers," he said. "Only questions."

To Lisa, Adi's interest in history, politics and what was happening now, and his way of linking them together like this, was new. It was as if he was laying out the pieces of a puzzle in order to bring some fresh understanding to what was going on around them, including the possibility of a future that was free of corruption, hate, propaganda, repression or terror.

"Hey Adi, are you becoming political?" Lisa teased.

Adi laughed. "Maybe," he said. "Look out!"

"Maybe all artists are political one way or another. Whether they like it or not, think they are or not." Lisa said.

There was still much to do but Lisa was curious about one of the paintings that was simply titled *R A Kartini, fourth wife of the Bupati of Rembang, 1879–1904*. Here, floating beneath the surface of the rice field, there was a grave stone with her name, dates of birth and death, and next to it, the words, "Pahlawan Nasional Indonesia" National Hero of Indonesia. Next to that was an image of a young woman wearing a white lace-trimmed kebaya and earrings. Then underneath it all, "Died in childbirth," then some lines from a letter she had written in which, he told her, she condemned polygamy in the aristocracy and promoted education and social justice for the people.

Lisa was fascinated. "Are you saying she was an outspoken critic of polygamy but she was married off to a bloke with three wives and then died a year later?"

"Yes."

"Just twenty-five! That is so tragic. Was she a feminist?"

"Yes, Kartini made equality for women important in Indonesia."

"Well, if we have a daughter we'll call her Kartini," Lisa said, and waited for him to tell her the next title.

Adi looked up in surprise. "*Betul,*" he said, and pulled out the photo of the next painting.

Part Five

Sydney
July–September 2012

Chapter 46

Slashing rain, flapping wipers, shoving wind. The elements poured out their anger as Adi and Lisa drove the hour-long journey from Darlinghurst to the crematorium – across the Bridge and north via a web of expressways whose overhead signs were blurred by sheets of water. July: the worst time of year in the city. It had not stopped raining since they arrived two days earlier, and it was bitterly cold. Snow was falling in the mountains and on the tablelands and the city had shrunk into itself; no one wanted to venture out unless they had to. Cafes closed early, taxi drivers complained about the lack of fares, and the chill penetrated their bodies no matter how many thermal layers they put on.

Adi had never been to Ryde but Lisa seemed to know which lane to be in to make the right exits. For two days, they had been involved in helping to organise the funeral. Adi still hadn't met Marj's son William, his wife, or the grandchildren, but Akira had been having discussions with him by phone about the order of service. He said that William seemed agreeable enough when Akira informed him that Marj always said she wanted *Amazing Grace* sung at her funeral.

"Perhaps we should call it Amazing Marj," Akira joked.

When Akira asked Adi if he wanted to speak at the funeral service, he said no. The Boys said they weren't up to it either, and so Akira said he would do the honours, but they would have to help him write it. During his fifteen years in Australia, Adi had not been to an Australian funeral and he hoped he could remain calm. Since the news of Marj's death, it was as though a sour fog had settled on the world. Even when flashes of deep red or blue cut through the grey, it caused him to feel drained of energy.

After they turned into the gates of the crematorium, Lisa and Adi found themselves in a large garden. A signpost pointed the way to the different chapels, all with floral names, and pointed them in the direction of a car park. The rain was pelting down even harder when they got out of the car and, as they made a run for it, they saw Akira getting out of the van he had rented to bring Lisbeth, the children, Archie and Bert. He'd let them out at the chapel entrance and was struggling with a gusting umbrella that pitched and turned inside out. It was a futile effort and, when he saw Lisa and Adi running, he threw it on the ground and took off after them.

In the chapel foyer they were met by Marj's son, William, and then Akira, Adi and Lisa joined Lisbeth, Eloise and Frank who were already sitting in the pews at the front. The day before, they had gathered at the Darlo Boarding House for lunch and to share stories about Marj, with Akira taking notes to help him write the eulogy. Archie had gone first, but broke down as he tried to tell the story of when he and Marj first met, and at the sound of his weeping, Eloise got up from playing with Frank on the floor to pat him softly on the back until he calmed down.

People had been bringing casseroles and cakes to the house, local business people and people Marj, Archie and Bert had known for a long time, as well as Adi, Akira and Lisbeth's friends. All came with solemn faces, tears and words of comfort.

When everyone was around him Adi felt safe, anchored, but now, waiting there in the chapel for the service to commence, his throat ached in anticipation of what was to come. The painting chosen by Gerardo for slow auction on the Grove Gallery website sat on an easel at the front of the chapel and there was a piano on the left. A double bass lay on its side and a clarinet waited on its stand. At the front was a glockenspiel on a low table and, in the row behind them, he glimpsed two musicians who dipped their foreheads when he caught their eye.

Adi's hands were cold and he tucked them inside the sleeves of his jacket. On his left, Lisa's orange kid leather gloves glowed and, on his right, Eloise stretched out her legs to show off her new lime green gumboots with a frog face on the front. Next to her, Frank had on gumboots too but his were shiny red and looked like an old-fashioned train engine. They were three spots of colour in the otherwise drab chapel and his gaze shifted back and forth, from one to the other. Otherwise, it was just blues and greys all around, and he could feel without turning around that the rows behind them were filling up with mourners. He'd just learned that word "mourners" and he found it strange and evocative, like a loud, sad moan.

A rustle of movement at the back brought everyone to their feet as the coffin was wheeled down the aisle. Archie and Bert were leading and William and his two teenage daughters followed behind. When it came to rest at the front of the chapel, William stood a framed photo of a smiling Marj on the top. The photo drew Adi's attention and every time he looked its way he saw Marj's colour, the soft musk pink of who she was, hovering above the coffin.

They remained standing as Akira played the opening bars of *Amazing Grace* and Lisbeth's voice soared over them, inviting them to sing along to the words printed in the order of service. Then the first slide came up on the screen of Marj as a little girl, maybe two or three, sitting on the bare back of a horse, with her father's arm around her, and with his other arm bent up under the horse's neck. He'd seen the picture before but now he saw the horse was a pony, perhaps a grey, but it was hard to tell because of the sepia tones. Whose horse was it? Where was that? Where did she grow up again?

When they were seated, William welcomed everyone and offered a chronology of Marj's life. He touched on her youth, growing up in the bush, the move to the city for work, her stint driving tractors in the Women's Land Army in the war. He spoke of the sacrifices she made to raise him and paid tribute to her commitment to his education. He finished by saying how much Marj would be missed but he did not say by whom.

Akira spoke next and began by explaining that he would be referring to her as Bu which, he explained, was the Indonesian word for mother. He described her kindness and generosity, her stand-in role as parent, along with Archie and Bert, for any occasion he or Adi had on, her role in the lives of his and Lisbeth's children, Eloise and Frank. When Akira mentioned his daughter's name, Adi heard Eloise sniff several times and then felt a warm, soft hand seek out his own. He caught hold of it and held on tight as Akira spoke of Marj's capacity for love and tolerance, her willingness to drop everything if someone needed her, and her favourite saying – it's always best to give people the benefit of the doubt.

"It's possible that Bu had faults and if she was here I'm sure she'd tell you what they were. Some of us thought she worked too hard, sometimes we thought she could or should think less of others and more of herself, but that was who she was. She was fiercely loyal and if she loved you she would brook no criticism of you – even if you deserved it! And I think I can say that for those of us who knew her well – Marj will live in our heart always."

Akira announced that William's daughters, Caitlin and Bridget, would read a poem they had written for their grandmother, and then the band would play a composition titled *Rainy Day at Marj's*.

When the girls had returned to their seats, the band members moved toward their instruments, and Eloise released Adi's hand and walked over to pick up the sticks on each side of the glockenspiel. When she was ready, Akira nodded and she began tapping out the melody. Then Akira signalled to the bass player who caught up the tune and began to improvise, while Akira moved down onto the floor and plucked slow haunting notes from inside the piano. The clarinet notes soared, and the sounds it made wrenched Adi's entire body, and absorbed the racket of wind, rain, and the thrashing trees outside. The music drew them up out of their daily lives and worries, set them loose from their loss and grief, and slowly deposited in them a settled calm and peace. When, at a further nod from Akira, Eloise began tapping out the notes of the melody on the glockenspiel, there was a silent communal drawing in of breath in the chapel.

Everyone took their time to return to the room as the last notes lingered and faded, and in the stillness that followed Adi saw the colours of life begin to glow with a full radiance. He felt lighter as if he had shed an old, papery skin, seen it pixelate and vanish. In his left hand, he felt Lisa's orange-gloved hand holding his and he gave it a soft squeeze; in his right he felt Eloise's hand slip back inside his own. He did not remember her returning to her seat but now, without letting go, they stood up and walked towards Marj's coffin.

Eloise let go his hand and went and stood at the head of the coffin. With her hand covering her mouth, he saw her whispering urgent messages to Marj through the lid, and felt his throat constrict as he looked on. When she was finished, she turned to her father and raised her arms for him to lift her up. She buried her face in his shoulder and did not look up until he had walked outside and well away from the chapel.

Marj's love, her spirit, flowed in and through them as they moved down the aisle and out of the chapel. The rain, which had settled into a steady drizzle, slid off their umbrellas and splashed onto the ground as they made their way across the road to the wake.

Chapter 47

On an unseasonably hot and windy September day, Adi and Lisa sat in the bow of a Manly ferry – felt it lift and fall as it made its way across the harbour. Adi was excited to rediscover the way the ferries disclosed new views and experiences of the city from the arteries and veins of the harbour. On the water, sailing boats were scooting by on the wind, with their sails flapping as they went about and then filling out as they caught up the wind again. The crowd of small craft, with one or two sailors hanging out over the water to keep the sail full and the boat on a straight course, were a contrast to the larger sailing boats that glided by, the skipper at the wheel, and the guests relaxing with a drink in hand.

"Look at us," they waved, and the passengers on the ferry returned the gesture.

"This is good too," they replied.

There was goodwill in the way people related on the water, as if the sky, sun, wind and water filled them with an idle friendliness. No appointments or meetings, no hurry up, schedules or agenda. Gaiety and shining colour – the rippling silver gusts of wind on the water, exuberant spinnakers, orange life jackets, rust red roofs rising up the harbourside hills, tracts of grey-green vegetation – and then there was the way it all dulled when the sun locked behind a cloud. As they passed the Heads, the cliffs that rose like sentinels where the Pacific Ocean entered the harbour, a watery swell bulged towards them and pushed and pulled at the heavy old ferry – showered the outside decks with cold, salty spray, wet the clothes of the passengers, and coated their skin and lips with the taste of salt.

At Manly Wharf, Lisa led the way up The Corso, a pedestrian mall that stretched less than half a kilometre from the harbour wharf to the ocean. There were outdoor tables and chairs, a tiny amphitheatre, slow moving tourists in hats and shorts, and young backpackers, skin red from the sun, who moved in chattering shoals of German, Swedish, French or Italian language. The mood and flavour of the place was so different to Darlinghurst that Adi felt like he had landed in another country.

At the end of The Corso they crossed the road to an avenue of tall Norfolk Island pines. On the beach, the sand was a shimmering yellowy-white and their bare feet made a crunching sound as they walked to the water's edge. The receding tide had exposed a steep sloping sand bank and a crisp breeze was made even more chill when it skimmed the breaking waves. With pants rolled up, they strolled along the water's edge, jumped the waves, and turned and ploughed up the bank when the water became too deep. As the tide pulled out, it sucked the wet sand from beneath their feet and, like little children, they used fingers and toes to draw pictures and words in the sand and then watched with satisfaction as the incoming waves washed them away.

In the flotsam and jetsam at the high tide mark there were piles of tiny shells, blue bottles with luminous clear bubbles and long blue tentacles, and random clumps of bubbly seaweed pods. Higher up the beach, thick green plastic wheelie bins, with "Do The Right Thing" labels stuck on them, were dotted along the beach at regular intervals. The air was saturated with spray. Sea gulls strode on red stilts, pecking at possible food scraps, then squawked and fought over any morsels they found. Further north, the beach arced around and two red and yellow lifesaving flags marked the safe area for swimming. A lifesaver sat on a tall seat between the flags to keep watch on the bathers, and several more sheltered inside a three-sided waist-high canvas windbreak that was open on the side closest to the water. From time to time they too cast an eye over the swimmers.

There were a dozen or more bathers in the water, diving under the rolling waves, or body surfing. Boogie board riders, mostly young boys and girls, were trying to catch waves outside the flags, and further out to sea a group of surfers sat waiting on their boards for a wave. Those still on the beach sat in groups, or lay sunbaking or reading on their towels, their bodies sticky and gritty from sunscreen and sand.

Lisa and Adi turned their attention to the surfers that were gathering beyond the breaking waves. At first they could see only four, but more and more were arriving at the water's edge. Wearing black wetsuits, and with their boards tucked under one arm and tied to a black rubber line at the ankle, they walked into the water. When it was up to their waist, they hoisted their bellies onto their boards and began paddling, reaching out with one arm and then the other, propelling themselves out to sea and letting the incoming waves wash over them.

From the back, each time the swell bulged into a wave, two or three surfers set off, pulling powerfully with their arms to stay ahead of it, and then gathering speed as the wave caught them up and thrust them forward. Then they were up on their feet, standing or crouching, and even disappearing inside the rolling tube before emerging and flicking themselves up and away as the wave continued on to the shore.

Adi was thrilled at the surfers' skill. "Is this what Mack does?"

"Yes it is."

"Does he surf here?"

"Not really. He mostly goes to the southern beaches now. Y'know, Bronte, Bondi or Maroubra. It depends where the best waves are."

"It looks difficult."

"Yes, you need good balance. It's like an addiction, they start when they're kids. You see men in their fifties and sixties still surfing up this way. Women too."

"I'd like to do this. Are there sharks out there?"

"Yes, probably."

"They're not scared?"

"They are, but in actual fact not that many people are attacked. Maybe two or three a year – that's all over Australia."

Some of the surfers rode the waves effortlessly, others capsized when the wave washed over them.

Suddenly Lisa gasped and pointed at a grey fin in a breaking wave. "Oh my god, did you see that?"

Adi looked in the direction of her pointing finger. "Shark?" he asked.

"Yes ... No, look, dolphins."

A pod of seven or eight dolphins swept joyfully out of the top of a cresting wave and then glided down its curving underbelly as if racing the surfers. Lisa and Adi laughed and Adi grabbed for his camera but it was too late – the visitors had gone.

Adi began to make sand castles and Lisa helped at first, but then she sat watching as he let the wet sand dribble from his hand, creating Gaudi-like fortresses that were no sooner built and admired than they were dissolved by a swirl of water. They moved further up the beach and he began digging a large hole in the sand, which he fashioned into the shape of a reclining chair. He pulled a sarong from his backpack, placed it over the end and invited Lisa to sit on the chair, with her head resting on the sarong. He helped her to get comfortable and then began pushing the dry white sand up and over her lap, legs, feet and chest until all that remained was her head. With wet sand brought from the shore, he began shaping a sand sculpture around her.

Lisa lay with her eyes closed. It was a lovely feeling, like being a kid again. As Adi put the finishing touches on the sculpture – tiny shells to make a mound of Venus – two passing older women looked on and recollected how they used to go in sand sculpture competitions all the time when they were kids.

When he called on her to open her eyes, Lisa saw large round breasts, rounded belly, strong almost masculine legs and arms. Even her nipples and hands were portrayed in detail, probably the feet as well, as much as the slightly damp sand would allow. Adi asked her to stay still while he took half a dozen photos, and then continued photographing as she began to stand, causing the sculpture to fracture and the sand to fall away. Behind her, there were the jumbled remains of an emptied grave.

She'd forgotten Adi's ability to infuse even the simplest activity with a creative impulse, and she found herself imagining the images he had been recording, from all sides of the disrupted sand sculpture, and their possible interpretations.

Since their return, they had acquired a new regard for the moments they spent together and she felt energised by his company. Art making was not something precious, not something that only artists do. It was the attention given to the moments of beauty and wonder that catch hold of us, the ways we choose to live with one another and with the earth, and in all the acts of kindness given and received in our lives.

"Marj was an artist in her own way, you know," she said.

"Yes," he said, as though surprised that she had only just made this discovery.

"I think she's smiling down at us."

"Probably … "

And he reached out and lightly dusted some grains of sand from her cheek with his fingers.

Acknowledgements

In response to a plea by Anthony Wong to write more parts for Asian actors in Australia, I began writing a filmscript in 1997 which was subsequently workshopped with dramaturg Timothy Daly. In 2011, I was granted a scholarship at Western Sydney University to study for a Doctorate of Philosophy in Creative Writing under the supervision of Professors Anna Gibbs, Nicholas Jose and Dr Maria Angel. Some of the ideas in the filmscript made their way into the creative component of the PhD which became the novel, *The Colour of Things Unseen.*

I thank the writers, academics, staff and postgraduate students at WSU for their generosity and support. I appreciate the friendship and professional encouragement offered by Melinda Jewell and others, including Felicity Castagna, Jen Craig, Claire Scobie and Jane Skelton. I am also indebted to a long list of Indonesianists and other scholars for their contribution to my research. I wish to thank all those who read my novel for their critical comments – including my PhD supervisors and examiners, Melinda Jewell, Nita Karianpurwanti, Ida Lawrence, Jan Lingard, Margo Moore and Sue Spence; Murray Robertson for sharing his perceptions about "thinking in colours;" Cheryl Robson, editor at Aurora Metro Books, for her insightful editing.

In Indonesia, Nita Karianpurwanti facilitated a conversation with four artists and Self Rumbewas and Nita translated the recorded transcript. Thanks to Pranoto for permission to use his painting on the cover and also for all the stories shared over the years, and for introducing me to our family and other friends. Mas Hartono's wonderful description of batik-making is a treasure.

Many people have offered assistance and I thank: Kerry Martin, Wawan, Mbak Mifta and the family in Dongkelan, Linda Kaun, Joan Suyenaga, Christine Cocca, Maudi Maria, Harto and the girls, Anita Scheeres and Ketut Yuliasa, Yuni Alfiah, Monica Proba, David Reeve, Eko Bambang Wisnu, Adji and Intang, Seno; and Sue, Alister and Alex Spence for the music, the reminders that art matters and for opening a door into Sydney's jazz scene; and to Sydney's Australian-Indonesian community and Suara Indonesia Dance, for the friendship and joy. And last, but not least, I'm grateful to: Kerry Pendergrast, Emil and Tahlia Raji, the families in Kliwonan, Janet de Neefe and Ketut Suardana at Ubud Writers and Readers Festival, Marie Flood, John Hayman and Ida Lawrence. Thank you for your belief and support.

Twitter @aurorametro
Facebook.com/AuroraMetroBooks

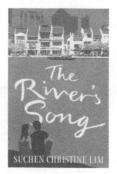

To find out about other titles from
Aurora Metro Books
please visit our website

www.aurorametro.com

CPSIA information can be obtained
at www.ICGtesting.com
Printed in the USA
LVHW030917010721
691577LV00007B/1132

9 781912 430178